STAY THE NIGHT

Kamau stroked his chin. "I must say, though, that I am not sure what you mean by chemistry. Explain more, please."

Adana took a deep breath, thought for a moment and said, "Okay, this is the deal. Chemistry is that insatiable urge to have someone near you, with you. You're drawn by the touch, the feel, the smell of that someone. At some point, being with that special person is as essential as the body needing water." She looked into his eyes, searching for a glimmer of awareness. "Do you understand?"

Kamau looked at the passionate woman across from him and thought that she could easily inspire insatiable urges. He responded, "I think I am beginning to. In my world, it is always assumed that in time any two reasonable people will come to honor and respect one another and thereby form a bond that is unbreakable."

Adana answered in a tone that was both warm and longing. "Kamau, the bond that I'm describing goes beyond the attachment of friends or business partners. What I'm describing is a physical yearning that in some cases clouds good sense and is strictly emotional. The head rarely leads. It's all heart."

Also by Chilufiya Safaa

The Art of Love

Passionate Encounters

A Foreign Affair

Published by Dafina Books

Stay The Night

Chilufiya Safaa

Kensington Publishing Corp.

http://www.kensingtonbooks.com

DAFINA BOOKS are published by

Kensington Publishing Corp.
119 West 40th Street
New York, NY 10018

All Kensington Titles, Imprints, and Distributed Lines are
available at special quantity discounts for bulk purchases for
sales promotions, premiums, fund-raising, and educational or
institutional use. Special book excerpts or customized print-
ings can also be created to fit specific needs. For details,
write or phone the office of the Kensington special sales
manager: Kensington Publishing Corp., 119 West 40th Street,
New York, NY 10018, attn: Special Sales Department, Phone:
1-800-221-2647.

Dafina and the Dafina logo Reg. U.S. Pat. & TM Off.

ISBN-13: 978-0-7582-1974-9
ISBN-10: 0-7582-1974-1

First mass market printing: December 2010

10 9 8 7 6 5 4 3 2 1

Printed in the United States of America

*To my muse, the ever-present one
who never leaves me, and to Sahib-Amar Khalsa,
without whose magic fingers, this manuscript
and two others would never have come to fruition.*

Dear Reader,

Adana's story concludes the journey of the Terrell sisters. I hope you enjoyed traveling with me, not just on the four romantic jaunts but also to the marvelous places in Africa, the Caribbean and Europe where the characters lived, worked and played.

It was my desire with this series to provide a different image of Africans throughout the diaspora and to serve as witness to the sacredness of the union between man and woman.

The characters came from the divine place from whence all creation comes, and I will be forever grateful to have had them embody my soul for short periods of time.

Love, peace and blessings,
Chilufiya Safaa

P.S. I love hearing from you as you travel with me. E-mail me at: *speakersdream@hotmail.com*.

I saw him, ebony-hued with bittersweet chocolate shards of light bouncing off of radiant burnished skin

I saw him, sinewy muscles rippling with rhythmic movements and quiet strength

I saw him staring in deep concentration with light flashing in catlike eyes holding secret thoughts

And then

He saw me

—Safaa

Chapter 1

Nairobi, Kenya

Mist hung as if by magic in the early morning air. The gray-colored Kenyan sky opened and released clear droplets of warm rain that drizzled gently down to the thirsty, rust-colored earth. Kamau Mazrui stood stoically alone inside the enclosed structure of the Mazrui family mausoleum. As the rain dropped softly to the ground, so did silent tears drop down Kamau's clenched, square jaw. The painful memory of the loss of his wife, Yasmin Mazrui, once again pierced his heart like the reopening of an old wound. He stood motionless. Even the air dared not stir as he stood mute, questioning silently what he could have done to prevent his wife's untimely death. Yasmin Mazrui's life had ended a year earlier in the crash of the small Cessna aircraft she had been piloting, but Kamau's need for her still lingered. The void left by his wife's absence wrapped around him like silken ribbons, reminding him of a touch that could no longer be felt. Kamau stood, knowing he would never see, hear nor feel Yasmin again. The void eased through him, leaving cold, empty traces of longing and regret. Rapid-fire questions lasered through his consciousness. *Was there a word that should have or could have been said? Could more have been done to stop her from piloting the plane alone? Why was her life taken? Why was he deprived of her beauty, intellect and humor? If they had not quarreled before her business trip about her wanting to pilot the plane without him, would she have been more focused and consequently still alive?* The barrage of muted questions had no answers. Feeling the moisture from tears landing on taut, chiseled, deep-mahogany-colored cheeks, Kamau wiped them away quickly with the back of his strong, dark hand. With one motion, he denied their existence. The end of Kamau Mazrui's momentary expression of sorrow was released in a breath that emanated from a body that had become defined by grief.

As if by rote, Kamau quickly looked at the octagonal face of his custom-made Cartier wristwatch. The time that registered brought him back to the realities of his current existence. In less than an hour, he was expected to host a breakfast meeting for businessmen who, like himself, wielded substantial power around the globe. Among the men attending would be his father, Judge Garsen Mazrui, and his older brother, Keino Mazrui, a highly successful international entrepreneur. For the sake of the family, Kamau knew he could show no signs of lingering grief. It was not his desire to have anyone show concern or pity for him. The isolation he felt shrouded him as he lifted dark, hooded eyes once again to read the golden plaque on which was etched YASMIN MAZRUI, BELOVED WIFE. He took a deep cleansing breath and slowly exited the mausoleum. Leaving the structure, Kamau noted that the rain had stopped, and the sky had returned to azure laced with chalky-white clouds making their way lazily across the heavens.

Moving his well-toned, solidly built body with grace and precision, Kamau Mazrui placed one elegantly crafted, meticulously polished, leather Italian lace-up shoe in front of the other. Having made his way across the manicured grounds on which the mausoleum stood, Kamau unlocked his four-door, late-model Bentley with the remote. Entering the driver's seat, he was encased in a soft cocoon of burgundy leather that became another refuge.

He placed the key in the ignition and turned his wrist slightly. The powerful engine responded with a barely perceptible hum. With an automatic motion, Kamau pressed his foot on the accelerator. The elegantly designed driving machine moved forward, gliding so smoothly Kamau barely felt the road. With skill and precision, he steered the touring sedan and sped along familiar highways, heading toward what he hoped would be the ultimate distraction—his work.

The streets of Nairobi were congested as Kamau Mazrui maneuvered the steel-gray Bentley along the stretch of roadway leading to the Meru Gentlemen's Club. The Meru Club had been founded decades before by his paternal grandfather. The Mazrui patriarch had always declared that the club had been erected as a barrier against the vulgar and the mundane. In contemporary times, its use had become more complicated. The vulgar and the mundane were open to loosely held interpretations. The major reason for the meetings held at the club in modern times concerned business; some would have conjectured that a certain level of business by its very nature lent itself to vulgarity and to the mundane. And so with every accelerated motion of the sedan, Kamau Mazrui moved momentarily away from the grief that permeated his soul to the ruthlessness that often characterized the world in which he operated as the principal attorney in the Mazrui law firm.

As he continued to steer the car in the direction of the club, the symbol of strength and timelessness erected by his grandfather soon became visible. It was a massive building that mimicked the Georgian architecture popular in eighteenth-century Britain. The sight of the structure released in him a calm assurance that connected him mentally and emotionally to the power of his grandfather, the patriarch of the dynasty who had conceived of and constructed the building he saw before him. At this time in his life, only his ancestral connections gave him the strength to persevere.

Kamau Mazrui wheeled the luxury automobile into his reserved parking space, and immediately a valet was on hand to open his door. Kamau pressed a lever to open the trunk of the car, stepped out, retrieved his flawlessly crafted leather briefcase and walked into the gentlemen's club with the air of pride, competence, arrogance and confidence that surrounded all of the Mazrui men. He entered the building and found within its well-preserved walls the sense of peace he craved. There was a refined splendor in the large, opulently decorated rooms. They were separated by their functions. Some were used for gaming; some for dining; some for meetings; and others for lounging with a favorite cigar, glass of port, snifter of brandy, pipe, periodical, book or the daily news. Conversations were to be had on any subject, from the ridiculous to the sublime. Kamau welcomed the smells of aged leather, rich tobacco, freshly brewed coffee and the faint fragrance of lemon from highly polished African and European antique furnishings. He was calmed by the watchful eyes that stared down from the ornately framed portraits of men like his father, grandfather and great-grandfather, men who had prevailed and thrived in spite of personal tragedies. It gave him comfort to know that such strength was his birthright. As Kamau entered the vestibule, he was greeted by the hall porter, a wizened, elderly gentleman who informed him that his father and brother had already arrived. He thanked the porter who had served the Mazrui family and the Meru Gentlemen's Club for three decades, and then made his way to the room he had reserved for the meeting.

As Kamau entered the room, Garsen and Keino Mazrui saw him, stopped their conversation and encircled him warmly in the familial embrace that was their custom. After the greeting, each man positioned himself in one of the high-backed chairs encircling a round table constructed of gleaming ebony wood inlaid on the surface with geometrically shaped mahogany pieces.

Judge Garsen Mazrui observed his son Kamau with more intensity than usual as the three of them discussed the fluctuating global markets and made light of recent political scandals. The judge watched Kamau go through the motions of emptying his briefcase of well-ordered file folders in preparation for the meeting. Kamau distractedly lined up the files perfectly on the table in front of him while conversing with his father and brother. Judge Mazrui noted that although it had been a year since his daughter-in-law's death, his son's eyes still held the look of one caught unaware by a tragedy that defied explanation. Keino, too, tried to unobtrusively observe his brother. It pained him that he could not help his beloved sibling find peace. Keino was well aware that although Kamau performed his normal duties as efficiently as ever for all the world to see, his brother wore his pain as close to him as one of his well-tailored suits.

Judge Mazrui changed the subject from stocks and bonds to more immediate concerns. While looking at his gold pocket watch, he asked, "Kamau, how many of our colleagues are joining us today?"

Still organizing the files in front of him, Kamau responded, "Approximately ten." He stopped positioning the files and added, "They should start arriving shortly." With the thumb and index finger of his left hand, Kamau stroked his full, well-groomed mustache as he continued speaking. "I have been informed that everyone invited will join us." He added with a slightly cynical grin, "Time in Africa is, after all, cyclical. Despite modern advances, some cultural practices never change."

Kamau's statement amused Keino, and through his laughter, Keino responded, "My brother, you are so right. African time will always be African time." He gestured, lifting his hands into the air. "Throughout the diaspora it is the same."

Just as Keino finished his sentence, a number of the businessmen scheduled to arrive walked into the room. These men were representatives of a number of African countries. As emissaries of their various city-states, they had come to the Meru Gentlemen's Club at Kamau's request to serve as the founding members of a continental African strategic planning entity designed to set policy to unify political and economic systems across the continent. Greetings were extended and small talk was exchanged. Shortly, the remainder of the group arrived, and Kamau took charge as waiters entered as if on cue, carrying trays of food that they placed on skirted buffet tables. Gone was Kamau's early morning melancholy; in its place was a driven, laser-focused attention to detail. His only purpose at that moment was to preside over the meeting with the commanding presence that was the hallmark of Mazrui tradition. As the morning clicked by at a rapid pace, filled with eating, lighthearted banter and serious business transactions, Kamau's sadness turned to the solemn focus and the passion and persistence that had forged his reputation as an internationally renowned corporate attorney. With the heightened decibels of his voice, he guided the men forward to the accomplishment of their stated goals, pushing thoughts of Yasmin for a time further back into the recesses of his mind.

Chapter 2

Virginia, USA

Adana Terrell stood in the empty courtroom where in two hours she was scheduled to begin the trial preliminaries of her newest case. Years before, she had developed a ritual of standing in the vacant courtroom in which she was to appear to breathe in all of the joy she felt when practicing the art of being a jurist. Adana couldn't remember a time when she didn't want to be a lawyer. She was living her dream. She was a partner in the prestigious firm of Wilkes, Willis, Burkes, and Terrell. A smile eased across her narrow face. A deep sigh parted ruby-colored lips as she tilted her head back, causing her short, precision-cut, fine, raven-colored hair to fall back, resting on her head in perfect layers. The lock of hair that normally stopped at her cheek, almost covering one eye, fell back, exposing round eyes that sparkled and glistened. Feeling a sense of peace wash over her, Adana closed her eyes and wrapped her arms around her torso. In her mind's eye, she envisioned herself facing the jury and hammering away at them with arguments so compelling her client would be acquitted. Just as she envisioned herself uttering the last sentence of her summation, the vision was shattered. A familiar voice that prickled her skin pierced the silence.

"I see you're still practicing that ritual of yours."

She felt as if the proverbial splash of cold water had been thrown in her face. Adana's body tightened, her eyes opened slowly and she stared with deadly precision at the figure standing before her. Adana could not mistake that voice. She would never forget it. There he was, cocky, flashy, with a hint of slick hiding beneath an extremely expensive wardrobe. She wondered what she had ever seen in him. Adana hated to think that her preoccupation with work and the pursuit of her dream had allowed her to fall for the shallow pretty boy Jeffery Scott, Esquire, who was now standing there leering at her. But it had, and now he was thrown back into her life as her adversary in the firm's latest case.

Adana straightened her slender, shapely form to its maximum five feet nine inches and, with the ruby-colored nails of her left hand, flicked a strand of hair from her cheek, turned her back to him and began walking in the opposite direction.

Jeffery watched her walk to the defense table, and for the zillionth time, he regretted losing the spectacular woman he saw before him. As always, she was impeccably dressed. Adana's black St. John knit suit tastefully hugged every curve, the white silk blouse and three strands of white pearls touched places he longed to embrace, and the matching pearl earrings and black three-inch stilettos brought back memories of the heat and passion Adana had always evoked in him.

Adana's silence spoke volumes, causing Jeffery to feel tremendous exasperation and a loss of control. With a clipped tone that sounded as though he were examining a witness, Jeffery asked, "Are you going to answer me?"

Having finished placing previously reviewed briefs back into her leather briefcase, a cold, exacting Adana responded while picking up the briefcase from the table. "No, Jeffery. No small talk, no answered questions. I only intend to speak to you when we are actively involved in matters pertaining to this trial. Until then, leave me the hell alone." With head held high and composure intact, Adana left the courtroom, leaving Jeffery frozen where he stood.

His eyes followed her. The corner of his mouth lifted in a sly grin. Jeffery shook his head and reminded himself that though he had lost one round, he wasn't giving up. Jeffery Scott felt he had been given another chance, and this time Adana Terrell was not going to slip away. He turned his attention to the documents he intended to review and silently assured himself that the lady lawyer, his worthy adversary, would once again be his.

Adana was steaming. The intensity of the anger was causing her head to pound and her ears to ring. Clenching her teeth, she muttered to herself, "What in God's name have I done to deserve this? What have I done? I am going to have to work for weeks with a man who deceived and humiliated me."

Walking became her release. The heels of her stilettos clicked rhythmically as she hurried along the marbled halls of the courthouse, moving as quickly as she could away from a piece of her past she wanted never to remember. Jeffery Scott was a constant reminder that though she was an accomplished attorney, when it came to choosing a man, she, Adana Terrell, was clueless. Jeffery Scott, the fast-talking, New York–bred manipulator, had more game than Adana had ever encountered. As she walked, she thought to herself, *Adana, you were played like a fiddle.* She needed to run, to punch something, to scream, to curse Jeffery. None of those things were options at that moment, so she hurried on to the parking garage where she had left her car.

Adana crossed the busy street facing the courthouse, taking deep breaths, hoping to calm herself. She quickly entered the concrete slab constructed to house automobiles of every imaginable size, shape and color. Adana found the numbered stall where she had parked her car, and as she slid into the driver's seat, she grabbed the steering wheel of the two-seater Mercedes-Benz with both hands, rested her head on it and wept. The tears weren't for Jeffery or for the loss of the relationship. The tears were because, in her mind, she had been played royally. Adana Terrell hated to lose, and she hated being duped. Both loss and deception left her feeling vulnerable, and being vulnerable was not something she handled well. With Jeffery she had missed every sign. Denial had been her middle name. The ability to judge correctly was the cornerstone of her chosen profession. The fact that Jeffery Scott was ever a fixture in her life left her questioning herself on the most basic levels.

With the windows rolled up and the parking garage seemingly empty, she threw her head back and screamed as tears flowed down her face. She yelled until her throat was raw, asking, "Why?" A small voice deep in her soul whispered, *You know why. Jeffery was easy. You didn't really give him your heart. You only gave him your time and not a lot of that. You didn't invest your soul, Adana. You've never done that. Your pride is wounded—put away your pride. You gave nothing; you got nothing in return.*

The tears slowed. She opened her glove box and retrieved a small travel case of tissues and began using her rearview mirror to repair the damage done to expertly applied makeup. As she tissued her cheeks and chin and blew her nose, she thought of the words that had come to her, and she said aloud, "I gave as much as I could. I don't know how to give any more, and I refuse to psychoanalyze my reasons. Besides, he was the wrong man to give anything to." She reapplied her makeup hurriedly, ran a comb through well-trained strands and said softly, "Pull it together, Adana."

She looked at her slender, gold Piaget wristwatch. "In one hour and twenty minutes, you need to be back in that courtroom operating at the top of your game, so stop sitting in your car babbling to yourself like the village idiot. You need to kick Jeffery where it really hurts—in his legal briefs."

She smiled, took a deep breath, turned the ignition key and headed in the direction of the home of her maternal grandmother, Lillian Gardener Chatfield, known as Mimi to her granddaughters. Of the four granddaughters—Adana, Amara, Cassandra and Afiya—Adana was the one who felt most closely tied to Lillian Chatfield. The two shared a great deal in common. Adana was merely a more modern version of her maternal grandmother. Lillian Gardener Chatfield was a Washington, D.C., socialite with old money and old ideas about life and how it should be lived. Traditions were her bread and butter. She was unnerved daily by the unraveling of societal norms. Lillian was especially dismayed by what she perceived as the African American community spiraling out of control. Her family was proud to have traced its American lineage back to the 1600's, to free landowning blacks in Virginia. All of her life, she had been imbued with a pride she did not see being passed on to future generations. Mrs. Lillian Gardener Chatfield was known to be uncompromising in the statement of her opinions.

Adana enjoyed her grandmother. Even when she did not agree with her, the way in which her grandmother structured her life and held on to her beliefs gave Adana a certain sense of peace and calm that she relished in stormy times. Adana's parents, Drs. James and Ana Terrell, were also rocks for her, but there was something special about Mimi.

Adana headed across the Potomac in the direction of Georgetown, knowing that she had just enough time to have an early cup of tea and a calming chat before heading back to court. Suddenly it occurred to Adana that she should call her grandmother. After all, Lillian was not one to sit at home idly. Her social activities kept her quite busy. Adana reached into the console, found her cell phone, flipped it open and pushed a button that dialed her grandmother's number.

On the second ring, Adana heard a refined, cheerful, "Lillian here."

Adana smiled. "Hi, Mimi, this is Adana. How are you?"

"Why, my sweet darling, I know your voice! I know who you are. I am not so old that I can't distinguish the voices of my grandchildren." Lillian laughed, ending her whimsical chuckle with a long sigh.

Adana's lips turned in a smile as she replied to her grandmother, "I know, Mimi, you're as sharp as ever. I have some time before court, and I thought I'd drop by for tea and a chat. Are you going to be home?"

"Of course, my darling child. Everything will be ready when you get here. It will be so good to see you."

"All right, Mimi, I'll see you in about ten minutes."

Adana snapped her cell closed, smiled and sped a little faster in the direction of her grandmother's home. The sights and sounds of spring permeated the air as Adana cruised along the Virginia highway in the direction of Georgetown. Cherry blossoms exploded from trees and hung in riotous variations of pink and alabaster. She lowered her window, needing to feel the warm breeze on her skin. The tingling warmth pushed thoughts of Jeffery Scott from her consciousness. Within minutes, she drove on to a tree-lined Georgetown street, peppered with historic brick structures filled with stories to tell of people of means and privilege. But while many of those considered landed gentry had long since gone and their progeny had abandoned the old ways and the timeless buildings, Adana's maternal grandmother held on with the tenaciousness of a foxhound.

Adana parked in front of the garage, which was located on the corner of her grandmother's home. The expansive redbrick building sat on a corner lot surrounded by expertly cared for rosebushes of various varieties and colors. Adana walked briskly up the walkway and rang the elaborately encased doorbell adjacent to the carved burl-wood door that marked the entrance to Lillian Gardener Chatfield's home.

Adana rang the doorbell twice. Mrs. Alma Battle, Lillian's housekeeper companion, answered the door. Mrs. Battle was a woman of immense strength and character. Although she had not completed college, she was gifted with an inquisitive mind and a voracious appetite for knowledge. Alma Battle had been widowed early and left without family. Her employment in the Chatfield household had been a blessing for both women. Though Lillian Chatfield and Alma Battle had dissimilar backgrounds, their sensibilities were well matched. Mrs. Battle greeted Adana with a cheerful, "Well, hello there, lady barrister. How is the commonwealth's finest attorney?" Not waiting for an answer, she embraced Adana tenderly and continued. "I'm so proud of you. I feel like I'm your grandmother too. I keep up with you in the daily news. I see you've landed yourself another high-profile case."

Adana smiled and melted into Alma's rose-scented embrace. It felt so comforting, so totally accepting. At that moment, she needed the reassurance of a comforting embrace. Mrs. Battle released Adana and said energetically, "Your grandmother is waiting for you."

Adana gave Mrs. Battle's soft, spongy upper arm a gentle squeeze and thanked her. She walked down a hallway that was carpeted in richly textured Persian rugs and entered a parlor elegant in its simplicity. Lillian heard her granddaughter enter the room and turned from the silver tea service she was arranging.

Smiling, she walked toward Adana and embraced her lovingly. "Sweetheart, it is so good to see you."

Once again in the loving, welcoming embrace of her grandmother, Adana felt the same assurance and comfort she had felt hugging Alma Battle. The scent of Chanel in the air surrounding Lillian stirred memories of Mimi's sleepovers when she and her sisters were children. Memories of the scented bubble baths, the silk nighties, the perfectly pressed sheets and the down-filled mattresses that she and her sisters sank into and laughed and whispered and giggled late into the night until they fell asleep. In spite of Mimi's insistence upon old-fashioned manners and strict proprietary behavior, Adana, Cassandra, Afiya and Amara always felt loved, and the ritualistic order of Lillian Chatfield's life always made Adana feel safe.

With twinkling eyes and a look of deep satisfaction on her face, Lillian looked at her granddaughter from the top of her stylishly coiffed head to the tips of her stiletto-clad toes. Almost as if thinking aloud, she uttered, "I had no idea when your mother was born that she would give me such beautiful, accomplished granddaughters and that they would bring me such joy. All of you, each in her own way, is such a treasure. I feel so blessed to have been able to live long enough to see my bloodline stretch into the future." Lillian stopped, took a breath and gestured to a nearby antique silk-upholstered chair. "Come over here, sweetheart, and join me. Have a seat."

Adana sat opposite her grandmother, who eased down on a French love seat positioned near an intricately carved rolling tray that held the heirloom silver tea service that had belonged to Lillian's grandmother. Adana smiled, thinking that for as long as she could remember, she had seen Mimi pour tea from that set. Adana released a breath that was a mixture of relief and subliminal sorrow. She said to her grandmother, "Mimi, it feels so good just to relax. I'm so glad you are home. I used to be able to run over to Afiya's house if I needed a quick retreat." A hint of sadness colored Adana's eyes as she spoke. "The house is still there, and I have a key, but it must have been Afiya's energy that created the calm and tranquility, because it's not the same."

With a studied glance, Lillian looked up at her granddaughter while pouring their tea. "I know you miss your sisters. You girls are all so close."

Adana picked up her cup and saucer and gently stirred the steaming tea with a cool silver spoon. "I really do." The corner of her mouth lifted in a wistful smile. "Even though Afiya and I argued often, I really miss her. Some days are harder than others." Adana took a sip of the savory tea. It slid down smoothly, warming her throat and calming her spirit. Adana's voice broke a little as she said, "All three of them come back and forth, but Africa is really home now for all of them."

Lillian watched Adana sip her tea and listened to

her granddaughter describe what she knew to be her loneliness.

"Amara is in Nairobi, thoroughly involved in rearing her twin sons and keeping her hand in her consulting business. Cassandra is in Addis Ababa rearing one son and"—she smiled—"she and Ras are trying daily to create a brother or sister for Kebran. Her design business has really flourished globally since she and Ras are now combining their talents on a number of projects."

Lillian added a lemon slice to her tea and continued to listen. Adana went on with a flourish of her hand. "And then we have Ibra and Afiya traveling the world buying and brokering art while rearing that little woman they produced." Adana's eyes lifted and a smile went from ear to ear as she gushed about her niece. "Mimi, you have to admit it—isn't she the prettiest little girl you've ever seen?"

Lillian added more sugar to her tea and smiled. "She is beautiful. She is the best of both her parents." She touched a corner of her mouth with her linen napkin and joked, "It sounds as if you miss your niece more than you miss her mother."

Adana's laughter had a trace of sadness. "From the day she was born, I've had a special connection to Miss Fara Diop, and I do wish I could pop in on her every day. And I miss seeing my nephews too. They are all growing so fast, and they're all so bright and full of life. Sometimes I feel as though I'll never catch up. We have our gatherings but—"

Adana's grandmother stopped her midsentence and completed the thought. "It's just not the same."

The trace of a smile on Adana's lips did not reach her eyes as she spoke. "I'm sorry, Mimi, I didn't come over here to bore you with my own personal pity party."

She placed more sugar in her porcelain teacup and gently stirred.

"It's all right, Adana. I understand missing those you love."

An imperceptible mist covered Lillian Chatfield's eyes as it often did when she thought of her beloved deceased husband. Daniel Joseph Chatfield had been her world. Lillian served herself one of the small delicate teacakes Mrs. Battle had baked, placed it on a small pristine white china plate, looked at Adana and inquired, "How is the new case going? It's being written about in all of the papers."

As Adana started to answer her grandmother's question, it struck her how beautifully Mimi was aging. Lillian was striking, with a shock of perfectly coiffed silver hair placed in a French roll, with wispy bangs covering her forehead. It was a style she had worn for as long as Adana could remember. She was dressed in a teal-colored spring dress. The collarless neckline was enhanced by the single strand of pearls she wore almost daily with matching earrings. Her honey-colored skin glowed, free from the creases of time.

Adana came out of her reverie saying, "We're going to win this one, Mimi."

Lillian took a sip of the fragrant tea, swallowed and asked, "Why are you so sure?"

Adana lifted a pastry from one of the elegant serving dishes. "I'm sure because, one, my client is innocent and, two and most importantly, I know we can prove it."

Adana took a bite of a morsel that melted in her mouth. She savored it and asked jokingly, "Did Ms. Alma put all of the sugar and butter in the house in these pastries? These are sinful."

Lillian took a bite and smiled, allowing the rich,

buttery concoction to melt in her mouth. "Alma has perfected baking to an art form."

"That she has," was Adana's satisfied response as she took another sip of warm tea. Feeling a sudden sense of urgency, Adana placed her cup and saucer on the nearby serving tray and stood. "Mimi, I need to run back to court. This case has me a bit anxious even though I know we'll win. I want to get in there again and steady myself before the judge walks in from his chambers." Adana distractedly fingered the pearls lying coolly around her neck. "I'm taking the lead on this one, and it has to be right."

Still seated and holding her teacup on her saucer while listening to her granddaughter, Lillian Chatfield's studied response was, "I'm surprised at the level of your concern, Adana. That's not like you. Is there something different about this case?"

Adana took a calming breath and walked quietly over to a picture window that held a view of her grandmother's carefully cultivated English garden. "Mimi, have you ever made a mistake that trailed you like a bad dream?"

Lillian placed her teacup and saucer on the serving cart and quietly folded her hands in her lap. Lillian's gaze held a look that Adana could not read as she said, "Sweetheart, there are probably few adults living who have not made mistakes that haunt them." Lillian smiled and asked tentatively, "Do you have a particular mistake in mind?"

"Jeffery Scott is lead counsel for the other side in this case, which means that I will have to fight hard every day that I am in that courtroom not to put Jeffery on trial for fraudulent activity in his impersonation of a human being."

Lillian uttered a soft, deep laugh that brought a smile to Adana's face. "Sweetheart, I have no doubt that by the

time you are through with Jeffery, he won't know what
hit him. You have faced much tougher opponents and
won. Besides, you know all of Jeffery's weaknesses. You
know all of the buttons to push to make him revert back
to being a first-year law student."

A smiling Adana listened to her grandmother with a
mixture of surprise and admiration. "Mimi, until this
moment, I didn't realize you had a devious bone in your
body."

"Some might call it devious. I call it self-preservation."

The two women shared a comfortable laugh at Jeffery
Scott's expense, after which Adana kissed her grandmother good-bye, said her good-byes to Mrs. Battle and
headed back to court.

Chapter 3

Nairobi, Kenya

Kamau found himself rambling through a house that felt much too large. It was a house that was no longer a home. It had been built for a family. The expectation had been that he and Yasmin would rear their children there. Kamau knew he had to move. Where the house had once held laughter and heated debates, it now held haunting memories and flashes of grief. It was closing in on him.

Since Yasmin had been chosen as his wife by his parents, they had learned to love each other. It had been a quiet, comfortable love. They had shared common goals and a love of practicing law. Their work together connected them emotionally and intellectually. For the two of them, that had been enough. Yasmin had been a strong, independent woman, and though Kamau had admired her strength and independence, he knew that in the end, it had been her stubbornness and her willful disregard for caution that had caused her death. He missed her. In six years of marriage, they had developed a rhythm, and now he was out of sync. Kamau had to hold in the raw emotions of rage and sadness he felt as he walked into the master suite of his desolate home to shower and change in order to be on time for the celebration of his mother's birthday.

Driving the short distance to his parents' home, Kamau was oblivious to the magnificent terrain, the profusion of flora and fauna and the peace that reigned in the countryside. The peace and tranquility that floated outside of him was in direct contradiction to the battle that was raging internally. Kamau used the drive to focus on the celebration for his mother and to calm his spirit so that his family would not be exposed to his pain. As he drove, he willed himself into a place of peace and calm. He knew that was the gift his mother wanted, and it was a state of being he wanted to find again permanently.

Because Kamau's mind was otherwise engaged, the drive to his childhood home seemed shorter than usual. Before he knew it, he was easing his Bentley into the circular driveway and parking it next to the sleek automobiles of his brothers—Keino, Kaleb and Aman—and a host of other relatives and friends. He knew they were all wondering silently if he would make an appearance. Family gatherings and late, lonely nights were, after all, the hardest times for him. They should have known, though, that regardless of circumstances, he would never miss an opportunity to celebrate his mother and her time on earth. After parking the car, Kamau opened the driver's door, placed one carefully shined black leather lace-up shoe on the paved driveway, took a deep breath and set an expression on his face that was as close as he could come to a smile. Kamau stepped from the car, lightly eased his shoulders back and walked with his spine erect to the front door of his parents' home. The door was opened, and Kamau entered to a throng of Mazruis and joyous guests.

It was early evening, and the Mazrui clan, along with the Selassies and other guests, had gathered to celebrate Adina Mazrui's sixtieth year. The room was swirling with activity. Ethiopian melodies, the music of Adina Mazrui's homeland, played softly in the background. Aromas of delicacies from around the world filled the air. The aromas were as intoxicating to the nostrils of the guests assembled as the laughter and the welcomed conversations were to their ears.

Adina Mazrui was the first to see Kamau as he moved into the room, walking to his own rhythm. Each of her sons made her feel such an overwhelming sense of pride. It occurred to her in that moment that Kamau had been aptly named, for his name meant "quiet warrior." When his eyes locked with his mother's, his full, sensuous lips, framed by a meticulously groomed mustache, lifted in a small smile that softened his square—often clenched—jaw. Adina Mazrui stretched out her arms, reaching to embrace her son, and noticed instantly that the smile on his lips had not reached his eyes. She embraced her son and whispered, "Kamau, I am so happy that you are here."

"Mother, I would not have missed this celebration."

Kamau kissed his mother gently on her taut, smooth cheek. Just as he ended the kiss, he felt a tap on his back. His brother Kaleb, a pilot who was also the family comedian, announced in pure comedic style, loudly enough for everyone to hear, "That's my mother—you are not allowed to touch her. You know she loves me best. Besides, I have it on good authority that you were found on our doorstep and our parents took pity on you. So don't get too familiar with my mother."

The family and friends listening could not contain their laughter. Kamau responded, laughing, "Kaleb, our parents should never have let you come home from boarding school."

Keino yelled out, "Kamau, you're right. I tried to tell them, but for whatever reason, they wanted him."

Aman added, "He certainly was a thorn in my side. To this day I'm psychologically scarred because of the reprimands I had to endure because of Kaleb."

Now the room was filled with gales of laughter. Kaleb had led the way, and his brothers, following his lead, had made what could have been an awkward moment light and easy for Kamau. Kamau was embraced by each of his brothers and his father, and then he was at ease to continue around the room to speak to and embrace family members he had not seen in far too many months. Kamau chatted with the children of Kaleb and Aman and with Ras and Cassandra's son, Kebran. He held and played with Keino and Amara's twins and found he could now actually engage young Mr. Kebran Selassie in conversation. It pleased him that Ras and Cassandra were having such success rearing Kebran. He thought of how difficult it had been serving as general counsel to Ras and having to fight him daily in order to get the job done. He was pleased to see that it had all been worth the challenges initially presented.

As Kamau found his way to the heavily laden hors d'oeuvre table, he heard a familiar voice behind him ask, "Okay, man, so how are you these days?" Kamau turned to find Ras, the first cousin he loved like one of his brothers and with whom he had fought constantly since they were children.

"Ras, truthfully? I am as well as can be expected. How would you be if you lost Cassandra?"

Ras was deeply touched by the mere contemplation of

the idea. His solemn answer was, "My mind and my heart cannot handle the thought."

"Exactly. That is exactly how I am these days, trying to get my heart and my mind to handle the thought."

Ras, now with a note of deep understanding in his voice, responded, "If you ever need anything, you know where to find me."

The two men looked directly at each other as Kamau said, "I appreciate the offer."

Kamau and Ras both felt a weight lift that allowed them to continue making small talk about business, sports and politics as they helped themselves to hors d'oeuvres. As the evening progressed, toasts were made to Adina Mazrui by her husband, Garsen, her sons and a host of relatives and friends. A libation was poured to the ancestors, and a lavish sit-down meal of various East African and European dishes was served. Laughter rang throughout the house. Adina Mazrui was basking in the love of her friends and family while her adoring husband and sons periodically looked her way to make sure that she was enjoying the evening. They had no reason to be concerned. Adina Mazrui could not have been happier.

At the end of the evening, as Kamau was saying his good-byes, he looked for his parents and found them in the family library exchanging parting embraces with General Selassie and his wife, Amara, who had flown in from Addis Ababa, Ethiopia. The Selassies were Ras's parents, and Amara Selassie was Adina Mazrui's sister. Kamau entered the room just in time to exchange a farewell embrace with his aunt and uncle.

When the Selassies left the room, Adina Mazrui said to her son, "Kamau, come and sit a moment with us."

Kamau took a chair, positioned directly in front of the sofa on which his parents sat. As Judge Mazrui gazed at his son with a look that held tenderness and compassion, he said, "My son, having you here tonight was good. The evening would have been incomplete without you."

Kamau stroked his mustache and smiled halfheartedly. "I would not have missed a celebration for my mother under any circumstances."

Adina Mazrui's soft eyes probed her son. "Kamau, how are you? Is your heart healing? I feel I don't see enough of you to judge or to help, to be a source of comfort."

Kamau's eyes narrowed as they sometimes did when he was deep in thought. "I am often asked these days how I am." He lifted his hands into the air. "What can I say? I lost my wife—how should I be? Is my heart healing? Mother, that is a question I cannot answer, because it implies that one day it will be healed. I am not sure that one ever completely heals from the death of a loved one. I think, though, the time will come when I will learn to accept it and live a normal life in spite of the tragedy." He took a deep breath. "In the meantime, I am convinced I need to make some changes."

It was Garsen Mazrui's turn to question his son. "Do you know what these changes are that you want to make?"

"I am clear about two of them, and I need to discuss both with the two of you."

With a gentle command, Judge Mazrui stated, "Go ahead, we are listening."

Kamau crossed his legs and settled comfortably back into his chair. "I am making plans to cut back at work. For the next two months, I need time to reflect and to re-organize my life. I also need to move, and in order to give myself time to relocate, I would like permission to use the family vacation compound until I find a place.

I need a change that will help me to see my future more clearly."

Adina Mazrui gently squeezed her husband's hand as he spoke for both of them.

"Of course, son, you may have both of those things and anything else you can think of that will make this transition easier for you."

Feeling as though a burden had been lifted, Kamau said, "I should have done this sooner, but I thought work would remedy my loneliness and that time would heal all wounds." He laughed cynically. "Well, for me, neither of those things has been true."

For the first time in months, he felt as though his direction was clear. He had stated aloud what had been in his head for weeks. With a plan for the revamping of his personal life, Kamau left his parents' home with his spirit a little lighter.

In another part of the exclusive suburban enclave in which the Mazruis lived, Keino and Amara Mazrui were lying in bed, recapping the evening's activities. Keino cradled his wife and whispered in her ear, "You looked beautiful tonight, my sweet."

Amara purred her thank-you and snuggled closer. Her husband's wispy breath in her ear never failed to arouse her. She could feel the sensual heat from his body clothed only in his pajama bottoms, rubbing against her long, silk, spaghetti-strapped gown. The relaxed, gentle tones in which Amara spoke soothed her husband's spirit.

"Your mother really looked happy tonight, and she was so excited to see Aunt Amara." She took a long, slow breath. "I don't think it was a surprise, though, do you?" Amara moved slightly, her limbs stroking the long length of her beloved husband. She felt his heated arousal as he answered while raining kisses down her back.

"No, she wasn't surprised."

Amara turned to face Keino, then wrapped her arms around his neck, touched his lips gently with hers and asked with desire permeating every syllable, "Keino, how are we going to help Kamau get through this grieving period?"

Keino, slightly preoccupied, stroked his wife's face. "My love, I wish I had an answer. We will keep reaching out until one day he will tell us what to do. Until then, our hands are tied."

Keino started slowly kissing Amara's lips. She answered each touch with a slow, seductive movement of her body while placing feathery strokes with her slender hands from his dark handsome face down to his fingertips. Keino shuddered and took the kisses deeper. Amara whimpered, eased her head back on the soft down-filled pillows and freed her arms from the thin straps holding her silk nightgown, leaving uncovered breasts aching to be touched. Keino responded to her need with tenderness, skill and passion. He had laid claim to every inch of his wife's body countless times. Every encounter surpassed the one before. The years had deepened their connection. He wanted her as much as he ever had, maybe more. As he nipped lightly the tender peaks that had lovingly nursed his children and brought him maddening pleasure, Keino whispered, "Amara, I love you. Do you know that I love you?"

Her tortured response was, "Yes, Keino, yes, yes!" With each intoxicating whirl of sensation, she allowed herself to succumb to delicious tremors, leaving her melting with every stroke of his magical erotic touch and ready for all the love he had to give. Keino slowly removed the rest of her gown, leaving a trail of kisses everywhere the fabric had touched. Then he slipped out of his pajama bottoms, leaving himself fully ready to join his wife on their blissful journey. With deep kisses, deep thrusts and hammering hearts, they loved until sleep became their refuge.

Chapter 4

Virginia, USA

Adana Terrell entered Judge Fullwood's chambers with all of the flair and confidence of an experienced litigator. She was exactly on time for the meeting, but Jeffery Scott was already sitting in the judge's office when she arrived. Adana placed her briefcase on the floor beside a leather chair with nail-head trim that was next to Jeffery in front of the judge's desk. She sat down and crossed her legs, leaving Jeffery a view of two long, shapely appendages accentuated by three-inch stilettos. Adana's fire-engine-red, custom-designed Carolina Herrera suit hinted at her curvaceous figure without revealing its secrets. The fiery red made her bronze skin glow. The suit was accessorized with a delicate ruby pendant that hung from her neck on a gold, exquisitely linked chain. Her earrings matched the pendant. Adana sat looking straight ahead, ignoring Jeffery Scott and waiting for the judge to enter his chambers. Jeffery sat mesmerized by the woman he still loved. Had Adana cared to look, she would have seen his warm brown eyes staring seductively.

He spoke in a low, husky tone. "Good morning, Adana. You're looking as lovely as ever."

An exasperated Adana released a long, audible breath, turned her head slightly and studied him. Just as Jeffery was about to react to Adana's cold response, a fully robed Judge Fullwood made a loud entrance.

"Good morning, Counselors."

"Good morning," Adana and Jeffery answered in unison.

"All right, Counselors, after what could have been a legal meltdown in my courtroom yesterday, I felt it necessary to meet with you both in chambers so that I might reiterate some of the ground rules of etiquette in my courtroom. Let me start by saying, Mr. Scott, that your courtroom blunders were unbecoming of an officer of the court. You appeared to be more concerned with Ms. Terrell's comportment than you were the arraignment. Whatever buttons she's pushing, you had better find a proper response. I refuse to sit in my courtroom and watch the law being improperly practiced."

Adana sat with a barely concealed smirk on her face as Judge Fullwood reprimanded Jeffery for slipups she knew she had caused. She had been fighting dirty the day before, sending veiled signals to Jeffery that only the two of them could recognize, a look, a way of moving, a strategic placement of a hand on a hip. All gestures that seemed perfectly ordinary to any onlooker but that held special meaning to Jeffery Scott. After all, they had devised those signals together, ways of communicating with each other in the courtroom so that no one else would know. Since Adana had repeatedly refused to speak to him, Jeffery came unglued when he recognized those signals in court. He became as confused and befuddled as a courtroom novice. So focused was he on Adana's sensual gestures that Jeffery neglected the rudimentary procedures expected in the defense of his client. He made a complete fool of himself for all the world to see, leaving Adana as cool as the proverbial cucumber. Having had an evening to recover, Jeffery was once again the consummate professional.

He responded to Judge Fullwood. "Your Honor, I admit to being a bit distracted. I assure you it won't happen again."

"See that it doesn't," was Judge Fullwood's quick response. "Now, Ms. Terrell, I understand that you would like to request a change of venue for this trial."

"Yes, Your Honor."

Adana couldn't finish her statement before Jeffery forcefully interrupted. "Judge Fullwood, Ms. Terrell has no grounds for a change of venue. A change of venue would imply that every juror in the pool from which we select has in some way been prejudiced against her client. That simply is not the case."

Adana's steady voice eased into the discussion. "Judge, if I may state my case more clearly."

"Have at it, Ms. Terrell."

"My client is a female Kenyan national who happens to be married to a Libyan. She has been accused of using her insurance brokerage firm to help her husband finance arms deals. First of all, her husband has not been convicted in a court of law, but he has already been tried in the press and convicted—hence my client will be seen as guilty by association. Secondly, both my client and her husband are Muslim. In this political climate and with a view of the White House evident from the steps of this courthouse, her chances of receiving a fair trial are jeopardized."

Judge Fullwood leaned back in his chair, stroking his

chin while silently considering Adana's rebuttal. "Ms. Terrell, though I tend to agree with your assessment of the situation, I am not sure a change of venue is the answer. I am going to deny the request for a change of venue and rely on your skills as a first-rate litigator to select those among our jury pool who will be willing and able to see that your client gets a fair trial."

Though disappointed, Adana offered a confident, "Thank you, Your Honor." While Jeffery and the judge finished their business, she rose from her seat, retrieved her briefcase, left the judge's chambers and started contemplating her new strategy. She was lost in thought, walking as if on autopilot, heading to her car, when she felt his presence. He had an apologetic smile on his lips that turned into an almost irresistible grin. Her frustration was unmistakable, and the lingering hurt she felt when she thought of her past relationship with the man standing there looking at her spilled over in her voice as she said with deadly calm, "Jeffery, I really want you to leave me alone. If there is anyone on earth I don't want to see, hear or speak to right now, it is you."

"Adana, I'm sorry things didn't go your way in there, but you owe me for yesterday. You caused me to make a complete fool of myself. Adana, look." He touched her arm and smiled. They were trapped, looking directly into each other's eyes. Jeffery softly took Adana's hand. She quickly removed it from his grasp.

"Adana, you need to know that I will always love you."

"Jeffery," she said slowly and deliberately, as though he were a child, "I know you have a hard time remembering things." Her tone rose slightly. "After the entire time we were dating, you didn't remember that you had a wife in another state." Adana took a breath and continued making her words as precise and as clipped as she could make them. "A living, breathing wife, Jeffery. A woman you had pledged your life to. I want you to remember to leave me alone."

Jeffery set his briefcase down on the marble floor of the corridor in which they stood and began gesturing with his hands as he spoke. "Adana, you would never let me explain that Celeste and I were separated. The fact that we were still legally married was merely a technicality."

Adana was miffed at herself for even talking to the man who had deceived her. He made her acutely aware of how vulnerable she could be with him. She almost shouted, "Jeffery, just stop. You were still sharing a house together for God's sake. The home I thought was yours was a second residence, your play den for unsuspecting women like me who were too busy to pay attention."

Jeffery lowered his voice and his eyes. "Adana, you have the wrong idea about me. You would never let me explain that Celeste and I had a platonic relationship. There was nothing happening between us anymore. There hadn't been for months. I swear to you it was purely platonic."

Adana laughed, releasing any number of the emotions Jeffery had stirred in her. Her laughter slowed and she took a long, cleansing breath before responding to her ex-lover. "Jeffery Hamilton Scott, the word *pure* or any derivative thereof should not be in your vocabulary."

Smiling in a way that lit up his eyes, causing them to smolder with lingering memories of Adana, Jeffery responded, "Adana, you always were a handful, but whenever you use my full name, I know I have a chance."

He removed her briefcase from her hand, set it down, took both of her hands in his, held them and pleaded longingly, "Adana, please, just let me take you out to dinner tonight so that we can really clear the air." He gently stroked her shoulder. "You never allowed us that opportunity. You found out about Celeste and headed for the hills. I got no chance to plead my case. You owe me that."

Adana, recovering from a momentary loss of focus, removed her hands from the warmth of Jeffery's touch, stepped back, picked up her briefcase and stated as calmly as she could, "I owe you nothing, Mr. Scott."

Jeffery answered in a low, smooth voice filled with sensuality, "I'm in trouble again. I've been reduced to Mr. Scott."

As he searched her keenly observant eyes, he thought he saw a hint of warmth. Adana hesitated for a moment before saying, "If I go to dinner with you, will you promise to leave me alone and confine our conversations to the reason why you felt the need to deceive me?"

Almost too quickly, Jeffery answered, "You've got a deal. I'll pick you up at seven."

"No, you won't, Jeffery! This is not a date. We are bringing closure to a *pitiful* situation. Just tell me where to meet you."

The name of what had been their favorite restaurant rolled off his tongue as smoothly as silk. "Ernie's."

Adana shook her head and countered, "Pick another place."

Jeffery replied with a boyish pout, "I like Ernie's."

Adana replied pensively, "I do, too, but I think that's getting a little too familiar."

Jeffery touched her soft, warm face ever so gently. "So you do still have good memories of our time together?"

Holding back laughter, Adana responded, "Don't press your luck, Jeffery. That one good memory is long gone."

Jeffery threw his head back, releasing a burst of sultry laughter that rippled through him. As Adana started to leave, he said, "St. Romain at seven."

Adana nodded in the affirmative and walked away. Jeffery stood taking in every curve until she disappeared.

Adana eased behind the wheel of her sporty Mercedes-Benz, turned on a Nancy Wilson CD and let the sultry songstress glide her all the way home. As the familiar strains of Nancy's classic "Guess Who I Saw Today" floated through the speakers, Adana's mind drifted to Jeffery. Why on earth had she agreed to meet him, and why for dinner? She knew she took some perverse pleasure in seeing him beg. Seeing him grovel gave her some modicum of satisfaction. The question was, why did it give her satisfaction? If there were no feelings left, what difference did it make? Pushing aside all well-reasoned arguments, Adana decided that she just needed to hear whatever rationale Jeffery was going to concoct. It had taken so long to get over him. The question was, had she really been successful? Time would tell.

Adana pulled up to her two-car garage, pressed a remote that gently lifted the large door and drove into the garage, closing the door behind her. Turning off the engine and quieting the melodic tones of her favorite songstress, Adana released a breath she was unaware she was holding, got out of the car and walked into her home.

All of the Terrell women expressed themselves in their homes. Adana was not an exception. Anyone observant enough to recognize it would have discerned that the Adana Terrell presented in her home was very different from the staid, controlled picture she presented as the youngest member of Wilkes, Willis, Burkes, and Terrell. In her home, Adana expressed her love of family, tradition and beauty. It was also the one place her love of being a woman was unabashedly displayed. Elegantly framed portraits of both sets of grandparents hung in her study amid flawlessly installed crown molding and chair rails. Above an elaborate fireplace mantel in the living room hung an oil portrait of her parents, posed with Adana and her sisters when they were children. Throughout her home, strategically placed in harmonious arrangements, were music boxes collected from her travels around the world. Several were antiques. One was especially dear to her because it had been a gift from her sister Amara. The fabrics on sofas, chairs, settees and windows were soft, warm and luxurious. Silks, satins and brocades were in tasteful abundance. Contemporary African and African American art hung throughout her home, most purchased from her sister Afiya's gallery.

Adana continued into her home, stopped in the foyer and picked up mail from the day before that was still lying on the marble-topped commode where it had been placed. She removed an intricately carved bronze letter opener and began methodically opening piece after piece of unsolicited junk mail, which was promptly discarded in a nearby red-lacquered hand-painted wastebasket.

The silence in the house felt good. Adana enjoyed her solitude, understanding clearly the difference between self-imposed solitude and waves of periodic loneliness. She walked upstairs to the master suite and began to indulge in what had become her daily ritual. She removed every piece of clothing that she wore, loving the feel of her bare body. When she was completely nude, she slipped on a silk robe and walked through her dressing area, deciding what to wear to dinner with Jeffery. Adana smiled, thinking that whatever she wore would have Mr. Scott salivating. The ringing telephone snapped her back to reality. Adana retrieved the cordless from its cradle and read her sister Cassandra's number on the caller ID. Adana pushed the TALK button, walked to her chaise lounge, made herself comfortable and said, "Hi, sis, how are things in Addis?"

Adana looked at the jeweled-faced clock on the table beside her, did some quick calculations and before Cassandra could answer, Adana asked hurriedly, "Cassandra, is everything okay? You're up really late."

Adana could hear a soft sniffle as Cassandra said, "I wish I could say everything is fine but it's not."

Adana threw an angora cover over her feet and asked slowly and softly, "What's wrong, Cassandra? Are Ras and Kebran all right?"

Cassandra's voice broke. "Everybody is fine but I am not fine. I'm just so sad. I can't stop crying."

"Why, Cassandra? Why?"

Cassandra started her labored response. "I just went to the doctor again today, and after what seemed like the hundredth test, they still can't find anything wrong, but I still can't get pregnant."

Cassandra sobbed uncontrollably while Adana worked to console her. "Cassandra, I had no idea you were going through this. I wish you had said something sooner so all of us could have been there to support you."

Cassandra, talking through sobs, answered, "I didn't think it would come to this. I thought it would all work out if we just gave it enough time." Releasing another torrent of tears, Cassandra almost screamed, "It's been a year and nothing has happened. I just don't know what to do or say. Ras has tried to be so understanding. He made sure he had the tests as well and he's fine. He keeps saying we're in this together and that it will happen in time."

Cassandra took a deep breath and asked with panic echoing in her voice, "But what if it doesn't? Adana, what if it doesn't happen?"

"Slow down, Cassandra. You're putting the cart before

the horse. First of all, you said the doctors can't find any problems with you or Ras, and second, a year really isn't a long time in the grand scheme of things. From everything I've read, it takes the body time to adjust after you go off the pill. You know that. You also know that the more you worry and stress yourself out, the more difficult it is to get pregnant."

"I know all of that, Adana, but I also know that there are women who get pregnant at the drop of a hat, stress or no stress. There have even been cases of women getting pregnant on the pill. I just want to conceive and give birth to Ras's baby. Is that too much to ask? Yes, we have Kebran, and I love him, but I didn't have the experience of giving birth to him."

"Cassandra, you know it's not too much to ask, and it will happen. I know it will." With a soft smile in her voice, Adana continued. "Sooner than you think, Kebran will have a little brother or sister."

With tears slowing, Cassandra responded, "I hope you're right, Adana." Cassandra sighed, feeling better after having vented to one of her sisters.

Adana asked, "By the way, where are Ras and Kebran while you're up doing your late-night prowling?"

Cassandra answered with soft laughter. "You know this house is so big I could ramble around all night and no one would ever hear me. Ras and Kebran are sleeping. I came down to Ras's study to call you. That way I have no fear of awakening either of them. Thanks, Adana. I do feel better. I guess I just needed to rant and rave." Cassandra shifted the focus of the conversation to her sister. "Are you in for the evening?"

Adana answered slowly, "Well, to tell you the truth, I'm on my way out in a couple of hours."

Pleasantly surprised and excited, Cassandra responded, "Adana, don't tell me you have a date."

"I won't tell you that because it is not a date."

Slightly disappointed, Cassandra said, "Oh, business, I should have known."

"Well, not exactly business."

"Adana, it's not like you to be so indirect, so mysterious. Come on, sis, what are you hiding? If it's not a date and it's not business, what is it?"

Adana hesitated and then spoke. "When I tell you, I don't want to hear any laughter no matter how ridiculous it sounds."

Now Cassandra's curiosity was really piqued. "Okay, I'm listening."

Adana spoke rapidly, hoping on some level that if she said it quickly, it wouldn't sound so wrong. "Well, I'm having dinner with Jeffery."

Cassandra didn't think she had heard correctly. "Jeffery? Did you say Jeffery? Jeffery who?"

"You know Jeffery who—Jeffery Scott, that's who."

"Adana, I'm speechless, and laughter is the last thing that comes to mind." The barrage of questions came next. "What brought this on? How long has this been going on? Are you two back together?"

"No, no, nothing like that. We are opposing counsels on my latest case, and in true Jeffery form, he has been hounding me since the case began, and no amount of rude behavior on my part seems to drive him away. He says he wants to clear the air. He wants to explain. So I decided to let him grovel. I need to be entertained tonight."

A concerned Cassandra said, "Be careful that the price you pay for your entertainment isn't too high."

"I can take care of myself."

Now it was Cassandra's turn to be the loving, consoling sister. "What I know, Adana, is that you can take care of everyone else. I also know that you are top-notch at taking care of your material needs, no question, but we all worry about who's caring for your emotional needs, your emotional life. You seem to forget, Adana, that there are tender loving places in you that long to be touched and held."

Adana responded quietly, "I don't forget."

"I said you seem to forget. And no matter how much you insist to the contrary, I know you want what we all want—a loving partner in your life who makes you want to sing, dance and smile at just the thought of him. I'm not fooled, Adana, I know you and I want you to be careful."

With tears in her eyes but bravado in her voice, Adana answered, "I hope you know that I am going to be fine and so will you, Cassandra. Love you—bye."

Cassandra knew when her sister had heard all she could take, so she answered, "Bye, Adana, love you too."

Adana placed the telephone gently into its cradle, got up from the chaise and made her way into her spacious bathroom to wash away melancholy thoughts and get ready to meet Jeffery.

Approximately two hours later, with Cassandra's words still ringing in her ears, Adana pulled into the valet parking section of the St. Romain Restaurant. Her car was attended to with the usual fanfare afforded the patrons of an upscale venue. Adana entered the romantically lit restaurant wearing an off-the-shoulder black dress that skimmed over her curvaceous frame, stopping at a length designed to show her long, slender, shapely legs to their best advantage. The only pieces of jewelry she wore were diamond earrings and a matching diamond bracelet. With a soft piano being played in the background, Jeffery sat at a table waiting. He had instructed the waiter to keep at the ready a bottle of vintage champagne. He was in the mood for a celebration—after all, Adana had consented to see him socially. Jeffery considered that a sign of progress. Adana had gone from outright hostility to sharing a meal. Yes, he thought to himself, that was progress.

Jeffery was as dapper as ever in an impeccably tailored, lightly pinstriped charcoal suit, complemented by a dark, pure silk tie speckled with minuscule white geometric patterns matching the white linen handkerchief in his breast pocket. He sat with his legs crossed, revealing expensive black leather slip-on shoes. When the maître d' showed Adana to the table, she and Jeffery were both flooded by memories of days gone by when times were different and the sights, sounds and aromas being experienced would have signaled an evening of implied promises and closely guarded dreams. Jeffery stood while one of the attending waitstaff pulled out Adana's chair.

"Good evening, beautiful," Jeffery greeted her.

Calming herself from the unexpected wave of emotions she was experiencing, Adana replied softly, "Hello, Jeffery."

As soon as they were seated, Jeffery signaled the waiter for the champagne. He then reached over and lightly touched Adana's hand. "Thank you, Adana, for coming tonight. We need this time for conversation. I believe we can fix whatever damage has been done. Sweetheart, we can fix this. We need to fix whatever is keeping us apart."

As Jeffery's plea ended, a waiter walked to the table and began to pour the champagne. Adana and Jeffery sat looking at each other, lost in their own thoughts. The waiter left the table, Jeffery picked up his glass and Adana followed his lead as he toasted, "To us."

Adana lifted her glass slightly, as did Jeffery. Each took a slow sip of the exquisitely mellow liquid. As the effervescent bubbles eased down her throat, Adana's mood shifted. Something was not right. Something was wrong, out of sync. The setting was beautiful, she was dressed to the nines and Jeffery was as fine as he had always been, but something was wrong. As they sat there surrounded by all of the beauty and the ambience, Adana felt more lonely than she had ever felt.

She placed her glass on the table and smiled slowly. "Jeffery, I'm going to go now. Although this is all very beautiful, and I am sure there is a lot we could both say, I know it doesn't matter anymore. You are the wrong man, we are in the wrong place at the wrong time. It is too late, Jeffery. Whatever was is a distant memory, and the essence of what we have left is memories. Nothing more. Just memories. And to be quite honest, most of my memories concerning you aren't good. Oh, there were a few lovely meals, a few moments of lust disguised by whatever we wanted to call it, but when the fog cleared and we looked at what we had, we had nothing, Jeffery, nothing to build a life on. I want a meaningful partnership—maybe not a marriage but at least a relationship with someone I can trust to tell me the truth. You're not the one. You're not the one."

A stunned Jeffery Scott sat and watched as Adana left the table. He finished his glass of champagne, sat back in his chair and wondered what his next move would be.

Chapter 5

Nairobi, Kenya

Perspiration ran in rivulets down Kamau's muscular body as he dared the tiny racquetball to hit the floor of the Mazrui vacation compound racquetball court. His feet pounded the floor as he glided quickly at just the right moment to slam the ball mercilessly into the backboard. The pristine white tennis shorts and polo shirt he wore were in stark contrast to his burnished ebony skin. The dripping perspiration illuminated cinnamon highlights in his lustrous appendages. The rippling muscles in his arms and legs did his bidding as he powerfully and masterfully, with unrelenting velocity, took out his lingering anger, rage and sadness on a racquetball.

The move to the Mazrui family vacation compound had been a good decision. He felt free from constant reminders of Yasmin, and he had time to clear his head without the distractions of pitying and prying eyes. Kamau had taken up residence in the main house. There were several homes on the property—enough lodging for the entire Mazrui clan if the need or desire ever arose. The setting was breathtaking. It had been dubbed the "Mazrui Paradise." Almost every imaginable species of bird and variety of flora and fauna could be found there. The sounds of the birds, the views of green, rolling hills, the profusion of vividly colored flowers and tall, full majestic trees gave Kamau a sense of tranquility he could find nowhere else. All of his young life, he had taken for granted the beauty and the peace of the place. He could not have known it would come to be his refuge.

When Kamau had finished his conquest on the racquetball court, he headed for the shower. He discarded his damp clothing and walked his bare body into a large enclosed glass shower. After adjusting the water temperature to a heat that only he could tolerate, he sat on a custom-designed marble bench that faced the downpour of water emanating from a number of different shower nozzles. He sat with his legs wide apart, his arched feet flat on the warm marble beneath him with his head dropped toward the floor. With eyes closed, he allowed the water to pound on his strong neck, powerful shoulders and athletically sculpted back. Kamau lathered his body with a cool, lightly scented body wash and laid his head back. He then stood and allowed the cascade of water to flow over pectoral and abdominal muscles, over rippled thigh and calf muscles, landing on the shower floor, changing the water into streaks of teal and sky blue, picking up the hues of the carefully placed marble.

When the water had massaged his tense body into a more relaxed state, Kamau turned off the torrent, dried himself hurriedly, put on a lightweight linen robe, tied it at the waist, slipped into his favorite supple leather house shoes and found his way into the expansive restaurant-sized kitchen to indulge in one of his favorite pastimes—the preparation of food. Kamau had always said had he not chosen to practice international law, he would have been a chef in a major venue somewhere in the world where his love of gourmet food preparation and presentation would have been greatly appreciated. He had specifically asked that the compound house staff be given a vacation while he occupied the premises. Kamau knew he needed the time to immerse himself in a few of the activities that brought him satisfaction— preparing food engaged all of his senses, and for a time his thoughts were suspended in a place where loss of any kind was a distant memory.

As Kamau chopped, arranged, basted, boiled and baked, preparing more food than he could consume in one meal, the distant ringing of the telephone brought him back to the present space and time. Unaware of who was calling, Kamau answered with a slight bit of annoyance. "Hello."

Hearing the trace of annoyance in Kamau's voice, Adina Mazrui said tentatively, "Son, I'm sorry to disturb you."

A contrite Kamau answered, "Forgive my tone, Mother. I was preoccupied here in the kitchen." Kamau's voice became a bit lighter. "I'm preparing what I hope will be a meal fit for a king." He smiled, a rare occurrence for Kamau.

"Son, I was really just calling to see how you are doing. Are you managing well without the house staff?"

"Yes, Mother." His words became more distant as if in faraway thought while speaking. "I have arranged for cleaning once a week, but I can handle my daily needs. I have a Realtor coming tomorrow to place my house on the market and to help me locate a new residence. Keino says the guy is really good at what he does. Supposedly he knows the market well and can sell anything, so perhaps this can all be over fairly soon." Kamau hesitated. "At least the resolution of my housing dilemma will be completed."

"Well, darling, that is progress. I hope it goes well. I know you also want to spend the next few weeks in as much solitude as you can, but remember, my son, you will always have a family that loves you, and our arms are always open to hold you."

Kamau was touched deeply by his mother's expression of love and caring, and he hoped she understood his heartfelt, "Thank you, Mother."

"Good-bye, son."

The telephones were placed in their respective cradles almost simultaneously. Kamau resumed chopping, stirring, inhaling aromas and reveling in the textures around him. Adina Mazrui sat in her richly upholstered chair and wept for her son.

Chapter 6

Virginia, USA

Adana sat in the partners meeting of her firm. Being the youngest, the only female and the only person of African ancestry was not without its challenges. Making partner had been one hurdle, remaining in the loop had proven to be another major challenge. Though it was clear to everyone associated with Adana that she was bright, articulate and an expertly competent litigator, her decisions were far too often questioned when other partners were given carte blanche. She sometimes wondered if her six-figure salary was compensation enough for the aggravation of the constant battles she had to wage with what was supposed to be her team. She sat listening to Richard Wilkes, the founding partner, drone on about her pro bono work and how, though their pro bono efforts were supposed to assist the community at large, he didn't see why they could not help the community by doing more pro bono work for more prominent society members and while doing so, shed the spotlight on Wilkes, Willis, Burkes, and Terrell.

Adana refused to listen to another self-serving pitch. She interrupted with all the command of her courtroom persona. "Richard, pro bono publico is precisely what it says—for the public good. Everyone at this table is thoroughly familiar with that particular Latin phrase, and nowhere in the spirit of that phrase is the self-serving notion of embellishing one's own accomplishments or serving a faction of the community that doesn't need it implied. If I have missed something, please let me know. Until then, I will choose pro bono cases based on merit, not on whether they will bring positive press to Wilkes, Willis, Burkes, and Terrell."

Her remarks were greeted with silence. Finally, with a sarcastic quip, Richard Wilkes asked, "Is there any confusion here about where Adana stands on this issue?"

Richard Wilkes had pushed for Adana's inclusion into the firm as partner not only because of her skills as a litigator, but also because her ancestry would bring to the firm the needed publicity as a progressive, diverse, multidimensional entity. Richard had not bargained on Adana's insistence on being heard and on forging her own path, whether or not she left feathers ruffled in her wake. He had hoped that being a partner would temper her insistence upon always doing what she saw as the right thing. Richard Wilkes felt most often that right was highly overrated.

Hearing no response, he continued. "Since it appears there is no consensus to be reached here, let me just say this—pro bono work aside, for the sake of the firm, let us make every effort to continue to involve ourselves with the upper echelon of this city's society for the lion's share of our work. That's where the revenue exists to support our firm, and the reputation we have worked hard to earn requires that we maintain a certain level of participation with the movers and shakers of this community. Shall we table this subject for discussion at a later time?"

There were affirmative nods around the table, and Peter Burkes interjected, "Adana, excellent job thus far on the new case. I am certain that soon you will have to handle the press as they attempt to try this case in the media. It was a good move to try for a change of venue, and even though it wasn't granted, I believe our chances of winning are still good."

Adana replied, "I was disappointed to say the least about the judge's decision, but this team has fought tougher cases and won."

Richard Wilkes slapped both hands quickly on top of the mahogany conference table and said loudly, "That's the tenacious Adana Terrell we all know and love."

The smile on Adana's face was a mask for an emotion her partners could not read, and the partners' smiles had less to do with congratulatory expressions for Adana than for the visions of dollar signs and the possibility of fame dancing in their heads. They all left the conference room and returned to their respective offices. Adana walked past her administrative assistant, saying, "Kathy, please hold all of my calls for thirty minutes."

Kathy's answer was a quiet, professional, "Yes, Ms. Terrell."

Adana walked into her corner office, closed the door behind her and went over to the wall of windows that provided her an unobstructed view of the city skyline. She folded her arms and lightly stroked the elegantly constructed knit of the pearl gray suit that she wore. There she stood, surrounded by all of the trappings of the power she had longed for, worked hard for, feeling an uneasiness that she could not shake. Adana shook her head, hoping to clear it, and silently said to herself,

Pull yourself together, Adana. You have work to do. She removed her jacket, placed it on a nearby brass coat rack and walked to her leather chair. She sat down at the ornate antique desk, which had been a gift from her sister Cassandra, whose interior design firm had decorated Adana's office to perfection. Sitting still for a moment, fingering the three-stranded smoke-gray pearl necklace she wore, Adana allowed herself to breathe deeply for a few seconds before plowing through the mountain of paperwork on her desk, waiting for decisions to be rendered based on the seriousness of the matters they contained.

The piece that caught her eye first had been flagged as urgent by her assistant. Adana recognized the familiar form. She opened it and would have screamed if she had thought there was no chance of being heard. Jeffery Scott had entered a motion to the court to suppress the most important piece of evidence she had to substantiate her client's innocence. Adana was livid. This would mean another delay in bringing the case to trial and getting Jeffery out of her life. Adana slammed her fist on her desk, got up from her chair and paced, muttering under her breath words damning Jeffery Scott to hell. She walked, feeling the plush carpet beneath her cushioning the stilettoed path she walked. Adana walked until her anger subsided and her focus returned. She said aloud, "Why am I angry about this? Jeffery knows he can't win. This is a ploy to buy time. I won't let his sophomoric games rattle me."

She sat back in her chair, released a long breath, reached for the telephone and dialed her sister Afiya. It was early evening in Dakar, and she hoped she would catch Mrs. Afiya Diop at home. After several rings and a short conversation with the Diop resident houseman, Adana heard Afiya say playfully, "Ms. Adana Terrell, how are you? Are you still the finest litigator in the state of Virginia?"

"Hey, sis, I'm hanging in here. But on to more important matters. How is my niece?"

Afiya's face glowed as she eased into a peaceful, caring smile thinking of Adana's love for the rambunctious little girl she and Ibra had produced.

Laughing, Afiya said to Adana, "That little woman is keeping her parents busy. Especially her father. That little girl has Ibra Diop wrapped around her little fingers," she quipped, "and I mean all of them. You should see him hopping around here at her beck and call, and she can't even talk. I shudder to think what is going to happen when she tries to out-think him."

They both laughed at the thought of Ibra and his beloved daughter matching wits. Afiya's laughter became a smile in her voice as she asked, "Adana, did you call just to check on Fara?"

Adana quickly responded, "Well, that was the most important item on my agenda, but it is also time for our sister gathering, and since I am the designated coordinator, I thought I had better feel everyone out for next week. It's Amara's turn to host, so we'll be in Nairobi." Adana clicked her manicured nails on the top of the desk. "It seems I have a break in my schedule, so the timing is perfect."

"It's good for me. Ibra and I don't have any buying trips scheduled, and little Miss Diop will be fine with her daddy, because of course he will have all the help in the world. I'll be there—just forward the details."

"Oh, Afiya, that's great. Let me call those other two globe-trotting sisters of ours and work this out."

"See ya."

"Kiss my baby for me."

"Will do. Love you, Adana."

"Love you, too, Afiya."

Adana contacted their other two sisters, Cassandra and Amara, and all agreed that the following week they would descend upon Keino and Amara Mazrui's Nairobi residence and spend a few days relaxing and catching up as only close sisters can. Adana then stopped to call her parents. Not having spoken to them in a week, an infusion of the ever-present energy and wisdom of Drs. James and Ana Terrell was much needed.

Dr. Ana Terrell picked up the ringing telephone, happy that the caller ID revealed her eldest daughter's number. "Adana, how are you? I'm glad you called. You were just on my mind a moment ago. Your dad and I were just talking about your new case. We must have conjured you up." Ana laughed her lilting, pretty laugh.

"Hi, Mom." Adana relaxed into her mother's warm laughter. "I've been thinking of you and Dad for a few days now, but I've been working so hard I haven't had a real moment to spare. How are you two?"

"You know your dad and I are fine. James is as busy as ever with his professorship. He truly enjoys the mental gymnastics that he can engage in with his students. You know James would walk miles for a good debate."

Adana laughed, thinking that pitting herself against her father's analytical mind and winning debating tactics had more than prepared her for law school and the courtroom. Coming out of her reverie, she heard her mother continuing to say, "I have some very interesting clients this year. I thought I was growing weary of listening to problems I felt powerless to solve, and then like magic I get a group of people who show me that progress is possible."

"That's great, Mom." Adana's voice lowered. "Satisfaction is so necessary in one's chosen profession."

Listening between the lines as Ana always did when communicating with her children, she asked Adana, "Are you satisfied, darling?"

With a feigned reprimand, Adana responded to her mother. "Okay, Mom, I'm not one of your clients. Stop psychoanalyzing my statements. I don't need therapy just yet. Okay?"

"I am not psychoanalyzing you, Adana. I am sensitive to the moods and nuances in the behaviors of my children, and I just sensed something, so I thought I would ask. Am I forbidden to ask questions?"

"Now, Mom, you know you can ask questions." Adana stopped and laughed. "You just may not get the answers you want."

Ana laughed with her daughter, enjoying the exchange. "That's okay, daughter of mine. I may not get the answers at the time I ask the questions, but I get the answers eventually. So what else is new?"

Feeling as though her mother had left a perfect place to segue into a different subject, Adana rushed on. "Well, I just talked to Cassandra, Amara and Afiya, and we are all going to meet in Nairobi next week just to relax and unwind."

"Oh, that sounds good. I know you girls miss being near each other. Thank God for planes and modern technology. James and I are planning a little jaunt next month to stop in on all three of them and enjoy those grands of ours and give James a chance to walk around for days, proudly saying 'my sons Keino, Ras and Ibra.'" Ana Terrell stopped for a moment and then began to speak as though thinking aloud. "We love the husbands our daughters have chosen. They couldn't have done better. They are all such honorable, loving men. Our daughters are well cared for in every way."

"You're right about that, Mom." Adana decided in an instant to end the conversation, because she knew her mother was on the way to steering the discussion to whether or not her eldest daughter had any plans to contemplate marriage and family. Adana did not want to have that conversation. "Mom, I've got to run. I love you. Give Dad a kiss for me. See you Sunday."

Ana looked at the receiver as she heard the dial tone. "That's all right, Ms. Adana, Mommy has nothing but time." She smiled and hung up the phone.

Adana decided that a momentary release from the never-ending obligations of her chosen profession was in order. She needed a quick break. Buzzing her administrative assistant, she said, "Kathy, I'll be out for the rest of the day. I will check my messages. If there is anything pressing, just alert me and I will handle it. I will be here in the morning at seven, but I won't need you until nine."

"Yes, Ms. Terrell. I'll see you in the morning."

Adana left the office, got in her car and headed in the direction of one of her guilty pleasures. Adana loved classic films. The old black-and-whites, vintage cinema. They appealed to that quirkiness in her psyche that required rightness, order and beauty. She had found an off-beat theater in an upscale trendy area of the city that featured only vintage films. She parked her car, walked to the ticket window, saw that *Casablanca* was showing and purchased her ticket. She walked into the small, cool, darkened movie house and found a comfortable seat in the middle of a theater that was empty except for two other people. Adana sat in the cozy darkened room, enveloped in a cushioned seat with legs comfortably outstretched and head resting on the high-backed chair, waiting for the screen to be illuminated so that she could be transported to another place and another time.

Chapter 7

Nairobi, Kenya

Salima Banda stood in the offices of the premier real estate agency in the city. As one of the Barclay Agency's top-selling agents, it was not often that she was called into the owner's office; when it happened, it was always important. Victor Barclay, a Liberian who had found his way to Kenya years before and made a fortune in real estate, was not one to engage in idle chatter. Victor opened the door to his office and almost yelled, "Come in, Salima. I need to talk to you."

Victor was an energetic dynamo, ambitious and extremely driven, and his office reflected his kinetic energy. The furnishings were good quality but purely utilitarian for him. There were stacks of papers, listings and files in what appeared to be odd placements in precarious arrangements on tabletops and chairs. As Victor paced around the room, it struck Salima that he was as thin as a rail, with a face that was hollowed out where cheekbones should have been. He chain-smoked absentmindedly, not finishing one cigarette before starting another. Salima sat down as Victor talked.

"Salima, I have an assignment for you. We have a job to do for the Mazrui family."

Now Salima's curiosity was really piqued. Mazrui was a household name in Nairobi. She listened intently.

"It seems that the Mazrui brother who lost his wife in the plane crash that was plastered across the papers last year wants to put his house on the market and find new living quarters. His brother Keino, whom I've found properties for in the past, asked him to call us. Keino wanted me to give him personalized attention. I now have a conflict, and I need to go to Uganda, so I called Keino this morning to let him know that I am sending my best agent to assist his brother."

He stopped, took a long drag from his cigarette and said through a cloud of smoke, "That premier agent is you, Salima."

Salima swiveled slowly in the chair in which she sat, her eyes following Victor's pacing. "If you think I can handle it, I'll get right on it. When is he expecting me?"

Victor took another drag from his ever-present cigarette. "He is expecting me today—at three o'clock—so when you get there, explain the situation and give him the attention that he needs. I don't really know all of the details. You can get those when you see him. I do have a file with some preliminary details. You can have that."

"Fine, Victor. I'll take care of it."

Salima left the office, and as Victor had directed, she retrieved all of the pertinent information from the Mazrui file, packed her briefcase and headed to her late-model Peugeot with only an hour to spare to be on time for the meeting with Kamau Mazrui.

The drive was pleasant. As a Nairobi transplant born

and reared in London with parents from Malawi, Salima was seeing a part of the Kenyan landscape she had never seen. The trek up to the Mazrui compound was awe-inspiring. It was not lost on her why it had been nicknamed Mazrui Paradise. Salima thought what a beautiful way to live. She had seen many properties around the world. She was sure there weren't any better than what she saw in front of her. Perhaps some that equaled it, but none better.

Kamau sat on the veranda of the main house, mesmerized by the sweeping views of the forest below. He was steeling himself in preparation for the process of tying up the loose ends of a phase of his life that was over. The ringing of the doorbell almost startled him, causing a momentary rush of adrenaline as he lifted himself from his chair and walked to answer the door.

Kamau opened the door. Salima stood frozen in the doorway. She could not help herself. For an instant she could not move. He was so elegantly handsome in a flowing magenta tunic with matching gauzy pants and black leather sandals. As he stood in the doorway, the light from the panel of windows behind him streamed through the room, catching him in a halo of light hitting the magenta garments and bouncing the flecks of sun off radiant, burnished skin. This man, Kamau Mazrui, was so beautiful. The pictures she had seen of him in newspapers had not been able to capture what she saw standing before her. Salima heard his velvety, steel-laced voice ask, "May I help you?"

Kamau was puzzled by the presence of the young woman with skin the color of the earth and shoulder-length auburn hair standing speechless on his doorstep. He quietly asked again, "May I help you?"

Salima took a breath, collected herself, extended her hand and said, smiling, "Please excuse me. I am Salima Banda from the Barclay Agency. I was sent by Victor Barclay to help you list one property and find another."

Kamau shook her hand, stepped aside and invited her in. Salima noted that the interior was as breathtaking as the exterior. Kamau, walking with a maddeningly sensuous stride, led Salima to an open-air sitting area. He gestured for her to sit. She sat and crossed one trouser-covered leg over the other.

Kamau sat and began speaking in a quiet, deliberate monotone. "Forgive the question, Ms. Banda, but wasn't this meeting to have been conducted by Victor Barclay?"

Feeling like a starstruck schoolgirl, Salima could not believe the visceral reaction she was having to Mr. Kamau Mazrui. She answered while trying to focus, trying to keep the electricity that was flowing through her body from short-circuiting all of her systems. "Mr. Mazrui, I hope you will forgive the change. Victor sends his deepest apologies and asked me to assure you that I am quite capable of assisting you in this matter."

Somewhat disappointed but not wanting to delay any further, Kamau said, "I see. Well, Ms. Banda, let us begin."

Salima smiled. "Fine. And, please, call me Salima. Now, tell me, where would you like to begin? With selling your present home or locating another residence before putting it on the market?"

"In actuality, Ms. Banda"—Kamau continued to use her last name, not easily letting go of formality—"I would like to work on both projects simultaneously. I have accommodations currently, so lodging is not a problem, and I can have the house ready to be shown as soon as is humanly possible."

Salima and Kamau worked for more than an hour, outlining Kamau's needs and wants for a new residence and completing a marketing strategy for selling the home that he and Yasmin had shared. All the while, Kamau Mazrui had no idea that the lovely Salima Banda was attracted to every move of his body, every gesture of his hands and every sound that floated up from his muscular throat, but something told her that the man she found hauntingly attractive was off-limits.

Chapter 8

The Terrell sisters were together again in Nairobi, Kenya. As Keino Mazrui left his home, he was smiling in amazement at how much joy the sisters brought each other. The four women were assembled in Amara and Keino's great room, planning ways to spend their precious few days together. Adana was the first to bring order to the discussion.

"Now, ladies, let's bring some order to this madness. I'm going to write while we throw out suggestions. Once we have the suggestions all down, then we'll pick the highest rated ones by vote and I'll take care of scheduling."

Afiya threw her hands in the air, laughing, and yelled, "Oh my God, Adana, this is not a business meeting! We came here to relax. Why don't we just wake up every morning and just do what moves us? I don't want to be on a schedule."

Cassandra and Amara were both laughing at Adana and Afiya, who never failed to find a reason to disagree. If it had not been clear to both of them, and everyone who knew them, that they loved each other more than life itself, their propensity to argue would have been tragic.

Amara took the opportunity to add her opinion. "All right, you two, as usual, somewhere in the middle of both of your extremes there is an answer. I suggest we make Adana's list and then go with Afiya's flow."

Everyone laughed and agreed with Amara.

Adana asked, "Okay, so what do we want to do?"

Cassandra said wistfully, "I know I want a massage every day."

"Amen to that," was Afiya's response.

Amara added, "I can have the staff from the Meru Gentlemen's Club make room for us at the club or we can have them come here."

"Let's do both," Afiya said.

Adana's loud retort was, "Afiya, choose one or the other."

Smiling, Amara interjected, "No one has to choose. We can really do both. We'll just play it by ear, okay?"

The unified response was, "Okay."

Amara stood up. "All of this discussion has made me hungry. I have planned a feast for us. Let me tell Mrs. Bana that we are ready to eat. I hope everybody is hungry."

"I am" was heard all around. Amara left the room and asked her cook to serve the luncheon she had requested. Amara had selected a meal that included all of their favorites. Enough vegetarian dishes for Afiya, enough meat for Adana, enough seafood for Cassandra, Ethiopian doro wat for herself and enough chocolate for everyone.

Amara's household staff arranged a buffet in the great room, and the sisters gathered at a lavishly appointed table and enjoyed the delectable meal. As her sisters chatted, Adana picked up a knife and fork and sliced into a tender piece of prime rib, gingerly dipped the piece into a savory sauce and allowed the morsel to melt in her mouth. After taking a sip of white wine, she heard Cassandra ask, "Adana, how is the case going?"

Adana placed her fork on her plate and took another sip of wine. "It would be going better if I could get rid of that ridiculous Jeffery Scott."

Afiya and Amara yelled in unison, "Jeffery Scott!"

Adana laughed. "I see Cassandra hasn't had time to fill you two in on my latest adventure."

Cassandra said, "While you're talking about the case, fill us all in on what happened on your date with Mr. Scott."

Now it was Afiya's turn to jump in. "Adana, don't tell me you're seeing that man again. After all the things you've said about him. What ever possessed you to start dating him again?"

"Afiya, will you stop acting like I'm on trial and give me a chance to tell you my side of the story?"

Afiya sat back in her chair, folded her arms and waited.

Adana continued. "First of all, Jeffery and I are not back together. It is not my intention to ever have him in my life again." Adana twirled her fork distractedly on her plate while talking. "I had not seen or heard from him until this case. He is the attorney for the company that is accusing my client of securities fraud." She placed the fork back on the plate. The china sang as the silver touched it. "From day one, he has been acting like a wounded lover. I finally decided to go out with him just to get him to leave me alone. I couldn't even make it to the appetizers. I just left him there sitting in the restaurant."

As Adana took a breath, Cassandra said, "I think he deserved that."

Amara asked, "Have you heard from him since the restaurant?"

A thread of hostility eased through Adana's voice as she answered. "I heard from him, all right. He filed a motion to suppress the best piece of evidence I have for my case, which, of course, throws us into a delay. He knows he can't win. He just did it to cause me aggravation. Jeffery knows the judge is not going to rule in his favor."

Afiya responded, "Wow, sis, you needed this little mini-retreat."

Adana replied, "I think we all need these few days for very different reasons." Adana continued eating while discreetly looking at Cassandra.

Cassandra saw the look the others missed, took a long deep breath and said, "I have something I need to say. We have always come to each other whenever we've needed support, or just to vent, and we never fail to be there for one another. Well, I've been going through a trial of my own, and I just recently shared it with Adana."

The room became still as Amara and Afiya tried to mentally process what Cassandra could possibly be referring to. "For the past year, Ras and I have been trying to have a baby, and nothing—nothing—is happening." Tears started to roll softly down Cassandra's cheeks. "We have taken every test known to man and nothing is happening."

Afiya and Amara, sitting on opposite sides of Cassandra, reached over and touched her hands.

Amara voiced everyone's sentiments. "Cassandra, you know we love you, sweetie, and we're all here for you."

Afiya added, "And you know it will happen. Don't worry, don't stress. Relax and let it happen."

They were all teary-eyed, feeling Cassandra's longing and frustration. Adana was the first to regain her composure. Smiling, she said, "Just look at us. Don't we make a pretty picture all sitting here with tears in our eyes? If Keino walked in here now, he would call an emergency family meeting."

The sisters laughed while drying their eyes. Adana had described perfectly Keino's tendency to fiercely protect not only his wife and their offspring but also her sisters and the rest of his family. He refused to see any of them unhappy if he could fix the problem.

With a smile of satisfaction, Amara said, "You know, Adana is right, so Afiya lighten our mood. How is life in Senegal?"

With a twinkle in her eye, Afiya answered, "Life in Senegal would be perfect if I could banish my mother-in-law to a faraway secluded island."

Now the sisters were laughing again at the humor of anyone banishing Mariama Diop to an island or anywhere else. She was not a woman one could quietly put away. Momentarily forgetting her own problem, Cassandra asked, "Hasn't she gotten any better?"

In an exasperated tone, Afiya responded, "I don't know what that woman wants me to do. I can't be reborn and become Senegalese. I know I'm not what she envisioned for her precious son, but one of these days it will dawn on her that Ibra is now my precious husband and he's not going anywhere and neither am I."

Amara interjected, "I thought things would change when the baby was born."

"Oh, she loves her granddaughter. She would just like to erase me as her grandchild's mother. Sometimes I feel sorry for Ibra. He is constantly putting his mother in her place and reminding her that I am his wife, Fara's mother, and the only woman who makes decisions in our home. She can be so rude."

With a slight wrinkle in her brow, Adana asked, "So how do you handle her? That must be difficult to live with."

"Well, I make sure I don't see her that often, and when I do, I pick my battles and I make sure I win. Thank God Ibra's father and sister are on my side. Ibra keeps saying she'll come around, and I keep saying as long as he loves me and continues to make love to me the way that he does, his mother will become a distant memory."

Now the four sisters erupted in gales of laughter. As the laughter slowed to wistful smiles and soft chatter, the sisters added more of their favorite dishes to their plates.

Adana spoke in a low voice, almost as though thinking aloud. "The three of you have no idea how really fortunate you are to have found the loves of your lives. This world is full of so many people who search a lifetime and never find what you have."

Amara, Cassandra and Afiya ate slowly, watching Adana with caring glances, listening carefully between the lines of what she was saying. Adana continued thinking out loud. "I don't think I'm ever going to have that experience. I'm not even sure I want that experience. God, you really have to give up so much. I mean, the give and take, the continual consideration of another person's thoughts and feelings, the juggling of schedules, not to mention parenting. I don't know how all of you do it day after day after day. Whatever the DNA molecule or gene is that makes what you do possible, it missed me. I really don't think I can love like that." Adana took a breath and picked up a forkful of salad.

While Adana ate, Amara's voice eased in slowly and softly. "Adana, as always when it comes to your personal life, you underestimate your abilities and you discreetly push away your desires by saying you don't have them.

Dear heart, sister of mine, you are one of the most giving people I know and almost as protective as Keino."

That remark brought a smile from everyone. Amara continued. "The problem is your love hasn't shown up in your life yet. When he does, it will all fall into place. You won't have to second-guess yourself."

The mystical Afiya added, "Adana, it really is true that when you hide from love, it won't find you. You have to be open to it. You deserve the kind of love you watch us experience, and I believe it's going to find you in spite of yourself."

Afiya lightened the mood again. "Since we're talking about sweet love, I think I'll have some sweet dessert."

Cassandra added, "I think I'll have more than one."

That elicited a chuckle from her sisters, who knew that of the four of them, Cassandra was the most figure-conscious. As they were getting desserts, Amara excitedly stated, "You will not believe who showed up at the women's association last week."

Her sisters looked in her direction.

Adana asked, "Who?"

"Makena Rono."

Cassandra gasped. "Oh my God, what on earth did she want?"

Amara's studied answer was, "I think she was just being nosy. The talk is that she is dating some poor, unsuspecting chap who worships the ground she walks on."

Afiya laughed and responded, "Poor guy, someone needs to put him out of his misery."

With dry wit ringing in each word, Adana stated matter-of-factly, "If he marries her, that will do it."

Cassandra added, "Makena is pitiful. That girl is always going to love Keino."

Amara smiled as she said, "The women in Nairobi are

standing in line for the Mazrui brothers, hoping one of them will revive the tradition of polygamy. I feel sorry for poor Kamau. Since Yasmin's death, the women have been hounding him. Some subtly and others just over the top—no tact, no class, no pride."

Cassandra asked, "How is he doing these days? It's been well over a year now."

Amara answered, "He is selling the house. He has moved to the compound, and Keino tells me he has taken some time off from the office. So I think he's healing."

Adana's mind seemed never to shut off from work. She blurted out, "Speaking of callous, I hope I'm not being rude, but I was hoping I could speak to Kamau while I'm here. It dawned on me last week that he practices international law, and the woman I am defending is a Kenyan citizen. I'd love to consult with him concerning the case. I need all of the ammunition I can get to kick Jeffery Scott's narrow behind."

Amara said, "Well, you know how the Mazruis are—anything for family, and you are family. Remember Yasmin had been dead a very short time when he dropped everything and came to help Ibra. I think it will be all right. I'll get his number for you later."

"Good, I think he can be really helpful, even though I think he's a real stick-in-the mud."

Afiya, teasing Adana good-naturedly, quipped, "Look who's talking—I'm not sure you come across as Miss Life of the Party."

The sisters once again had a laugh at Adana's expense.

The sisters spent the rest of the day lounging and playing with Amara and Keino's twin sons. The doting aunts were thrilled with the children's growth and their precociousness, and they continually raved about the physical beauty of the identical little boys. As the sisters planned the ways in which they would spend their days, Adana's mind strayed again and again to her omnipresent case.

The following morning, Adana awoke in one of the Mazrui household guest rooms. She sat up in the king-sized canopied bed with tousled hair and a body weary from too little sleep. Adana and her sisters had talked late into the night. After getting into bed, Adana had been unable to still her mind, and she tossed and turned until a fitful sleep overtook her. Deciding to call Keino to feel him out about consulting with Kamau, she slipped a peach-colored silk robe on her bare body. It trailed the plushly carpeted floor as she headed into the adjoining guest bath to prepare for the day.

After a long, leisurely soak, Adana followed through on her decision to talk to Keino about consulting Kamau. Her night had been so restless she had slept later than usual and missed seeing Keino before he left for the office. Adana grabbed a fresh robe and retrieved Keino's office number from her BlackBerry, but she decided a landline would give her better reception. She dialed the number and waited for the familiar ring and for the Kenyan-flavored voice on the other end of the line to say, "Mazrui Industries."

Adana responded, "Good morning, this is Adana Terrell, Mr. Keino Mazrui's sister-in-law. May I please speak with him?"

There was a quick "One moment please," and then Keino's mellow baritone. "Adana, my sister, how are you? I trust you slept well."

"I'm fine, Keino, but I'll be better when I win this current case. That's why I'm calling. I really hate to disturb you, but I discussed the issue with Amara yesterday and I'd like your take on it as well."

"Fire away, my sister. I will help in any way that I can."

"I need the expertise of an international lawyer. Not only is your brother Kamau an international attorney, but he is also Kenyan—and so is my client, though she is in the process of becoming an American citizen. Kamau's background is perfect for helping me make sure I have dotted all of my i's and crossed all of my t's. Do you think he would be up to consulting with me? I don't need much of his time. Maybe a few hours. What do you think, Keino?"

"Amara mentioned the situation to me this morning." The smile on Keino's lips was heard in his voice. "I am sure my brother will be happy to help you. In our world, nothing takes precedence over family. You are family, Adana. Kamau is currently living in the family vacation compound. I will give you the number to the main house where he is living and to his cell. He has been there a few weeks now. He should be itching to discuss anything having to do with jurisprudence."

Adana and Keino shared a lighthearted laugh at the thought of Kamau's love of practicing law. Keino gave Adana both numbers and they said good-bye.

Adana looked at the numbers she had written and wondered when she should call. Then she said out loud, "There is no time like the present." She dialed the number to the cell first. It rang again and again without being answered. Adana tried the house line.

Miles away at the Mazrui compound, Kamau was swimming laps and missed the ringing of his cell. As he stepped from the pool, wiping moisture from his face, he heard the ringing of the house phone. He walked to the area in the pool house where there was an extension, expecting a call from Salima Banda with properties to show him. Kamau picked up the receiver.

Just as Adana was about to hang up, she heard a smooth, relaxed, "Hello, this is Kamau."

Happy to hear an answer to her call, a delighted Adana said, "Hi, Kamau, this is Adana Terrell. Amara's sister. You may not remember me."

Kamau interrupted and very matter-of-factly stated, "I know who you are. I never forget people who question my abilities, as you did during a family meeting held to strategize about ways to help Ibra avoid being framed. I remember you."

Adana was immediately thrown off balance, but it didn't show in her reply. "Kamau Mazrui, that meeting was well over a year ago, but even so, had I questioned your abilities, I would not only remember the incident but also I would not be calling you now. Questioning your ability to practice law is very different from questioning statements in order to gain clarity. If I recall, I was trying to be very clear that my sister Afiya would not be implicated in any of the madness that was surrounding Ibra at the time."

There was silence on the other end of the line. Adana waited. In the mental game of chess they had begun, it was Kamau's move.

His clipped tones broke the silence. "Touché, Adana. How may I help you?"

"Well, oddly enough, I need to tap into those expert abilities that you think I question."

Kamau laughed a low, throaty laugh. He laughed so seldom the act surprised him.

Joining his laughter, Adana said, "I didn't realize I have comedic abilities. Please tell me what is so funny."

Kamau's only response was, "Adana, life has its comedic strains. I'm just laughing at the irony of me thinking all those months ago that you questioned my ability to practice law and here you are wanting to tap into the very ability I thought you were questioning. Life is full of misunderstandings."

As he finished the sentence, the last argument he had had with Yasmin about piloting the plane alone played out in his head. He willed the thoughts away and said, "So tell me, what do you need?"

"I need to consult with you about a case that has international ramifications. I don't think I'll need a great deal of your time, and since I have been told that you are not coming in to your office, I can come to you."

Kamau thought as he listened to Adana, *Another head-strong woman who insists upon getting what she wants the way she wants it.* He knew the type. He had been married to one, and he knew in his heart that he would never again involve himself on a personal level with a woman who could not yield. Kamau could hear that Adana Terrell was the walking personification of willful and obstinate. It was clear to him that she didn't trust anyone's judgment but her own.

"I have an appointment with a Realtor late this morning, so perhaps we can meet late this afternoon, or do you need more time to order files and documents?"

"Oh no, I brought what I need with me. I wanted to go over some things while I was here. Anything else I need I can retrieve through my laptop."

"Well, then, this afternoon it is, three-thirty."

"Great, thank you, Kamau—I'll see you at three-thirty."

Just as Adana hung up the telephone, she heard a knock at the door and a voice announce, "Ms. Terrell, breakfast will be served in half an hour on the terrace."

Adana thanked the faceless voice and began her ritual of dressing for the day. She opted for khaki-colored walking shorts with a matching boat-necked top cropped at the waist, with khaki-colored espadrilles laced up the calf. When she walked out onto the terrace, Afiya, Amara and Cassandra were already enjoying a leisurely breakfast. They all looked up when Adana walked out to join them. Afiya said, "Hi, sleepyhead, you must have been tired. You never oversleep."

Adana fixed herself a plate, choosing from an assortment of meats, fruits, pastries, eggs, teas, coffees and juices. "I couldn't get to sleep. I thought we had talked ourselves into a stupor, but when I got into bed, I just couldn't turn my mind off. I kept running the case over and over in my head. Oh, by the way, Amara, I ran our conversation by Keino this morning, and he agreed with you that Kamau would definitely help family. I called Kamau this morning, and after we got off to a very rocky start, he agreed to help me. I'm meeting him today at three-thirty."

Cassandra softly reprimanded her sister. "Adana, we all came here to rest. We were supposed to leave work at home."

With plate in hand, Adana walked to the table, sat and said, "This is an opportunity I can't possibly pass up. For the sake of my client, I need to pick Kamau's brain whenever I get a chance."

Afiya picked up a piece of melon and said, "I take it this puts a hole in our plans for today."

Adana responded a little guiltily, "Well, the three of you can still go without me. You know I've got to do this."

In a conciliatory tone, Amara spoke to her sisters. "Look, we can handle today while Adana takes care of her business. We know Adana and we know that if she doesn't go, it will be on her mind, and if she's preoccupied, she might as well not be with us."

Adana took a sip of a spicy Kenyan tea and said contritely, "I promise I'll make it up to you. I promise."

Afiya looked at Adana and, in a tone not disguising her disappointment, responded, "We're going to hold you to that."

Chapter 9

Nairobi, Kenya

Salima Banda was looking forward to seeing Kamau Mazrui again. She picked up her telephone and dialed his number. As the telephone rang, visions of him danced in her head. His voice woke her from her daydream.

"Kamau Mazrui here."

She answered with a perky, "Hello, Kamau, this is Salima."

Something about her familiar air grated on Kamau. It felt as though she had established a friendship where none existed. His retort was, "Ms. Banda, I was going to call you to reschedule our tour of available properties."

"Oh, Kamau, I'm not sure that is a good idea. Good properties in this market go very quickly, and I'd hate for you to lose out. There are at least four listed right now that might suit your needs, but they aren't going to last long."

"I appreciate your candor and your salesmanship, Ms. Banda, but I will just have to take my chances."

Knowing she had lost the round, Salima Banda replied, "In that case, I will give you a call later in the week to reschedule; who knows, perhaps by then I'll have even more properties."

"Thank you, Ms. Banda. Good day."

When Kamau hung up the phone, he made a mental note to discreetly replace Ms. Salima Banda as his agent—something about her made an already difficult situation even harder. Kamau went into the master suite, changed his clothes and headed for the racquetball court to do battle with a small inanimate object that was no match for his powerful arms and legs.

As the sisters headed out for pampering and shopping, Amara said to Adana, "The compound is about an hour and a half away from here. I've arranged for a driver to drop you off. You can call him when you are ready to come home and he'll pick you up."

"Thanks, sis. You three have a good time. I'll be back soon."

Afiya, Amara and Cassandra headed out the door while Adana headed to the room she was occupying to gather up the things she would need for her meeting. At promptly two hours before her meeting with Kamau, one of the house staff alerted her that a car was waiting to take her to the Mazrui vacation compound. Adana stepped past the opened car door that was being held for her and eased into the plush interior of the backseat of the late-model touring sedan. As she rode, she turned over in her mind again and again the presentation she wanted to make to Kamau so that he could show her the holes in her arguments. If he could find any.

As the car whizzed along, she found herself mesmerized by the countryside. The landscape was breathtaking. She could understand why Amara had fallen in love with the land of her husband's birth almost as deeply as she had fallen in love with her husband. As the driver slowed in front of the main structure of the sixty-five-acre compound, Adana realized that this vacation compound did not resemble any she had ever seen. The main structures were connected in the shape of a U, with outlying structures emanating from a central pavilion. The grounds were manicured to reflect the natural beauty of the area and incorporated designs of gardens Adina Mazrui, the family matriarch, had seen in her travels around the world. Adana smiled to herself. The Mazrui family truly knew how to take a family vacation.

The driver stopped the car, got out, came around and opened her door. Adana grabbed her things and stepped out of the car.

When he heard the doorbell, Kamau had just finished a shower and was slipping a simply tailored African robe the color of sapphires over his head. He put his feet into slippers of the same material and hue as the robe, and with an even, sensual rhythm, he walked toward the front door. Adana stood waiting in front of a heavy geometrically carved door reminiscent of the ancient carvings of Timbuktu. She took in the sights, sounds and smells of the Mazrui paradise. As she turned her head to watch the chauffeured car ease down the roadway, Kamau opened the door. Adana's head turned and she found herself staring into dark, seductive eyes embodied in a powerful presence. She looked at Kamau and felt an unexplainably familiar connection. Kamau had not remembered clearly the woman who stood before him. He had remembered what he had thought to be her dismissive arrogant attitude, but he had not remembered her loveliness, her appearance of softness.

Adana extended her hand and said in a low, composed

voice, "Kamau, thank you so much for allowing me this imposition on your time and space."

Kamau, rather than shaking her hand, instinctively enfolded her delicate hand in his two strong ones and said, "I hope I can be of help to you. Please come in."

As Adana walked past Kamau, her senses were filled with the aroma of the clean breezy fragrance he wore. The scent reminded her of miles and miles of white sands and blue ocean waters. Kamau directed Adana to a loggia, where there were two large marble coffee tables placed in front of long, intricately carved mahogany settees outfitted with upholstered white raw silk cushions and pillows. The loggia provided an unfettered view of the expansive property. Adana sat, simultaneously folding one hand over the other in her lap and crossing her legs. The crossing of her limbs caused the khaki-colored walking shorts to ease discreetly up her leg, painting a visually enticing picture of shapely legs entwined in khaki-colored satin ribbons. Kamau found himself drawn to the dance of the movements Adana unknowingly choreographed before him.

Assuming it was her show and not wanting to delay the business at hand, Adana placed her briefcase on one table, opened it and removed a small laptop and a stack of files. Before she could begin her spiel, Kamau, despite not liking small talk or unnecessary preliminaries, felt the need to engage in the time-honored African tradition of conducting social formalities of discourse and nourishment before attending to business.

He interrupted Adana before she could speak. "Even though I am here temporarily without a household staff, I would be remiss if I did not offer you refreshments of some sort. There are waters, juices, teas, coffees, fruits. Would you like any of those things?"

For a moment Adana was stunned. She sat staring at Kamau Mazrui, who seemed at that moment a contradictory mass of virility, arrogance and gentleness. Something about him soothed and rattled her at the same time. His gaze was soft, his voice hard, but his words caressed her like one of her cashmere throws. She answered with a slight hesitancy. "A sparkling water would be nice."

Kamau stood, and as he did so, he reminded Adana of an African Tao master whose every movement was a prayer. The sapphire-colored garments flowed as he walked, accentuating skin that was so dark and so flawless it almost seemed translucent. He walked a short distance to a well-equipped kitchen area off the loggia and returned with a bamboo tray holding two tall cylindrically shaped crystal glasses filled with sparkling water garnished with lemon and lime. Kamau set the tray on the table and sat down on a comfortable chair, facing the settee on which Adana sat. Thankful for the distance provided by the table that separated them, Kamau pondered what it was that drew him to the woman sitting in front of him, and then it happened. Adana picked up the glass nearest to her and savored the cool liquid with her eyes closed. It was just a small, quick gesture, an act performed by countless other human beings, but he had known only one other who had made it her habit to close her eyes when drinking something she savored—Yasmin.

Adana opened her eyes to place the glass back on the tray and found Kamau's eyes riveted to hers. "Is something wrong?"

Kamau's husky voice lumbered out an apology. "I am very sorry for staring. Please forgive me." He stopped, swallowed and spoke again in a tender murmur, "The way you closed your eyes when you drank your water reminded me of someone."

Adana smiled. "Old habits don't go away easily. I was told over and over as a child to stop doing that because it would become a habit that I'd regret when it slipped out at some inopportune moment. I guess my parents were right again," she said, smiling. "Don't you just hate it when your parents are right almost all of the time?"

Kamau's quick, terse answer was, "No, I count on their wisdom as elders."

Adana couldn't control her burst of laughter. "Kamau, until I spent time with you, I thought I was serious. You have cornered the market on seriousness. What I said was meant to be a joke. I know people joke in this part of the world."

Adana's retort amused Kamau. He sat back in his chair, and with a flicker of a smile in his eyes, he said, "Yes, people do joke in this part of the world, and on occasion I have been known to laugh." He paused and stated with mock seriousness, "Perhaps it was your delivery."

Enjoying the friendly sparring, Adana said with a flash of humor in her voice, "I see you do have jokes. Now let's find some humor in this case so that my client can laugh all the way home."

Kamau crossed his legs and relaxed into his chair, saying, "Barrister, the floor is yours."

Without blinking, Adana quickly became the consummate professional. "My client, Diani Bitak, a Kenyan by birth who is becoming an American citizen and has been living in the U.S. for six years, has been accused of using her insurance brokerage firm to launder money to finance arms deals in which her husband is involved. Her husband is a Libyan named Emir Al-Sanussi. I'm certain you have seen or heard his name plastered all over the international media."

Kamau nodded.

"First of all, as I have said countless times to anyone who will listen, her husband has not been convicted in a court of law. He has only been tried in the media, and there is no hard evidence to convict him."

Kamau stopped her. "So you believe your client is innocent of all charges?"

"She tells me that she and her husband are both innocent. I believe *she* is innocent. I have my suspicions about her husband's involvement in money laundering. It is quite possible that her brokerage firm could have been used without her knowledge. Her husband is the chief financial officer. She could very well be just another woman who put her life in the hands of a man who had no intention of protecting her interests."

Kamau heard clearly the undercurrent of mistrust as Adana talked about her client's spouse. He wondered if that distrust was specifically for Al-Sanussi or if it was a general distrust of the male species. Kamau decided to probe further, knowing that though his question might have little bearing on the trying of the case, he would gain insight into the workings of Adana's mind.

In a coolly impersonal tone, he asked, "Is it possible that your client"—Kamau paused for effect and slowed his speech, a technique he often used in the courtroom— "that your client's spouse is, as she says, innocent? Is it possible that he, too, is being erroneously characterized in the press?"

Adana stiffened, her body language shifting from relaxed to tense. She leaned toward Kamau slightly. "This man is the only person who had access and motive."

Kamau questioned, "Motive?"

"Yes, motive. One of Libya's most high-profile Muslim extremists is a relative of Emir Al-Sanussi. It is highly unlikely that an African who espouses adhering to his cultural tenets the way Al-Sanussi does would refuse to aid a relative." She took a breath. "No matter how risky."

Kamau nodded slowly and stroked his mustache, an unconscious habit whenever he was thinking. "And so you think Al-Sanussi would jeopardize his wife's well-being to aid another relative?"

Adana relaxed again and eased back into the cushions behind her. "What I'm saying is that in far too many instances, I've seen men profess undying love for wives and lovers only to toss them aside in favor of the next big thing. Emir strikes me as that kind of guy."

With all the command of a monarch, Kamau lifted his chin slightly and asked, "Is it because he is an African that you think he would disregard his wife's safety for other concerns?"

Sounding somewhat defensive, Adana quickly shot back, "My contact with African men has not led me to believe that they corner the market on that particular human failing. I'm talking about this particular man's character, not his national origin."

Kamau looked pointedly at Adana and replied, "I see, and so what is your strategy for the exoneration of your client?"

"My first line of defense, as I see it, is to separate my client from her husband in the minds of the jury. I tried for a change of venue but was unsuccessful. What I have to do now is not allow Diani to be tarred and feathered because of the perceived misdeeds of her husband. My investigator located a former employee who uncovered some expenditures that were suspect. When she reported them to Emir a month later, she was let go because of a 'company reorganization.' She made copies of the documents before she reported her findings to Emir. The copies are now in our possession, and following the trail they leave could go a long way toward exonerating my client. Unfortunately, opposing counsel has moved to suppress that piece of evidence."

"On what grounds?"

"Illegally obtained. He knows that he's just throwing up a smoke screen, and I know he knows that a judge is not going to rule in his favor, but in the meantime, the delays are wreaking havoc with my client's psychological state."

Kamau's voice was distant as he asked, "Is it possible that someone else had a motive, a reason for using the brokerage? Your focus on Emir may be misplaced, and you could be wasting valuable investigative time by not pursuing other persons of interest. It is always a mistake when trying a case to allow emotional prejudices to cloud your judgment."

Adana's eyes narrowed and her words were clipped and distinct as she questioned, "Is that what you think I'm doing, allowing my emotions to cloud my judgment? Is it possible that my powers of observation and my skill as a trial attorney have led me to certain well-founded conclusions?"

Kamau was undisturbed and unmoved by Adana's pointed barb. When he spoke again, his words were as cool as a mountain stream. "Your powers of observation I know nothing about, but given your position in a prestigious firm, I expect that you possess a level of skill beyond the ordinary. However, I trust my ability to hear beyond what is said, and based on our very brief conversation, the media seems to have painted a picture of Emir that has perhaps seeped into your psyche."

Adana sat momentarily stunned and speechless. It

was rare that she found herself in either state. She was furious. How dare he psychoanalyze her, and more importantly, how dare he impugn her good judgment? A controlled anger eased through as she spoke. "Kamau, though you have questioned my powers of observation, I am sure yours are beyond reproach. I am not, however, in any way appreciative of your attempts to play psychiatrist. I came here for a very specific kind of assistance with this case. If you would just stick to the agenda, I think a lot can be accomplished."

Kamau, never easily ruffled, leaned forward, picked up his glass and took a sip of water. He placed the glass carefully back on the tray, settled into his chair, crossed his legs and looked pointedly at Adana with sharp eyes that spoke volumes. "I am well aware of why you are here. I am not one to waste time. Whatever comments I have made have been purely in the interest of furthering your case."

The two sat silently, allowing a low-grade tension to fill the loggia. Without warning, warm drops of rain began to fall. Soft splatters trickled onto the open-air structure in which they sat. Adana became so engrossed in the rain and how suddenly it had come that she was almost startled by Kamau's touch as he said, "Come with me inside so that you will be protected from the rain."

Without speaking, Adana gathered up her things and followed Kamau inside. As soon as they entered the great room, the sky blackened and the rain went from gentle drops to a relentless downpour. Kamau saw a shift in Adana that he could not clearly read. As he watched her watch the rain, he sensed a vulnerability that he was sure Adana did not often display.

Adana sat fighting the tremors she felt crawling through her body. Taking silent, deep breaths, she hoped to erase the intense feeling of sickness that was sweeping over her. Only her family knew that because of a childhood incident, she was terrified of storms. Countless trips to behavioral therapists as a child had left her able to cope well as an adult, but she was not cured. She had not mentioned to her family her lingering anxiety and fear of storms. They all assumed that she had outgrown her terror of rainstorms. Adana had done nothing to correct their assumptions. She felt it was something she needed to handle. She refused to revert back to being the young child who had gone on a camping trip and had gotten separated from her group, lost for hours in a wooded area on a dark, stormy night. The following morning when rescuers found her, she was huddled against a tree, shaking and crying, having experienced a terror unlike anything she had ever known before.

Adana sat in Kamau's great room, struggling to bring her emotions under control. She wanted to run.

Seeing what almost looked like pain in her eyes as she clutched her throat, Kamau pulled a small upholstered stool in front of Adana, sat on it and took her hands in his. He looked at her compassionately and in a voice full of the strength she needed at that moment asked, "Adana, are you all right? May I get you something?"

Her breathing slowed. Her voice registered embarrassment and gratitude as she answered, "I'll be fine. Maybe it was something that I ate earlier. If you will just call the driver for me, maybe I can go back to Amara and Keino's and we can talk later."

As soon as she thought of driving in the storm, her stomach knotted again as fiercely as before. She need not have concerned herself with riding in the storm. Kamau's response took away the responsibility of that decision. "I'm sorry, Adana. The driver can't be called in this kind of storm unless there is an emergency. Everyone just stays put while Mother Nature puts on her show."

Feeling the tension float through her fingers as he held her hands, Kamau reassured her. "If there is anything you need, we are well stocked here. You will be safe."

Kamau was not sure why he suddenly felt very protective of the independent, often arrogant, high-strung woman who sat before him, but he did. He also knew that something more than disagreeable food had her in a state of high tension. As the rain continued to pour, the flora and fauna drank thirstily. The clay-colored earth sighed under the nourishing downpour. A clap of thunder and a streak of lightning caused Adana to tighten her grip on Kamau's strong hands. She closed her eyes, hoping to shut out the sights and sounds that filled her with so much fear. Holding her hands, watching Adana, Kamau examined her face, aware of his own feelings, which were a mixture of confusion, sympathetic compassion and an unexplained attraction. She sat with her eyes closed, her full, parted lips covered in a cocoa-colored gloss. Her cinnamon-colored skin appeared as soft as cotton, and her long neck led to the hint of cleavage that rose and fell with her every breath. Adana's hair, cut in the style of a 1920s flapper, was perfectly contoured to her head, every strand in place. Her eyelashes fluttered slightly with her next breath and so did Kamau's heart. He eased his hands from hers, not at all familiar with what he had experienced. He silently thought to himself, *Kamau, your seclusion is getting the best of you.*

In order to distract them both, Kamau stood and said,

"I am going to prepare tea for us. Perhaps it will help to calm your system."

Adana, not wanting to be left alone, stood on legs that threatened not to hold her and said, "I'll go with you."

With a skeptical look, Kamau asked, "Are you sure?"

Haltingly, Adana answered, "Yes . . . yes, I'm sure."

Kamau led the way to the restaurant-style kitchen. Momentarily focused on what she saw, Adana remarked, "The household staff must really prepare fabulous meals in here."

"They do indeed and so do I when the mood strikes."

Registering slight surprise, Adana asked, "You cook? Kamau, you are full of surprises."

Kamau's voice had lost its hard edge as he spoke. "Had I not been smitten with the practice of law, I would undoubtedly have been a chef living somewhere in the south of France, running my own private restaurant that seated no more than ten at a time." Kamau continued to speak as though reciting a well-rehearsed dream. "Spots would have to be reserved a year in advance."

Kamau smiled when he realized he had never told another living soul about that particular dream. He thought it must have been the rain. In his opinion, rain had a way of causing introspection even in the most self-absorbed souls.

From an ebony-wood glass-front cabinet, Kamau retrieved a brass box containing tightly sealed cups that held the special spices used in many Kenyan households to make tea. Adana watched quietly, deliberately trying to distract herself from the waves of anxiety that continued to wash over her. She noted that Kamau appeared so calm, so naturally tranquil as he prepared the pot of tea with the same strong, dark hands that had moments before comforted her so gently. His back and shoulders seemed broad enough to carry the weight of the world. Closely cropped hair lay like a black velvet blanket over a perfectly formed head. Kamau turned slightly to the side to add the spice mixture to the steeping teapot. Adana's eyes locked on a magnificent profile that displayed the sculpted cheeks and the strong jawline for which the Mazrui men were known. Her eyes followed the lines of a meticulously groomed mustache that ran over his full, sensuous top lip and spilled under his chin, waiting to be stroked. Adana noticed for the first time what other women noticed instantly. Kamau Mazrui was an incredibly handsome man. He possessed a raw masculine beauty that made a woman feel as though she could be ravaged and protected at the same time.

Adana swallowed and took a deep, audible breath. The anxiety slowed. Hearing the breath, Kamau turned toward her and placed a cup of the aromatic tea and spice blend in front of her. He stared at her, silently questioning, waiting for answers that he knew she would only provide in time. As the rain continued to pour, Adana picked up the cup and savored the scents of cinnamon, cloves, ginger and cardamom. The warmth was soothing. Looking up from the cup directly into Kamau's questioning eyes, Adana was struck by the unreadable emotion in them.

"Kamau, this is wonderful." And then she lied, "I'm okay now. I think it really was breakfast that disagreed with me."

Not believing the explanation, Kamau responded, "I hope you are better. This downpour seems to be a bit more fierce than was anticipated. If that is the case, then I want you to ride out the storm in relative comfort."

"What do you mean, ride out the storm? Isn't this just a minor rain? Isn't it going to stop soon?"

Kamau could hear the tremor in her voice. His voice was low and smooth. "This is the rainy season, so some downpours may go on longer than others." Kamau took a sip of his tea and sought to reassure Adana again. "As I have said, you are safe here. We have everything that we need."

Adana could not begin to explain to Kamau that what she needed was to be away from the rain, the storm and memories of a child lost on a cold, dark, lonely night. She just sat, drank her tea and said over and over in her mind, *You're fine, Adana. You're fine.*

Chapter 10

Nairobi, Kenya

The time seemed to pass quickly. Night was falling. The rain continued to pour, but more gently, giving Adana the hope that it would soon stop. Feeling very much as though he carried the responsibility for Adana's mental and physical well-being through the storm, Kamau offered, "Adana, if you do not mind, while you are continuing to allow your system to settle, I can review your briefs and any electronic notes you might have brought with you."

Relieved to have something else to think about, Adana responded, "Yes, please, and if you have questions, I can work with you. I think working will help me to feel even better."

"Fine."

Kamau thought to himself, *This woman is not one to let anything stop her.*

Adana placed the briefs and laptop on a nearby desk. While she logged on to retrieve notes she had compiled,

Kamau stood next to her. As she inhaled the cool breezy scent that he wore, Kamau, too, was engulfed in Adana's scent, which made him think of warm summer days and long hot nights. He backed up quickly, feeling as though he had been scorched by the fragrance. Adana didn't notice as she said, "This is everything. I'll take a few and we can review at the same time."

"Fine," was Kamau's only reply. He took a seat at the computer, and Adana took files with her across the room to a plush cozy couch where she began to unlace her espadrilles in order to read in comfort. She was unaware of Kamau watching as she untied the knots of each satin ribbon and slid them down her long, smooth legs. The picture Adana painted reminded Kamau of how necessary the right woman was to complement and balance the life of a man. The wonderful and wondrous contrasts of hard and soft, smooth and rugged. Watching Adana brought to mind once again the void that existed in his life.

Kamau got up, turned on soft, muted lighting and filled the room with the mellow sounds of John Coltrane. Hearing the first notes of the music, Adana looked up and smiled. It was one of her favorite recordings. Kamau noted her approval with a tentative smile of his own. They worked in companionable silence as the light glowed, the music played and the rain fell.

The restful mood was momentarily interrupted by the ringing of the telephone. Kamau picked up the extension near him and answered with a distant "Hello." Adana, hearing only Kamau's end of the conversation, could tell that family was inquiring as to their safety. The thought of their concern did not reassure her. If they were concerned, there must be a reason. Kamau spoke in his low, quiet and now-familiar tone.

"Yes, Adana is still here. We should be fine. We have

everything that we need. I don't know if the generator is working properly; I have had no reason to check it. Wasn't it recently replaced?"

There was a pause and then, "I see. If the need arises, I am sure I can take care of it. Yes, I will."

Kamau placed the telephone back in its cradle and turned to find Adana's troubled stare peering at him, waiting for answers to the questions the telephone call had raised. Kamau got up from his chair and walked toward Adana. Their eyes were locked in a silent gaze until he eased down beside her on the sofa, removed the brief she was holding from her hands, placed it on the coffee table in front of them and enfolded both of Adana's hands in his while he spoke. "It appears that an unusual storm front is headed our way. That was Keino on the telephone. The family was concerned that you might be traveling in the storm. I told him that you were still here."

As Kamau spoke, he could feel the tremors go from Adana's hands to his. He started gently stroking her palms. Once again, he instinctively felt the pull to take care of the fiercely independent and engagingly beautiful woman sitting next to him.

Adana stammered, "W-when is the storm coming? Tonight, tomorrow?"

Kamau answered quietly, "Tonight."

Adana was fighting not to fall apart. The terror she felt was real. She wanted to be home where she could manage in her own way, away from prying, questioning eyes. Here she was trapped, afraid to be alone yet not wanting to be seen in the state of panic that was quickly overtaking her. From a fog of repetitive silent affirmations that she was saying to herself, Adana heard Kamau. His deep, resonant voice was the balm needed at that moment.

"Adana, tell me if there is something I should know." Making it clear to her that he did not believe her disagreeable-food story, Kamau said, "When I mentioned the storm front, your bout with disagreeable food seemed to return. If there is a problem, there is no need to face it alone." The corner of his mouth lifted in what he hoped was a reassuring smile. He continued to hold on to Adana's trembling hands. "I am very resourceful, you know."

Full of pride and the hope that she could literally weather the storm, Adana lifted her head slightly. "Thank you, Kamau, but I am fine."

Kamau saw the faint glistening of unshed tears in her eyes. "Adana, Adana, Adana." Her name sounded like a song on his lips. "Please don't lie to me. I can feel you shaking. Your limbs are trembling." Kamau placed a strong, comforting hand on one of Adana's soft, smooth legs, still folded on the sofa. The slight tremor in her slender legs was not unlike that in her hands. Kamau didn't speak but gently stroked her trembling legs and looked at her with probing eyes. Unable and unwilling to answer the questions Kamau's dark eyes held, she eased away from his tender grasp, got up from the sofa and busied herself restacking the small mound of briefs she had brought for Kamau's inspection.

Kamau sat still, watching Adana as she examined each folder and every document attached to it and then neatly stacked them. Kamau understood the action as an unconscious way of bringing order to what felt like chaos. He left her to her task and walked across the room to his pipe stand, picked one of his favorite intricately carved pipes, filled it with his special tobacco blend, sat back in a plush chair designed to match the sofa, lit his pipe and relaxed into the time-honored ritual of pipe smokers the world over. He placed his feet on an ottoman in front of the chair, crossed his legs at the ankles and watched Adana through the aromatic stream of smoke.

Adana felt his gaze, looked over at him and said, "You don't have to concern yourself, Kamau. I'm not a child. I can take care of myself and I will be fine. Between the food and the stress of the case, my body is just reacting a little strangely."

With his strikingly handsome features composed and his dark seductive eyes lasered in on Adana, Kamau asked, "If that is true, Adana, how do you manage under the stress that I know must come with your job on a daily basis?"

Adana snapped, "I said it was a combination of things." Her tone softened. "I said I'll be fine."

Kamau gave an impatient nod of his head, put down his pipe, rose from the chair with the fluidity of a dancer and said, "Fine, I am going to check on the generator."

As he moved to leave the room, a wave of anxiety started to ease its way through Adana's body. A statement in the form of a hidden plea tumbled from her lips. "Kamau, I would feel more comfortable if I came with you."

Kamau shrugged and said in an offhand manner, "Whatever pleases you, Adana."

She hastily retrieved her shoes and followed the man who had become the guardian of her emotional well-being.

Kamau led an emotionally conflicted Adana down a winding back staircase that stopped in what appeared to be the bottom of the palatial structure. Kamau opened a door, and behind it appeared to be enough equipment to launch a space shuttle. Without waiting to be asked, Kamau explained that what she saw was command central for the compound. There were enough components to run a small city. Kamau also explained that from very young ages, all of the Mazrui brothers had been given the training necessary to operate and maintain the major machines she saw before her. Kamau spoke to Adana as though speaking aloud to himself. "Father thinks this generator needs replacing, and Keino says it was scheduled to be replaced next week. He's not sure it would serve as backup if the storm is too severe."

Adana almost whispered, "So what happens if the generator doesn't work?"

Kamau answered calmly and succinctly, "I'm here to make sure that it does."

Adana was almost frozen in place as she watched Kamau skillfully grasp tools she had never seen and examine the intricate workings of the generator. The strength and the power he exuded left her wanting to walk into his arms and release her fears to a man she was sure was strong enough to handle them. Instead, Adana closed her eyes and silently repeated over and over to herself, *I'll get through this. I'll get through this*. Her head was pounding. The beating of her heart was pulsating in her ears. Kamau's touch brought her back to the reality of where she was. He placed one of his masterful hands on each of her long, slender arms and gently turned her to face him. Adana looked up into smoldering eyes that were looking down into her glistening ones. There was so much compassion in his face as he almost pleaded, "Adana, tell me what I can do to help you."

The weight of the terror she carried gave way to the strength of Kamau's arms. Without thought, she leaned into him, placing her pounding head on his waiting chest. Without hesitation, he pulled her farther into his arms and wrapped her lovingly into the fragrant fabric of his garments. He stroked her silklike hair, and with feathery touches he massaged her back. Stroking her hair released in him a series of emotions that were at once familiar and unfamiliar. The pace was so rhythmic and so soothing that Adana wished it could go on forever. Kamau stopped, took her by the hand and led her back up the stairs. She walked slowly, mentally attempting to will her anxiety away while matching Kamau's methodical steps until they were once again in the living area of the main house.

Adana walked back over to the sofa. This time, instead of returning to the briefs, she once again took off her shoes, stretched out on the lushly upholstered couch, closed her eyes and hoped that she could anesthetize herself with sleep. After watching Adana remove her shoes and position her extraordinarily lovely limbs to prepare for rest, Kamau quietly left the room and walked to the kitchen to sedate himself with the preparation of food. He was certain now that Adana's malady had nothing to do with tainted food, or food that she had not digested properly. From all of the signs, Kamau knew that Adana's case of nerves had to be directly related to the storm. The rain was at that moment still beating softly against standing structures and dry earth. It would soon turn into a torrent, accompanied by claps of thunder and streaks of lightning. Whatever her response, he knew he would be there to see her through it.

Deciding to let his creativity have full rein, Kamau concocted a Moroccan chicken dish he had not tried before. The ingredients were combinations he knew well. From the restaurant-capacity refrigerator, he took mushrooms, three varieties of onions and tricolored bell pepper slices, and started washing and chopping. As he chopped, the rain poured more heavily. The drops hit the glass windowpanes with hammering thuds. Evening settled into nightfall as Kamau prepared his meal and Adana slept.

When Adana awakened from a short, fitful nap, she was startled by the pounding rain. Looking around, she found Kamau missing. Rationally she knew he had not left her, yet her irrational mind wanted to be sure. She called out his name in a voice laced with shrillness. "Kamau? Kamau!" Before she could utter his name a third time, he stood in front of her, saying, "I am here, Adana."

Standing there, his gaze was soft as he pointed in the direction of the kitchen. Kamau paused, giving Adana's brain time to absorb his words. "I only went into the kitchen to prepare a meal. I thought perhaps a nourishing dish to soothe your nerves would be helpful."

Feeling residual traces of fear and the flush of embarrassment for yelling out like a schoolgirl, as well as having a sudden, intoxicating attraction to the magnificent man who stood staring at her, Adana closed her eyes and spoke quietly, "I'm sorry, Kamau. I woke up and heard the rain, and I didn't see you. I thought the worst—I'm sorry."

Kamau's piercing eyes studied Adana's face, which was etched with weariness. He said, "There is no need for an apology. As I said before, Adana, you are safe here. I promise you. Come, sit with me while I cook."

Taking Kamau's extended hand, she walked with bare feet into the kitchen and took a seat at the granite-covered island to watch Kamau create a meal designed for the most discriminating palate. Leaning both elbows on the island, her chin resting in her hands, Adana momentarily forgot the rain and her discomfort. "Kamau, what sparked your interest in cooking?"

Turning a copper-bottomed skillet in semicircles, coating it with olive oil, Kamau answered, "From the age of two to twenty, a magnificent woman who was more family than employee was the lead chef for our household. I was always fascinated by the sights, sounds and smells that emanated from that kitchen. As children, my brothers and I ran through the kitchen, constantly swiping food and being severely reprimanded. We loved those verbal harangues that Muga would dish out. Her name translated means 'mother for them all.' She was indeed that. She made food interesting for me. I never lost the interest. She was around long enough to encourage my first attempts to prepare dishes." A tinge of sadness colored his tone as he continued. "We lost her a few years ago. Stubborn woman that she was, she had been ill for a while but refused to tell anyone until it was too late."

He placed chopped garlic and onions in the skillet, thinking about the fact that his beloved Muga was another woman for whom he cared a great deal who allowed her stubbornness to take her life. The thought made him look up from the sizzling skillet directly into Adana's curious eyes. Though he had not known her long, he had already experienced how willful, headstrong and obstinate she could be.

Unaware of Kamau's thoughts, Adana smiled and continued to watch as he turned his attention back to the meal he was preparing. With the precision of a surgeon, he started cutting chicken into serving pieces and placing them in the skillet. The falling rain continued to play in rhythmic splashes on windows and nearby skylights. It offered an auditory backdrop to Kamau's movements as he seasoned, chopped, sautéed and stirred.

The two sat listening to the sounds of sizzling food and falling rain. Adana watched Kamau's hands move swiftly with skill and caring. She noted that they were dark and smooth with long slender fingers ending in naturally tapered nails kept respectably short and immaculately clean. Adana wondered how hands strong enough to harness a generator could be gentle enough to prepare a meal or soothe a woman. And she had, indeed, found him to be soothing. Just his touch had made her feel safe and whole. She couldn't remember ever having felt that way before. To distract herself from thoughts of Kamau's hands and from the rhythmic falling of the rain, Adana pierced the comfortable silence with a question about the case.

"Kamau, I know you've only looked very superficially at the documents in the case file, but given that quick preview, what do you see as my chances of getting my client exonerated from these charges?"

Kamau turned his full body to face Adana. He leaned against the custom-made countertop, crossing his feet at the ankles. With brows knitted, he stared at her pensively, wondering if he was choosing the proper time to add to her further discomfort. Gesturing for emphasis with a carving knife, Kamau started slowly.

As he spoke, Adana was momentarily lost in the movement of sensuous lips that housed glistening white teeth. Instinctively she wanted to touch his lips with the tip of one finger and slowly trace a path in the shape of an O around his mouth, savoring the softness she knew she would find. Adana's unsolicited daydream was interrupted as she heard Kamau ask, "Do you really want my opinion?"

Without hesitation, Adana's slightly irritated reply was, "Of course I want your opinion. Do you really think I came all this way, sitting here braving the elements, to not hear the truth? I am trying to win this case, and I need someone with an international perspective to check to see if I have uncovered every possible loophole."

A half-smile eased across his face, and one naturally arched eyebrow lifted as he spoke. "It seems to me your focus on your client's husband as the guilty party is a mistake. Valuable time is being lost while the true culprit is getting away." Kamau turned back to finish browning the chicken pieces he had placed in the skillet.

Adana was speechless. His answer had not been at all what she had expected. She recovered her voice and in a tone filled with playful sarcasm replied, "Well, almighty prophet, give me the name of the guilty party."

Kamau faced Adana with a look that told her in no uncertain terms that he was not in a playful mood.

"Adana, if you wish to use my expertise in this case, I would advise that you take seriously the suggestions I make. I assure you I do not make them without thought."

Adana was no longer smiling. All of the levity she had felt dissipated. They glared at each other, each waiting for the other to turn away. A sizzling skillet claimed Kamau's attention. He turned to remove the carefully prepared poultry from the pan. Not only was the skillet sizzling but so, too, was Adana. She was seething. Her head felt so hot she could almost feel smoke being released through her ears. She swallowed hard, clenched her teeth, shot daggers with her eyes into Kamau's back and uttered silent profanities at his insolence and arrogance. As Kamau was continuing to arrange his meticulously prepared chicken on a platter, he was oblivious to the fact that Adana had left her seat at the island and stood near him as he placed the last piece of chicken on the serving dish. If he was startled, he didn't show it. Kamau looked peripherally at an angry Adana without turning his head. Her scowl was unmistakable. Kamau was enraptured in her heady fragrance, causing him to be less affected by the scowl as she read him the riot act in a tone that was barely above a whisper.

"Kamau Mazrui, I don't know who you think I am, so let me provide some clarity. I asked for your opinion not because I have none of my own, but because I wanted an equally expert opinion. I am extremely good at what I do, and I don't need to be reprimanded by anyone, least of all a man who appears to have the misguided notion that his opinion is somehow sacrosanct and if given to a woman should be accepted without question." She took a breath. "Well, I'm not the one, Mr. Mazrui." Pointing her finger in Kamau's face, Adana ended her tirade. "I am sorry you have no sense of humor, but do not ever again dismiss me as though I am a child who needs to follow your lead without question."

Adana turned and left the room, leaving Kamau standing over his carefully arranged entrée. A slow smile eased across his handsome face as he thought that he had just experienced for the first time in his life a woman pointing her finger in his face and chewing him out. Adana was pacing in the dimly lit sitting room, muttering to herself. That was what Kamau saw when he entered the room. He stood in the entryway for a moment, taken by the form of the beautiful woman he saw in front of him. The magnetism between them was undeniable—contentious but undeniable. His intense physical awareness of her pulled him in like pulsating music.

The shock of seeing him standing there as she turned ran through Adana's body. Remnants of anger and harnessed chemical attraction vied for dominance. She inhaled and a chill coursed through her veins.

His baritone floated over her as he said, "I suppose I am not as accustomed as I should be to having my opinions questioned by a woman."

In a calm voice, looking pointedly into the dark pools that were Kamau's eyes, Adana asked, "Is that an apology?"

With a huskiness lingering in his voice, Kamau responded, "If an apology will calm you enough so that you can join me in a relaxing meal, then an apology you shall have."

Adana shook her head, and her voice sounded weary when she said, "An apology is not just something that I want; it is something that I deserve, Kamau. Can you understand that?"

Kamau stated very matter-of-factly, "Intellectually I do indeed understand your point, but culturally it seems that we are disagreeing over a very minuscule matter and I have done no harm. I have merely stated my position in the way that a man should."

Adana, even more exasperated, shook her head, lifted her hands in the air and said, "Just let it go, Kamau, just let it go. Never mind, never mind."

Kamau, now slightly more aggravated, walked over to Adana, grabbed both her upper arms and looked directly into her large, sparkling eyes now filled with surprise. Without flourish or fanfare, he said, "Adana, I apologize."

Completely taken aback, all Adana could feel was the touch of Kamau's strong hands on her arms. Completely weary of a struggle of any kind, her desire was to wrap herself in his embrace and rest her head on his hard, powerful chest. Instead, she stared into Kamau's unreadable eyes as he fought feelings and thoughts of his own that were new to him.

He wanted to hold Adana, press her close to him, feel her body touching his. He wanted to linger with her in a dark, silent place, stroking her limbs and savoring her mouth. He wanted her. He had wanted his wife but not like he wanted Adana at that moment. It was all so new. Kamau abruptly let go of Adana's arms. She felt the loss.

In a voice now low and almost pleading, Kamau spoke. "Adana, join me for dinner. Perhaps we will both be less testy."

Adana walked slowly over to the beautifully set table Kamau had indicated. As she sat down in one of the two chairs placed at the table, the rain began to beat harder, and for a split second the lights flickered, threatening to go dark.

Kamau saw the terror flit across Adana's face. He rushed to ease her discomfort. "Do not be alarmed by the flickering lights. It's okay, Adana. Remember the generator works and"—Kamau hesitated for a moment as he looked around, opened a cabinet and brought out a candelabra and a box of candles—"if the power should fail us for a moment, we can eat by candlelight."

He smiled tentatively. Adana noted that the magnificent, rock-solid man in front of her could go from tyrant to teddy bear in a matter of minutes, and the ways in which he showed tenderness spoke to her heart. Kamau placed the candles in the candleholders and lit them. The soft ambient lighting brought a warm glow to an already dimly lit room. Kamau then went into the kitchen and returned with a large serving tray laden with the dishes he had prepared earlier. He placed each serving platter on a circular lazy Susan in the center of the table to be served family style. The aromas reminded Adana that she was indeed hungry, and the presentation of the food left no doubt that Kamau's food was a welcome complement to the table.

Kamau sat in the chair across from Adana, and with a deep, penetrating stare, offered politely, "Please, Adana, help yourself. I hope you enjoy."

Adana helped herself to Moroccan chicken, couscous, curried cabbage, and avocado and papaya salad. While she served herself modest portions, Kamau poured them both glasses of Sauvignon Blanc. He then served himself. Adana savored a delicate morsel of chicken accompanied by a forkful of couscous. The spices erupted in her mouth, revealing the sensations of sweet, tart, hot and peppery. After a satisfying swallow, she said, "Kamau, this is really wonderful. I was hungrier than I thought."

Kamau's expression was stilled and serious as he spoke. "I am pleased that you enjoy the food. It has been a while since I've shared a meal with just one other person."

Adana knew the reference was to his deceased wife, Yasmin.

"I'm sorry to hear that, Kamau. I imagine it must be difficult to recover from losing someone you love."

Adana didn't really expect an answer, but he surprised her. As he spoke, his exquisite face seemed a conglomeration of hard, soft, distant and revealing. "It is difficult. There are days when I feel as though I have awakened from a hellish nightmare. I try to resume my normal life only to find that what I hoped was a nightmare was, in fact, a real event and my life as I knew it has been radically changed, never to be the same again."

Kamau took a sip of the cool wine. Adana continued to listen. "My life had rhythm, purpose, meaning. I am now in search of all those things again. The man I was I knew inside and out." He gestured toward himself. "This man I am learning. In Africa, a married man has a specific place in society. One who marries and provides for a wife and family is truly living out his creed as an adult male. I had no idea how much I have internalized the tenets of my culture until these past months as I have tried to sort out my future and determine my place once again in the world of my ancestors."

When his sentence was finished, Kamau looked almost stunned, and then a flicker of amusement crossed his face. "Adana, it must be the rain. Once again I have shared thoughts with you that I have not shared with anyone else."

Adana placed her fork on her plate, took a relaxing breath and laughed gently. "I'm glad. It lets me know that you are human, and that's important because the way you behave most of the time leaves one to have serious doubts."

They both laughed—warm, comfortable laughter. As the laughter subsided, Kamau's face became almost somber as he asked, "Adana, why have you never married?"

Surprised by the directness of the question, she forced a half-smile. "I have to give you a very trite answer and say I never found the right man."

Kamau looked slightly puzzled. "I've heard Americans talk about finding the right man or the right woman. Please explain to me what this 'right' is, as you understand it."

Adana tilted her head and thought a moment. "Right is right, Kamau. I can't really explain it. It's more ethereal than I can put into words. You know what right is when you feel it. The two of you fit together, you share values, you have a chemistry that works—you can trust each other." Jeffery Scott flashed through her mind. "You just know when it's right."

Kamau stroked the velvety beard on his chin. "To me it is all so curious. You see, my wife was chosen for me, and all of those attributes you described were characteristics of our marriage. I must say, though, that I am not sure what you mean by chemistry. Explain more, please."

Adana took a deep breath, thought for a moment and said, "Okay, this is the deal. Chemistry is that insatiable urge to have someone near you, with you. You're drawn by the touch, the feel, the smell of that someone. At some point, being with that special person is as essential as the body needing water." She looked into his eyes, searching for a glimmer of awareness. "Do you understand?"

Kamau looked at the passionate woman across from him and thought that she could easily inspire insatiable urges. He responded, "I think I am beginning to. In my world, that has never been seen as an essential component for a marriage. It is always assumed that in time any two reasonable people will come to honor and respect one another and thereby form a bond that is unbreakable."

Adana answered in a tone that was both warm and longing. "Kamau, the bond that I'm describing goes beyond the attachment of friends or business partners. What I'm describing is a physical yearning that in some cases clouds good sense and is strictly emotional. The head rarely leads. It's all heart."

"You sound as if you have experienced this chemistry."

Adana's lips lifted in a slow, thoughtful smile. "Haven't been that fortunate, but you forget I have three sisters who have been seriously bitten by the chemistry bug. I've seen it in action and heard it described countless times."

"Do you envy your sisters' experiences?"

Adana laughed. "No, I thoroughly enjoy watching them love their lives. I suppose what they have wasn't meant for me."

Kamau wondered if her laughter hid tears.

Chapter 11

The two finished their meal with peaceful chatter and the backdrop of falling rain, deliberately staying away from conversation about the case, understanding instinctively that it would be better left for later in the evening. When the meal was completed, Adana offered to clear the table and clean the kitchen. She was feeling much better. Kamau had been a wonderful distraction. He decided to act as her assistant, showing her where things in the kitchen should be placed. While they worked together, they compared notes on the practice of law in their respective countries. They found many similarities, since both countries were rooted in the British system.

As the last cabinet door was closed, Kamau said to Adana, "I need to show you where you will sleep tonight. The rain is not letting up, and you will surely be here through the night." The thought of being alone in a strange room during the night in a torrent of rain left Adana feeling a bit nauseous again. She slipped her shoes back on, tied them, and followed Kamau down a long hallway and into a beautifully decorated room resembling a master suite. All of the bedrooms were designed with their own baths and dressing areas. Adana commented on the loveliness of the room and walked from one end of it to the other, trying to still her nerves again.

Kamau noticed the change in her mood but said nothing. It became crystal clear to him that the storm was the cause of Adana's anxiousness. He was at a loss as to what to do. He certainly couldn't offer to share her room, and besides, she had not admitted to being unnerved by the storm. Kamau offered quietly, "Adana, if there is anything you need during the night, I will be next door in the adjoining room."

He turned and walked out, leaving Adana feeling truly alone. She walked slowly around the room, thinking. She turned on all of the lamps, hoping that light would destroy her fears. She then turned back the covers on the bed and remembered that she had brought nothing in which to sleep. It had not been her intention to stay the night. She sat on an upholstered bench in a corner of the room and considered her options. She unlaced her espadrilles once again and placed them neatly by the bench, as if arranging her shoes would somehow buy her time and solve her problems. Adana sat for a protracted length of time, looking around the room, repeating affirmations in her head and finally getting up to pace the floor. She hesitated for a moment, deciding what to do, and then left the room and walked to Kamau's suite. Adana was so preoccupied with thoughts of the storm and finding something to substitute as a nightie that when she saw the door ajar, she didn't think to knock; she just walked in saying, "Kamau."

Her voice faltered at the vision before her. Kamau had just finished a shower and was leaving the bathroom with a towel wrapped at his waist. What Adana saw caused her mind to empty. The razor-sharp brain that never failed her, that clicked constantly, was on hold.

The only image that registered was of Kamau Mazrui standing there with the body of a trained athlete, moist from the streams of water that had been fortunate enough to touch every glorious spot on his burnished, ebony body. His chest and arms personified strength. His thighs looked as though they had been sculpted from blocks of bittersweet chocolate-colored clay. His perfectly arched feet held his glorious form in place as he stood stunned to find Adana in his room. Sexual tension layered the place where they stood like silken multicolored ribbons on a maypole. Adana felt warm all over; the moisture on his ebony flesh was intoxicating. His hand resting on the folded closure of his towel left her too full of emotion to speak. The hard shell that she had spent years building was shattered instantly as her eyes quickly registered the image of his rippled abdominal muscles cutting and folding with perfection into the barely visible tops of his thighs.

Kamau Mazrui, a man who rarely allowed himself to be vulnerable, stood in a most vulnerable state, but feelings of embarrassment and exposure were erased with a look into Adana's eyes. There he read pure unadulterated desire. The desire in her eyes caused his entire body to harden with a lust of its own. He was flooded with feelings that were new that overrode anything he had ever experienced. Currents of heat radiated between them as they stood with Adana's dormant sexuality being awakened and Kamau understanding for the first time in his life the meaning of chemistry.

After what felt like an interminable time, Adana stammered out, "K-Kamau, I'm . . . I'm sorry, I should have knocked. I was thinking . . . I mean, I wasn't thinking. I was preoccupied and I should have knocked."

Adana felt like a stammering idiot. Words failed her. She could barely remember why she had come into the room. Finally she took a deep breath and finished her hastily thrown together thoughts. "I really need something to wear to bed. I came to see if maybe there is something in the house that I can use."

Kamau, wondering if he could trust his own voice, swallowed, cleared his throat and answered, "I can offer you pajama tops that I own but do not wear. If you'll wait a moment, I'll get something for you."

"Thank you," was Adana's soft reply as she left the room.

All the way back to her room she silently cursed herself for being so stupid. Walking in on Kamau like that—what had she been thinking? She hadn't been thinking, that was the problem. The scene in Kamau's bedroom replayed in her consciousness. She whispered out loud, "What was that? What happened in there?"

A small voice replied, *You know*. She entered the bedroom, closed the door behind her, rested her back on the door, looked up toward the heavens and said, "No, please God, not this man."

She walked over, sat on the down-filled bed, drew her knees up to her chest and muttered, "Adana, what is your need to be attracted to difficult men?"

Kamau knocked at the door.

"Come in," Adana said tersely.

He opened the door and entered the room, carrying over one arm the articles of clothing he had promised. Though his body was now covered in a kimono-style floor-length robe the color of fresh raspberries, Adana could not erase the image of his bare torso from her mind's eye. She uttered a quiet "thank you" as he handed her the pajama tops.

Feeling the awkwardness of the moment and not sure what to do about it, Kamau walked closer to the bed, looked at Adana intently and said, "If there is anything else that you need, do not hesitate to let me know. I want you to be comfortable."

Feeling equally ill at ease, Adana answered, "Thank you, Kamau, I'm sure I'll be fine."

Kamau bowed his head slightly, turned and left the room, leaving the door slightly ajar behind him. Adana felt the fabric in her hand. Both pajama tops were made of silk, one the color of sparkling emeralds, the other indigo. She placed both garments on her cheek and enjoyed the cool, silky feel next to her warm face. She buried her nose in the fabric and inhaled Kamau's fragrant scent. Though he had said he did not wear the tops to his pajamas, Adana could still smell his scent and she could not disguise her body's reaction. She moaned softly, placed the pajama tops on the bed and started undressing slowly, placing her clothes and undergarments on the love seat at the foot of the bed. Mentally and emotionally exhausted, Adana slipped into the indigo pajama top, turned off the lights, and got into bed. A sheet was all that covered her as she dozed off listening to the rain, praying that it would not turn into the anticipated storm.

Chapter 12

Kamau sat in the room next door, wondering how the willful, sharp-tongued woman sharing his home for the night could evoke such feelings of longing and desire in him. He sat on top of the covers, a mountain of pillows behind his back, wearing only silk pajama bottoms. He reached for a copy of a law journal he had started reading the day before. As he read the first line, the words faded and Adana's look of unbridled lust appeared in his head. The look brought back memories of the sexual tension he felt when Adana had walked into his room unannounced. A wave of passion struck him to his core and sent him spiraling into thoughts he had never had about any woman, not even his beloved Yasmin. Kamau thought about Keino and Ras. Was the feeling he experienced with Adana what they had been trying to describe when they had talked about their wives? Was the emotion he was experiencing what kept Keino from committing to Makena Rono before he met Amara? How had Keino known instinctively that there had to be more?

Kamau placed the journal back on the nightstand. He

thought about Adana's fabricated bout of nausea and decided to leave his bedroom door slightly ajar in order to listen for signs of distress. He got up, opened the bedroom door, turned off the lamp, put his head on the nearest pillow and tried to sleep. Thoughts of how illogical his feelings were plagued him. He tossed and turned, thinking of how foolish he felt to have the magnitude of attraction he was experiencing for a woman who was everything he did not want in his life. Besides, how could he feel anything for anyone when Yasmin had been gone only a year? Kamau drifted off into a light, fitful sleep.

The wind and rain picked up speed. A torrential downpour began assaulting the palatial Mazrui vacation home in sheets, accompanied by claps of thunder and streaks of lightning cutting across the sky like jagged-edged swords.

Late into the night, Kamau was awakened by a woman's cry for help. Feeling slightly drugged with the remnants of sleep flowing over him, he followed the sound and found Adana in the fetal position, whimpering and crying, immobilized by fear. Kamau walked quietly to the bed, making his way in a darkness permeated by enough light to distinguish shapes and figures. He called her name softly. "Adana, Adana, I'm here."

Her answer was a muffled cry. Kamau reached the bed, sat on it and scooped Adana into his strong arms. He stretched his legs out on the bed and cuddled her. Adana hung on tightly; in that instant, Kamau became her lifeline. As she sobbed more deeply, Kamau stroked her hair, rubbed her back and kissed her forehead. He tried to console her with soft whispers of "I'm here, Adana. You're safe. I'm here." Her falling tears left moisture on his neck and chest. Kamau used his thumbs to gently help wipe away her tears. Those he wiped away were replaced almost immediately. Finally he just held her, rocking her slowly and gently attempting to ease her fears and provide the comfort he knew she so desperately needed.

After a time, Kamau heard a barely intelligible, "Kamau, I am so sorry." He reached over and, while still holding Adana, turned on the bedside table lamp, which emitted a warm glow. Compassion and fragments of an undefined emotion radiated from Kamau's face as he stared into Adana's pleading eyes. In low, deep, resonant tones, he said, "I told you you would be safe with me."

Adana lifted her head from the safe haven of Kamau's bare chest. She tried wiping the remaining tears from her eyes with the sleeve of the pajama top that she was wearing. Kamau studied Adana with a curious intensity. There she was, sitting in the middle of the bed looking ravishing with tousled hair, tear-streaked face and long, slender, perfectly shaped legs folded under her body as she attempted to dry her eyes. The act was pure, it was graceful, and sensuality emanated from every stroke. Adana was so distraught that it did not occur to her that the pajama top she wore was not completely buttoned, and though it left much to the imagination, Kamau was painfully aware of the fact that underneath his silk pajama top was nothing but beautiful brown honey-colored skin. Only Kamau's eyes betrayed what he felt. "Adana, if you are all right now, I'll leave you."

As Kamau moved to leave the bed, he felt a tender touch on his bare arm and heard a whispered, "Please don't leave just yet. I owe you an explanation. Please stay."

Kamau eased back onto the bed, resting his head on the headboard. Adana stretched out beside him, feeling an element of safety she had never felt with any man except her father. Though she knew she was totally vulnerable physically and emotionally, she sensed that Kamau would be as he had promised—her safety net. Kamau was pleasantly surprised to see the willful and abrupt Adana show a side of herself that was gentle and almost compliant. He settled back, crossed his out-stretched legs at the ankles, folded his muscular arms across his sculpted chest and waited.

After a deep cleansing breath, Adana turned to face Kamau and was struck by the beauty of soft golden light washing over his radiant ebony skin. For a moment she was stunned by the power of his masculinity. He sat there like a king in all of his bare-chested glory, waiting to be served by willing subjects. And at that moment, Adana felt very willing. The two stared deeply into each other's eyes as Adana spoke slowly and softly.

"When I was a very young girl, I went on a camping trip. It was meant to be an overnight excursion for a group of ten little girls and their mothers." Adana stopped speaking, swallowed and started again. "The area was considered very safe. The trails were well marked. We were split into groups. I was not in my mother's group, something she would blame herself for for many years."

Adana's speech slowed as if she were thinking aloud. "I was always a curious child, and I spotted a plant grow-ing that I had never seen before. It was so beautiful. I wanted to get closer. The leader of the group trudged on with the other girls and I stopped. I meant to stop for only a moment. I was only going to look at the plant. When I looked up, I was alone. I looked around, and every tree and bush looked the same. The silence was deafening. Occasionally there was the rustling of leaves or the chirp-ing of a bird, but silence like I'd never experienced was everywhere. The terror set in almost immediately. I became paralyzed with fear. I started running, only I got turned around and was running in the opposite direction of where the group leader had gone. If I had screamed, perhaps someone would have heard me and I wouldn't have been left. My throat was closed with fear. By the time I could scream, the group was long gone."

Tears began to stream again down Adana's cheeks. Kamau reached over and touched her hand and stroked it gently.

"For hours I was lost in the dark, and then it started storming. I just knew that I would die and never see my parents or my sisters again. They found me after a night filled with terror for everyone. It took years for my mother to ever speak to the group leader again, and needless to say, I don't go camping and storms still terrify me." In a tone that was as contrite as she could make it, Adana confessed, "So you see, I was lying about an upset stomach. I still come unglued if caught in a storm away from familiar surroundings."

Kamau once again wiped tears from Adana's cheeks with gentle strokes of his fingers. She melted into the hypnotic heat of each stroke. Adana's body began to yield to the burning sweetness of Kamau's touch and of his words. "Precious Adana, I am so sorry that you had that experience." A tentative smile softened his features as he said, "I wish I had been there to rescue you."

Adana smiled through tears as she responded, "I feel as though I'm being rescued right now."

The rain was falling in a rhythmic pattern as Kamau, in an act of raw possession, captured Adana's trembling lips. The heated moment left her surrendering completely to his skillful introduction to a kind of pleasure she had never experienced before. Adana felt a rising passion burning inside her; Kamau's hands were so gentle and so warm, his mouth so tantalizing. The kiss left her wanting more. She lifted her arms and placed them around Kamau's neck, pressing willing flesh against willing flesh, stroking silken fabric against hard, sable skin. The rain continued beating down, splattering windows and rooftops. Kamau moved his hands through Adana's hair and pressed his lips deeper onto hers, savoring the feel of her willingness to come to him. Her surrender left him spiraling with heat, fragmented thoughts and a growing desire.

The rain poured harder. Adana released sighs of ecstasy through parted lips as they were captured over and over again by Kamau's hungry kisses. The harder the rain fell, the deeper the torrent of Kamau's kisses captured Adana's heart, draining away her fears. They held one another, communicating only with touches and sighs and moans of ecstatic pleasure. Kamau moved from Adana's swollen lips to her neck. With head back and eyes closed, Adana willingly gave in to a wave of sexual desire that she did not recognize. She craved his touch, his scent, the hardness of his chest and arms, the sweetness of his mouth. The rain poured and poured. Kamau nibbled Adana's earlobes and sighed into her ears the sounds of searing need. Adana's answer was to ravish his neck and mouth while repeatedly stroking his arms and chest. Neither had any desire to control the pleasure they were experiencing. Kamau stroked Adana's silky soft thighs, running his hands under her pajama top, causing Adana to quiver with intoxication as he gently moved his hands over every inch of her firm bottom, slowly and completely as though committing it to memory. Melting and quivering, Adana sighed and then moaned. Kamau released the one button on her pajama top that was fastened and pulled Adana close to him. He wanted to feel her bare breasts against his chest.

The perfect contrast of Kamau's hard, solid, sculpted chest against Adana's soft, round, firm breasts sent them both scrambling out of control. Kamau outlined her full breasts with his fingertips and then with his lips, indicating his delight with his eyes and kisses of pleasure. Adana's nipples peaked and her breasts filled with the weight of desire. Kamau's fingers and mouth burned into her flesh, and she felt herself drowning in sweet agony. Her pleasure was pure and explosive. Her defenses were gone, and as the rain continued to pour, so did Adana's desire for Kamau. He removed the pajama top Adana was wearing. Adana unhooked the button that held the top of Kamau's pajama bottoms. Without words, he slipped the smooth fabric down his hard, rippled legs and discarded the pajamas.

Witnessing Kamau's desire for her come alive, Adana wrapped her taut legs around his hard, strong ones, sending waves of ecstasy throbbing through them both. With slow, measured strokes, Kamau moved his hands over every inch of Adana's waiting body. She mirrored his every stroke and touch as they explored each other for the first time, with a heat and passion reserved for new lovers. Their hearts hammered in sync, and shivers rippled through them like electric currents, causing Adana to repeat his name as though it were a mantra. Deliciously drunk on arousal, Kamau answered her call by lightly, lovingly biting every visible surface of her body, sending waves of pleasure to shatter her womb.

Their sense of time was lost as the rain poured. Kamau, on the edge of spilling his passion, enveloped Adana once again in a long, deep, slow kiss. Adana was floating, she was burning and her legs were moving involuntarily up and down Kamau's body. She arched and twisted in slow, circular movements. Kamau, wanting to prolong the newness of what he was experiencing, once again took each of Adana's firm breasts into his mouth. As Adana felt the heat of his mouth close around her breasts, her cries of pleasure sent his blood racing. They both wanted never to end the pleasure that was permeating every fiber of their being, every inch of their souls. They wanted to prolong the agonizing pleasure that enveloped them, yet they longed to close the distance between them. They read each other's minds. Kamau wrapped Adana's legs around his waist, she arched up and he filled her completely. Her gasp of delight caused him to question with his eyes whether he had hurt her. Adana's answer was to wrap her legs tighter and pull him into the seat of more joy than either of them had ever known.

The rain continued whipping the palatial home as Adana and Kamau went from long, slow, measured strokes to hammering, pounding rhythms. The sound of the thunderous sky was mixed with Adana's screams of dizzying pleasure. The loving was urgent. There were no words, merely sounds of ecstatic murmurs. All of the force and passion that was exhibited in Kamau and Adana's courtroom personas now ignited in bed in throbbing jolts of demanding, burning desire. Kamau dominated; Adana succumbed. He orchestrated; she followed his lead, wanting to be consumed by his passion. The pent-up frustrations, the deep longing for a burning, willing connection, blazed in a white-hot heat not unlike the lightning that was streaking across the sky. Control was exchanged for pure abandon. Their spirits knew each other as they instinctively desired completion and a continuation of the intoxicating lovemaking all at the same time. Pulses quickened, mouths throbbed, blood rushed, euphoria drugged them. Repeated shudders rushed through Adana like wide ocean waves as she screamed Kamau's name.

Hearing his name uttered in the throes of passion sent blood rushing to the top of his head. His body tightened and hardened more, filling Adana with pleasure beyond her dreams. The air swirled around them, the syncopated rhythm of their lovemaking threatening to halt their breathing. Unable to take more, Kamau spilled his passion, washing Adana's womb in the fulfillment of his pleasure. Neither wanted to let go.

In wordless bouts of arousal throughout the night, their hands moved like magic over each other, exploring, pulsating. Their bodies, bare and moist from urgent lovemaking tingled deliciously as they repeatedly writhed in relentless rhythms as they followed sensuous paths to ecstasy. They remained silently wrapped in each other's arms until sleep overtook them as the rain continued to fall gently.

As the dawn peeked over the horizon, it brought with it a clean, satiated earth and a clarity to Kamau's mind, which the night before had been clouded by the look, touch, taste and scent of the woman peacefully curled up next to him. Even though he was well aware of what he had done and why, he was still amazed that for the first time in his life, he had suspended rational thought and succumbed to pure emotion—the result of which was remorse permeated by guilt. Kamau stared at Adana, savoring the moment as if expecting it never to be repeated. He gently lifted himself from the bed, retrieved his pajama bottoms from the floor and walked like a bare African god back to his room. Once back in the room, he slipped into bed and was almost immediately enveloped by a feeling of aloneness that rivaled what he had felt when told of Yasmin's death. In a flash of rage, he repeatedly struck with closed fists the down pillows that filled the bed. Finally exhausted, he covered his face with a pillow to muffle the sound and released an utterance that was part battle cry, part rage, and part wounded soul aching from the loss of what was and the understanding of the impossible situation he knew he had created.

Chapter 13

The light streamed into the room where Adana slept and filled the space with soft golden rays that nudged her gently from a peaceful sleep. The light warmed her body, causing her to stir in a feline motion, stretching arms and legs slowly, easily, across the expanse of the bed, expecting even in a state of semiconsciousness to touch the supine body of the man who had the night before loved her into willing submission. With eyes closed and a dreamy smile on her face, Adana reached for Kamau and found instead air and down-filled pillows. With disbelief clouding her mind, Adana opened her eyes, sat up in her bed and looked around the room, satisfying herself that Kamau was indeed gone. Fighting the feeling of disappointment at not being able to savor the pleasure they had experienced the night before, she decided to shower and prepare for the long ride back to Nairobi.

Stepping into the steaming hot shower, she hoped that Kamau's abrupt departure had nothing to do with second thoughts. Yes, they had thrown caution to the wind. They had moved beyond anything either of them had expected, but they were consenting adults capable of making life-altering decisions. After all, they did just that for other people all day long. Adana smiled to herself as she thought of how she was rationalizing making love to Kamau Mazrui in a moment of weakness. She mumbled out loud, "Adana Terrell, attorney at law, now what are you going to do? You threw yourself at the man." She stopped, lathered her body and then continued aloud. "No, no, that was a mutual seduction." She replayed the lovemaking over in her mind, and dreamily she thought that the two of them had been like children in a candy store, feasting on their favorite sweets. As flashes of the passionate night floated through her mind, a sobering question eased in. If she was not ready for a committed relationship and Kamau appeared to be still suffering from the loss of his wife, where did that leave them? Adana shook her head, allowed the warm water to flow over her body and decided that no decision had to be made at that moment. She continued the shower, hoping that soon all of her questions would be answered.

Kamau had made his way to his favorite retreat—the kitchen. While Adana slept, Kamau had played racquetball, showered and thought endlessly about how to remedy what he saw as a very difficult situation. In the kitchen, he knew that he'd somehow find an answer among the pots, pans, aromas and textures. He was wrong. All he saw on the racquetball court, in the shower and in the kitchen were images of Adana. He could still taste her, feel her, smell her. He still wanted her, but he was also clear that his feelings were betraying Yasmin's memory and placing him in a position where the outcome could only be disastrous.

As he retrieved eggs from the refrigerator for what he hoped would be perfect omelets, Adana walked through the kitchen entryway and in a low, sensual voice said,

"Good morning, Kamau." The good morning he didn't hear, but his name reverberated in his ears over and over, reminding him of Adana lying beneath him, repeating his name in the throes of lovemaking. While holding an egg, Kamau's hand halted in midair. He uttered a husky "Adana." At the moment her name left his lips, he tried distracting himself by finishing the omelet. He cracked the egg and accidentally dropped it, shell and all, into the waiting bowl. His mouth curved in an unconscious smile. He left the half-cracked egg in the bowl, turned to the sink, washed his hands, looked up at Adana as she watched him and said, "Adana, we must talk."

She could tell by the look on his face that she was about to hear the answers to the questions that had been running through her mind. Adana kept her face as composed as she could while saying, "Fine, Kamau, let's talk."

She wasn't prepared as Kamau moved toward her with the same hunger in his eyes that she had seen as he had ravished her body the night before. He encircled her waist with his hands and possessively pulled her toward him, needing to feel the body that fit him like a missing puzzle piece.

Adana leaned into Kamau's sweet embrace and listened as his voice dropped in volume.

"Adana, for the second time in my adult life, I am at a loss as to how to handle a situation. The first time was the death of my wife, and now, because of a moment when I suspended rational thought, I have compromised us both. I am in no position emotionally to take on the responsibility of a relationship yet. I am drawn to you in ways I don't begin to understand. Even now you can feel what you do to me. You are an incredible woman, but I was not reared to toy with a woman's affections. Life is more precious than that. I should never have allowed last night to happen. Please forgive me for taking advantage of your vulnerability. It is not something I have ever done before, and I will never allow it to happen again. Please forgive me."

Though his words were full of contrition and denial, Adana could feel the heat from Kamau's body and his growing arousal matching her melting center. Pain and need were a lethal combination. Hearing Kamau's words left Adana grief-stricken yet needing to be loved by the man who had caused the grief. Hiding her hurt, she took a deep breath. Her chest felt as though it would burst. Her voice was soft and whispery.

"Kamau, I am not a woman who can be easily manipulated. Last night I was willing to be in your bed, in your arms, loving you with every fiber of my being. You made me feel things I did not know existed. You made me feel alive in ways I've only heard about. I haven't been compromised—I have been truly made love to for the first time in my life. But I am also not a woman who insists upon being where she is not wanted. I don't know what I want from you. I have said often enough that I don't want to be married. I'm not even sure what a relationship for me would look like. Let me assure you, though, that neither of us has been compromised."

She removed his hands from her waist, stepped back and said, "Please call the driver. I really need to get back to Nairobi."

Adana left the kitchen and went about collecting her things while waiting for the driver. Kamau called the chauffeur and sat in the living room, watching as Adana packaged case files and her laptop in order to make a hasty departure. Neither of them mentioned the case. The time had passed for legal collaboration. It had been tainted by collaboration of another kind. When the driver arrived, Adana stood in the doorway, looked back at

Kamau and said, "Thank you, Kamau, for your generosity in helping me through the storm—I'll never forget it."

A deep sorrow covered Kamau's face as he responded, "I need no thanks for protecting you and making you feel safe. I am grateful that I was able to hold you in my arms and give you peace of mind for however long. If there is ever anything that you need, please let me be the first person that you call."

Fighting tears, Adana's only reply was, "Good-bye, Kamau."

Chapter 14

The ride back to Nairobi was torturous for Adana. Conflicting emotions confused and frustrated her. One event with Kamau had caused her to question everything she had ever said about love and relationships. When she thought of how he made her feel, warm tears ran down her face. Wiping them away, she reprimanded herself for shedding tears over a man she hardly knew; then the avalanche of images floated through her head that were testaments to the fact that what she did know embodied everything she wanted in a man. Kamau was strong, honest, faithful, full of integrity, brilliant, gentle and kind. And, yes, she smiled through tears, he was arrogant, willful and a traditional stick-in-the-mud, but she knew that the way he had made her feel, whether in bed or in the kitchen, her life would forever be incomplete without that feeling. In that moment, she understood that he was the catalyst for all of her potential, he was that entity in the universe for whom she was fashioned, and she knew that she had found him and lost him all at the same time. Adana swallowed hard and bit back tears as she made the long trek back to Nairobi cocooned in the comfortable leather of the backseat of the chauffeur-driven car.

Kamau sat unable to move from the chair in the great room positioned across from the sofa where Adana had slept. He sat smoking his pipe and drinking a glass of Spanish port, wondering how he had managed to so thoroughly complicate his life—a life that was already in disarray before Adana Terrell showed up on his doorstep. Adana had turned everything upside down, rearranged his thoughts, his feelings, his physical reactions. He almost laughed as he thought she had rearranged his chemical makeup. His physical chemistry had reconfigured itself just to accommodate Ms. Adana Terrell.

Even as he sat in his comfortable chair, the thought of Adana's passion, the way she had come to him without fear, without shame, with complete unbridled joy and desire, made him feel whole as a man. Just the thought of her left him weak and wanting. The unanswerable question was what was he going to do about this new-found pleasure that was causing so much pain? He needed someone with whom to talk it through—someone who could offer balance and sanity to the situation. Keino immediately came to mind, but Kamau squashed the thought, thinking that he didn't need to involve Keino in something that he didn't even understand himself and couldn't explain if his life depended on it.

And so he decided that he could put in order those pieces of his life over which he did have control. Since the storm had lifted, he would put aside his uneasiness with Salima Banda and allow her to find him new living quarters. He also needed to review documents for the next meeting with a group of African dignitaries whose countries were considering coming aboard his newly formed international venture. Kamau had a great deal to accomplish in the weeks and months ahead. He hoped it would blur the constant thoughts of Adana.

Adana checked her slender gold wristwatch and knew that she would soon be arriving in Nairobi. She pulled out of her bag a mirrored compact and checked her face. It was clear of any makeup except for the mocha-colored gloss on her lips. The long ride had been a godsend, giving her a chance to compose herself before seeing her sisters again. She had promised herself that this time she would not share with her sisters her newfound passion— the calm, quiet, thrillingly sexual Mr. Kamau Mazrui. She didn't want to hear the onslaught of questions, didn't want to see the worried looks, didn't want to hear remarks that questioned her sanity. This bit of information she would keep to herself until there was a need to share. As quickly as the thought hit her, she had a flash of panic—suppose Kamau told Ras or Keino or any of his other brothers. As quickly as the flash of panic had arisen, it subsided when she thought that Kamau didn't want to appear foolish either. He couldn't explain what happened any better than she could, so she thought she was safe for a while. Adana took a deep cleansing breath and settled back to travel the last few miles to Amara's home.

When the car pulled into the driveway, Amara, Afiya and Cassandra walked out to meet their sister. As Adana stepped from the car, she was encircled in an embrace that filled her with comfort, love and joy. Through it all, there was nothing like her sisters. With teasing laughter, Adana said, "I need to get waylaid by a storm more often. I prefer this greeting to your usual." Adana started mimicking her sisters, "Slow down, Adana. Don't be so serious, Adana. Adana, we came to play not work. Adana, stop rearranging our lives."

"Okay, okay, we get the picture." Afiya's eyes sparkled as she talked. "We were so worried about you."

Amara chimed in, "Thank God Keino was able to get through to Kamau. When I saw how satisfied my husband was, I felt that you were in good hands."

Adana's mind flashed on Kamau's hands, the soft, gentle touch, the places they found on her body that made her ache and burn.

"Earth to Adana." It was Cassandra pulling Adana out of her daydream.

"Oh, I'm sorry, just thinking about work again, I guess."

Afiya took the case files from Adana's hand, saying, "That's your problem now. Work! Work! Work! Come on, let's get inside and figure out how to spend our last day together."

The sisters, laughing at Afiya making fun of Adana, walked into Amara and Keino's home. The next day the sisters finished their pampering rituals, talked, laughed, ate and played with Keino and Amara's twins before heading out on Mazrui company planes back to their respective homes, countries and continents, away from each other. Adana kept her thoughts of Kamau tucked deeply in her heart, using thoughts of him as her own private pieces of bliss.

After three months of being at home without any word from Kamau, Adana felt both blessed and cursed. Always anxious to dive into work, she knew it provided a much-needed distraction. She was never disappointed. As she walked past her assistant's desk, she was hit with a barrage of questions about scheduling upcoming cases. Adana answered succinctly and walked into the large room that had once been her sanctuary—her office. Everything was the same, but she wasn't. Adana settled in and began pouring through a never-ending list of e-mails and a stack of court cases, all of which seemed urgent. When she finally came up for air, it was two in the afternoon and her assistant was knocking on her door.

"Come in."

"Ms. Terrell, this came for you."

The efficient young woman walked through the door carrying a long gold box tied in gold satin ribbon. Adana's surprise did not show on her face. "Thank you. Please just put the box on the table near the window."

The assistant complied and left the room. Adana placed the Montblanc with which she was writing down on the legal pad. Folding her hands in front of her face, with her lips touching her index fingers, she sat staring at the box. She had no idea who could have sent it. It wasn't her birthday; it wasn't a holiday. A hopeful smile crossed her face. Kamau! Maybe the box was from Kamau. It appeared to be a traditional florist's box. Kamau was such a gentleman; sending flowers would certainly be something that he would do. Adana walked over to the box and lifted it, looking for a card—nothing. She untied the satin ribbon and lifted the cover from the box. It was filled with two dozen red roses. They were beautiful. The card was positioned on top of the bed of roses. Adana opened the envelope and read, *I miss you and I need you back. Jeffery.*

Adana wanted to scream, first from disappointment and then from rage. Jeffery infuriated her like no one else. He took so much for granted. She was seething, muttering out loud. "I told you, you self-centered moron, that I am through, finished."

Adana put the top back on the box, picked it up, carried it to her assistant's desk and said, "Kathy, please see that these get to a patient at a nearby hospital. Thank you."

The startled assistant's only reply was, "I will, Ms. Terrell."

Adana went back into her office to bury herself once again in the never-ending stream of paper that found its way to her desk. Working until her eyes were crossing, her hands were aching and her brain was feeling like mush, she decided to call it a day, or more accurately an early evening. She freshened up in the private bath adjoining her office and then packed a briefcase to accommodate at least four hours more of work once she found her way home. Walking down the carpeted corridor of the firm's suite of offices, Adana was feeling as though she had almost completed a very productive day. As she approached the glass doors serving as the entryway to the building, she could see them. A group of reporters—waiting. She was not in the mood but she was ready. The moment she opened the door, flashbulbs and microphones were thrust into her face. Ever the consummate professional, Adana smiled and quipped, "All of this for me?"

The flood of questions came. "Ms. Terrell, is it true that your client, Ms. Bitak, is funneling money to terrorists?"

"Is her husband the relative of a nationally known terrorist?"

"Are you withholding vital information that affects the security of this country?"

The questions enraged Adana, but she used the anger to fashion a passionate response that made everyone who cared about her proud, including Kamau Mazrui, who sat in a Washington, D.C. hotel room watching the news while he prepared for a meeting of his Continental African Strategic Planning Committee with newly recruited African dignitaries. Kamau had been in the hotel no longer than an hour when Adana appeared on television. He considered her appearance his welcoming gift. He noted that she looked weary but as beautiful as ever.

"Ladies and gentlemen, I am certain that you know that guilt by association should have died with Joseph McCarthy. It is a sad day in the history of this democracy when an innocent woman is tried in the press based on unsubstantiated charges and indiscriminate allegations. See you in court."

Adana continued walking amid continued questioning that she ignored. The office valet had brought her car around. Adana settled herself comfortably behind the wheel and drove away as cameras continued flashing.

Kamau picked up the television remote and touched the OFF button. He then picked up his briefcase, left the hotel room and headed for the conference room previously reserved for the meeting of continental Africans, whom he hoped would serve as venture capitalists for the international projects he had designed to bring unification and economic stability to Africa. But as he made his way to the conference room, his thoughts were of Adana. Three months of missing her had become more constant than mourning the loss of Yasmin, which left him with a nagging emotional mixture of guilt, remorse and longing.

Chapter 15

By the time Adana reached her home, her voice mail and personal e-mail were filled with congratulatory remarks concerning her handling of the press. A smiling Adana thought that though she handled public presentations well, she was essentially a private person, and public displays of any kind were not to her liking. Feeling the need for freedom, she removed every piece of clothing she wore and dressed in a red silk kimono. The cool, sleek fabric caressed her skin. Just as Adana had found a wonderfully relaxing position on her bedroom chaise, her doorbell rang. It startled her. She couldn't imagine who could possibly be at her door without calling. She decided to ignore the ringing, but the more she ignored the bell, the more persistent the ringer became and then the telephone rang. Somehow Adana sensed that the two were connected. She picked up the receiver. The caller ID read PRIVATE. Adana spoke calmly into the telephone. "Hello."

"Adana, I really need to see you, just to talk to you. I'm at your front door. I knew you were home. I saw you drive into the garage."

She knew the voice. "Jeffery, have you lowered yourself to being a stalker now?"

"Look, I just want to talk. I really messed things up with us, and I really need to talk."

"Nothing you can say is going to fix anything, Jeffery. It's okay, it's over! I've moved on and you had already moved on while we were together. Just go, Jeffery, just go."

"Adana, I can't go. I have to talk to you now. Please, just let me in."

"Look, I don't want you causing a scene at my front door. I have neighbors, and all I need is for the press to get a glimpse of you acting a fool at my front door."

"All you have to do is let me in, Adana. You know I don't give a damn about the press. Do you want me to call a press conference out here on your front steps? I can do that."

"Jeffery, just shut up. I'm coming down."

"I'm waiting." He smiled.

Adana was more furious with Jeffery now than she had ever been. He knew she hated public scenes, and he had the nerve to pitch a fit on her doorstep. She raced down her stairs, flung open her front door and spoke through clenched teeth.

"Come in, Jeffery."

"Thank you for the invitation."

"There was no invitation. I've had a long day, and I want you to say what you want to say and get the hell out. Do you hear me?"

"I must say, there was a time when you treated me far better than this display of rude behavior that I am becoming accustomed to."

"Jeffery, say what you came to say."

Jeffery turned slowly. "May I sit?"

"I don't care what you do. Just get done what you came for."

Jeffery sat on one of Adana's matching sofas, gesturing for her to sit across from him on the other sofa.

"Jeffery, I don't need to sit. Just talk."

"I won't start talking until you are sitting."

"You obstinate fool." Adana sat down. As she did so, she was unaware that the slits in her robe exposed her smooth thighs, long slender legs and bare feet with perfectly painted red toenails, a pure turn-on for Jeffery.

Almost salivating, he swallowed, took a breath and said, "Look, Adana, I know I was wrong. I should have been up front with you from the beginning, but to tell you the truth, I really didn't think it would matter. My ex-wife and I had an understanding, and though we were friendly, we had no sexual contact. It wasn't that kind of relationship. Why can't you understand that?"

"Jeffery, I understand. I understand that you were so selfish all you thought about was yourself. Did it ever occur to you that if I were going to be involved in a three-way relationship that I might want to be privy to that involvement? No, Jeffery, all you were concerned about was having what you wanted, when you wanted it, the way you wanted it. The women involved were just pawns. Who is to say there were only two of us? How many were there really, Jeffery?" She threw her hands in the air. "Never mind, don't answer that question. You might have to indulge in your favorite pastime—lying."

"Is there no reasoning with you, Adana? I invite you to dinner; you walk out on me. I send you flowers; you don't even acknowledge them! What more can I do?"

"Jeffery, read my lips—there is nothing you can do, nothing. I am finished, through. Whatever we had is washed from my mind, heart, soul. It's gone, Jeffery, gone, gone—now could you go too?"

Jeffery rose slowly from the sofa, and as an afterthought adjusted the cuffs of his dress shirt. "All right,

Ms. Terrell. The loss is just going to have to be yours, but if you ever need me, you know where to find me."

As Adana stood, he leaned over to kiss her. She turned her head and lifted her hand just in time to avoid the amorous good-bye Jeffery was hoping for. He headed toward the door, smiling and shaking his head. Adana followed him, encouraging his exit.

Taking two steps from the door on the way to his Lincoln Town Car, Jeffery was aware of a black limousine with tinted windows slowing down as it approached Adana's house. Not knowing what to make of it, but not finding it unusual given the neighborhood dignitaries, he got into his car and drove away. Adana noticed the luxury automobile, made a mental note of its presence, closed her door, locked it and went back upstairs to her bedroom, hoping that she had finally ended her verbal altercations with Jeffery Scott. She found herself laughing at his arrogance and his selfish persistence.

Just as Adana settled down once again, the shrillness of the ringing telephone shattered the momentary peace. Expecting that Jeffery was once again going to attempt to plead his case, she picked up the receiver with the intention of slamming it back down, leaving a dial tone reverberating in Attorney Scott's ear. In a split second, the caller ID caught her eye and she read MAZRUI, followed by a foreign telephone code that she knew did not belong to her sister Amara. Adana's heart started pounding in her ears. Heat rushed to her face as she breathlessly said, "Hello."

There was no mistaking the deep, rich, sensual, heavily accented response that came back. "Adana."

Inside her head, Adana was shouting, *It's Kamau! Oh my God, it's Kamau.* Hearing him speak her name caused her body to react, igniting pleasure points from her head to her toes. Her hand went to her taut stomach, holding it gently, helping to compose a voice she was not sure she still had.

"Kamau, how are you?"

The words of his studied answer wrapped around her like a cool ocean breeze.

"I have been busy trying to organize my life. I flew in to D.C. this morning to meet with a group of investors whom I have been trying to pull together for some time. It was a brief but very productive meeting."

Her thoughts were spinning. "Kamau, did you say D.C.? Are you in the area?"

His voice lowered and became more intense. "Yes, I am, as a matter of fact. I saw you on a news broadcast today. I had my driver bring me to your place to leave a congratulatory note. Your handling of the press was indeed impressive."

Kamau's voice then took on a deceptive calm and a distance Adana could hear.

"I didn't expect you to be at home, but as we drove by, I saw you standing in the doorway in your dressing gown escorting a gentleman caller out of your door. It did not appear to be a good time to leave a calling card."

The silence that followed was deafening. Adana was struck by the picture she and Jeffery must have presented as Kamau's car drove by, and a genius IQ was not required to imagine what Kamau had concluded. Her silky voice sounded so fragile to his attentive ear.

"Kamau, was that you in the limo that just passed my house?"

His answer was a cool, controlled "Yes."

Adana spoke in a tone that was almost apologetic. "You need to know that what you saw is not what it appeared to be, and I really would like to explain."

"I'm parked out front. Shall I come in?"

"Please."

"I'll be right in."

Adana rushed into her bathroom, freshened up her face and ran a comb through her hair. By the time she had combed the last strand, the doorbell rang. She took a deep breath and walked down the stairs, trying to contain the joy she felt knowing that she was going to see Kamau for the first time in too many months. Cursing Jeffery Scott under her breath, thinking about how he could have caused a monumental problem by his unannounced visit, Adana reached the door, clutched the doorknob, took another breath and opened the door. There he was, as magnificent in Western attire as he had been in traditional African garments. His face was beaming with a seductive smile that many found totally disarming. His beard had grown fuller and shaped his face like manicured velvet surrounding full, sensuous lips. An exquisitely tailored charcoal-colored suit, pristine white linen shirt and silk tie knotted Windsor fashion gave him a look of elegance and power. Posture perfect, he moved through the door with a grace and ease that said he belonged wherever he was.

Adana muttered hastily, "Come in, have a seat."

The two of them were equally unsure about how to greet each other. They were each torn between wanting to continue where they had left off the night of the storm, yet remembering the conversation they'd had before Adana had been driven back to Nairobi. Now they were faced with a conversation about Kamau seeing Jeffery leaving Adana's home in a way that implied more intimacy than Kamau wanted to contemplate when it came to Adana and another man. They had much to unravel.

Kamau moved into the living room. His steps slowed as he looked around, admiring the space that told him even more about the woman who had become a fixture in his daydreams. His smooth voice broke the silence. "Your home is as beautiful and as elegant as you are."

Suddenly aware of her bare skin under the robe she wore, Adana secured the sash a bit more tightly. "Thank you, Kamau. My home is my refuge, and I try to surround myself with things that I love."

Kamau positioned himself comfortably on the sofa opposite Adana. Legs crossed and hands resting in his lap, he talked and stared at her as though committing her face to memory. Though he was as taken by Adana's loveliness as he had ever been, he was more astounded by the way in which he reacted to her emotionally.

"I am still looking for a new home. The process has not gone as quickly as I would like." His voice trailed off as he thought of how ready he had finally become to complete the process of relocation.

"Kamau." His name floated through her lips. "I am sure you will find something soon. I've heard it said more than once that things appear in our lives when we are ready for them."

His voice was tender. "Does that apply to people as well?"

In a low, composed tone, Adana answered, "Yes, they say that it is true of people as well."

"Really?"

Kamau's one-word question was quietly spoken as his dark eyes studied hers. "When I saw you on the hotel's television, I knew I had to make contact of some sort. I remember clearly our last conversation, but I still needed to make contact. I needed to tell you how proud I am to know you. You are clearly a brilliant litigator and so lovely that thoughts of you sometimes take my breath away. I was going to be discreet and just leave a note, but when I saw the gentleman leaving your home and saw you dressed the way you were, I must admit"—his tone lowered and his diction became even more precise—"I really didn't like what I saw. For a moment I experienced something akin to rage until it occurred to me that I have no right to be angry about how you live your life. I think perhaps I was more disappointed than angry. Though I am unfamiliar with whatever it was I experienced with you, I know now that what we experienced bordered on sacred. In college I once heard a philosophy professor say that the erotic and the spiritual are at least intertwined if not the same. I did not understand that principle until I was intimate with you. Having said that, I think that when I saw the gentleman leave, I could not understand how if I felt what I felt, how you couldn't feel it too? And if you did, how could you contaminate the experience?"

Adana's eyes filled with tears. The tears flowed for a myriad of reasons—joy that Kamau had acknowledged the connection that she also understood, pain that he thought that she could discard so easily the experience of truly being loved and anger that Jeffery's selfishness had caused Kamau to doubt her. She allowed the tears to flow gently as she spoke.

"That man you saw leaving my home is not someone I am involved with. He is Jeffery Scott, opposing counsel on the case I talked to you about. We had a long-distance relationship three years ago. Jeffery turned out to be less than truthful about a lot of things. One of the things he was not truthful about was his lack of a divorce. Since we've been working on this case, he has decided all of a sudden that he must have me in his life again. Tonight I was here peacefully settling in for the evening when he showed up, making a scene at my front door. I decided to let him in so that the neighbors would not call the authorities. I don't need the publicity and I hate public scenes. As for feeling what you felt, Kamau

Mazrui, you were not alone. Your professor was right—with you, I understood that the spiritual and the erotic are the same. I have missed you so much."

Kamau reached into his breast pocket and handed Adana a small ecru-colored envelope. She turned the envelope over and raised the back flap, which had K. MAZRUI engraved in platinum. She lifted a card penned in Kamau's hand that read, *I miss you. I need to find a place for you in my life.* Adana's tears flowed more heavily. Kamau stood in one fluid motion and walked over to sit beside her. He removed his monogrammed handkerchief and began gently wiping tears from Adana's eyes.

She allowed herself to collapse in his arms. He held her close and with one strong hand took her face, held it gently and began a slow, thoughtful kiss that sent her swirling. Before she could recover, she felt the warm sensation of Kamau's full, sensuous lips against her neck. With eyes closed, Adana felt as though she were drowning in the sea of kisses he placed in pulsating points along the column of her long, delicate throat. Her lips parted to emit sounds of need and wanting, only to be met by Kamau's mouth covering hers again with a hunger that had been too long controlled.

Adana abandoned herself to the kiss, her arms encircled Kamau's neck and her robe opened enough for him to feel the soft bareness of her breasts and the willing peaks of her erect nipples. He couldn't resist easing the silken fabric slowly off Adana's smooth shoulders and pressing his mouth, burning with desire, over each waiting mound of her honey-brown flesh.

The fiery massage of his lips on her burning skin caused Adana to erupt in erotic sounds and to hold on tightly to Kamau's shoulders, allowing him full rein while he sent her on an ecstatically magical ride. He lowered her down on the plush pillows of the sofa, and after releasing the sash of Adana's robe, slid his hands with featherlike touches up and down the length of her smoldering body. With her heart pounding in an erratic rhythm, she clasped one of his hands. The look he read in her eyes was an invitation he willingly accepted as she loosely slipped on her robe and led him by the hand up the stairs to her bedroom. When they entered the room, Adana sat on the chaise and lightly tapped the space next to her with the palm of her hand, indicating that she wanted Kamau to join her.

He sat and pulled her close to him, whispering in her ear, "Our being together won't be easy."

She unknotted his tie. "I'm not asking for easy, Kamau."

He removed his jacket. "Adana, are you willing to allow us time alone away from all prying eyes, family and friends, until we figure out what we want to do?"

She started unbuttoning his shirt. "Yes."

"Are you sure? Solitude for me is an easy matter; for you it could be more difficult."

"I want to know the meaning of what we feel for each other as much as you do, Kamau, and I don't want to hear the inevitable questions like, is it too soon? Is it right? I don't want to hear the questions, and right now I don't even want to hear my answers. I just want to be with you whenever we can, however we choose." She helped him ease out of his shirt.

"Adana, you must remember the path we are walking is foreign to me. I know that Americans talk a great deal about love, and saying 'I love you' seems to be very important. I don't know if I can give you that."

Adana gently stroked Kamau's chest, which was the color of burnished sable. Her soft, warm hands sent slight shivers through his body as she said calmly and quietly, "I have not asked you to say you love me. All I ask is that you keep treating me the way that you do and make me feel the way that you make me feel. I've heard 'I love you,' and if it was love, it wasn't the kind that I needed, but I had never been made love to totally and completely until you breathed life into every part of my body in Nairobi. I want that, Kamau. I want that."

Adana's words released them both. They were free to be, free to explore without questions, without recriminations. Kamau led Adana to the bed. They both sat, and while he removed his Movado timepiece, his socks and Berluti leather lace-ups, Adana massaged his neck and back with long, sensual strokes interspersed with warm kisses and tiny bites on his neck and hot pulsating kisses on his shoulders and down his spine. Her bare body hugged his back, the rippling of his muscles playing on her taut abdomen, awakening all of her senses.

Kamau was drugged by her scent and the feel of her body on his bare back. He had never experienced being with a woman who gave herself to him so completely. Adana aroused in him a sexual appetite he didn't know he had. She ignited sensual, explosive currents that left him wanting more and more. He removed her hands from his back and stood up. As she watched, he removed every remaining garment that he was wearing and tossed them onto the chaise. He was so spectacular, his body dark, his strong muscles taut and sculpted to perfection. He was visibly ready to give her all of the pleasure that she desired. There was no hiding the fact that he wanted her. Adana slipped out of her loose robe and opened her arms to Kamau. He came to her without hesitation. They fell into each other's arms. Her soft curves molded to his muscular frame. His soft, velvety beard tantalized her as he kissed the hollow of her neck.

He whispered, "I want you. I need you," in her ear, leaving her breathless. He kissed her parted lips, burying his masterful hands in her hair, guiding the kiss.

Adana melted into him, stroking Kamau's back with palms and nails, leaving him with involuntary tremors that heightened his arousal. For the two of them, what they felt was far more than sexual desire. The pleasure they found was intoxicating. It took them to a dimension where neither had ever traveled. Their passion moved from gentle to raw, warm to burning, from cries of delight to surrendering moans. Kamau was lost in her taste, in her scent. With an underlying urgency, he moved his hands to her thighs. Feeling his touch, Adana parted her legs willingly, offering herself to him. She felt his powerful hands moving seductively in, through and around her center, ringing from her the nectar he craved. Adana's limbs shivered. She could not disguise her body's reaction, nor did she want to.

The urgent need she felt for him was revealed in her barely audible voice as she uttered, "Kamau, Kamau, please."

Barely able to control himself, his voice hardened with need, Kamau whispered, "Soon, my beautiful one, soon." He took one waiting breast into his mouth and then another, buying time for himself and sending Adana over the edge. Her cries of pleasure were unmistakable. As she trembled in glorious agony, Kamau blew wisps of air over her body, punctuating each soft, feathery wisp of air with gentle nibbles. Adana's body ached to be taken as only Kamau could. She called his name as he entered her with a powerful thrust, sending them both soaring. There was no time, no space, just magic. They loved as though they could never be satisfied. Time and distance had not diminished the powerful attraction that had begun on a stormy night in Nairobi. The distance had fanned the flames in each of them, leaving an insatiable hunger that threatend to devour them both.

Kamau did not recognize the man he had become

since his loving encounter with the intriguing Adana
Terrell. His need for her was unlike anything he had
ever experienced. She came to him with a freedom, a
sense of abandon and a desire to give him pleasure that
left him feeling powerful and untouched by sorrow of
any kind.

She made him want to love her thoroughly, marking
her body for eternity so that she would be able to respond to only him. He burned every inch of her with a
touch, a kiss, a nip, a nibble, a breath shattering her core
over and over again. Adana alternated between flying
to the heavens and spiraling down to earth. She wanted
Kamau to take her again and again. She wanted to be
ravished by his mouth, engulfed in his strong dark
hands, wrapped in his muscular legs and opened repeatedly to deep hard thrusts of his manhood. She wanted to
be absorbed into the pores of his onyx-colored skin. Her
fingers never tired of stroking the velvety soft richness
of the hairs on his head, mustache and beard. His smell
left her feeling intoxicated. Kamau had taught her the
meaning of being a woman totally captivated by a man
designed specifically for her and her alone. Their bodies
communicated when words were lost. Their vocal eruptions of ecstasy answered every unspoken question. In
the throes of passion, they knew they had to be together
wherever, whenever they could for however long.

Adana cried out her final release, and Kamau followed. Their bodies rode together the wave of electrical
current that united them for one final jolt. Kamau rolled
over, gently pulling Adana with him. Placing her into the
circle of his arms, he held her snugly, whispering, "You
leave me no thoughts except those of you. You take my
breath. You render me speechless. My heart wants to
stop when I enter you. You have opened a whole new

world to me. Please be patient with me and give me time to make sense of it."

Kamau lovingly stroked Adana's back and gently held her bottom, causing her skin to tingle at his touch and her heart to pound at evidence of his continued desire for her.

She kissed his full, waiting lips and said, "We have time. We have time."

His next caress was a command, and she willingly obeyed, opening herself up to receive again all of the pulsating power and pleasure that was Kamau. The love-making was less urgent; it was a slow, sensual dance. His body moved like a poem being written especially for her. Adana rode the wave of the rhythm while burning a trail of tantalizing strokes down the length of Kamau's firm backside. His beard became an aphrodisiac as he sensuously brushed the velvety strands of hair over her torso. He found her so delicate, so ready as he sank deeper into her. Adana was on fire. Nothing had prepared either of them for the sensations they aroused in each other. They feasted on the pleasure they had found until physical exhaustion lulled them to sleep.

The rest was short-lived for Kamau. His internal clock had been trained to keep him on track with the schedule of his extremely busy life. He had a plane to catch, and though it was a company jet and the pilot would surely wait for him, he didn't want to explain to anyone his reason for being late.

Kamau looked at the beautiful woman curled up sleeping next to him. He didn't want to leave her. He wanted her with him, but he also knew that the time was not right. They needed time for themselves before becoming the center of family conversations. They needed time to determine where they were headed and how they were going to get there. Kamau leaned over and gently kissed a sleeping Adana. She stirred slightly. He stroked her hair, and she slowly moved against him, easing her limbs awake. Kamau kissed each taut nipple and then her lips. Adana slowly opened her eyes. She smiled as she stared into the face of the magnificent man who had given her thrilling moments of unspeakable pleasure. She said dreamily, "I'm glad you didn't leave without saying good-bye."

Kamau stroked her face. "I will never again leave you without letting you know. I have a plane to catch, and if I'm late, there will be far too many questions to answer." He stopped, smiled at her and said, "Speaking of questions to answer, if I get on that plane with a new fragrance called Á La Adana, our secret will no longer be well kept."

Adana laughed softly and pointed Kamau in the direction of the master bathroom. Adana slipped on a robe and sat on the chaise, waiting for Kamau to complete his grooming ritual. In a matter of minutes, he was showered and as elegantly groomed as he had been when he first walked through Adana's front door.

When he was ready to travel, he sat beside Adana, took her hands in his and said, "I will be longing for you until I see you again. You will never be far from my thoughts or my heart. Adana"—he spoke her name as though it were a prayer—"you are burned forever into my spirit."

She wrapped her arms around Kamau, kissed his lips and whispered, "I miss you already."

Kamau stood, took Adana's hand and walked down the stairs to the front door. Once there, their embrace was tender, tinged with sadness and marked by the fact that they had to part so abruptly. Kamau tenderly kissed Adana's forehead and said, "I will call as soon as I board, and we will plan our next rendezvous."

Adana's smile flickered. "All right, be safe."

Their final kiss was as tender as their embrace. Kamau let himself out. Adana locked the door behind him and stood for a moment reliving the joy and pleasure she had experienced in Kamau's arms. It also became clear to her that for the first time in her recent memory, she had experienced something in her personal life that she could not share with her sisters. The thought left a lonely feeling, but she was sure that it was a small price to pay to have private moments with Kamau, away from prying eyes and offered opinions until the two of them decided what course to take. Adana walked slowly back up the stairs to her bedroom, filled her bathtub with lavender-scented bath salts and prepared for a long soak.

Chapter 16

As the limousine pulled up to the runway to meet the Mazrui company aircraft, Kamau glanced at his finely constructed timepiece. He had arrived within one minute of his scheduled departure time. His brother Kaleb was in the cockpit.

"Hey, Kamau, business must have been good for you to cut it this close. This is a first—Kamau Mazrui, the man who keeps everybody else on track, made his flight with only a minute to spare."

Kamau ignored Kaleb's observation. "Kaleb, I thought Mohammed was scheduled to pilot this flight."

"Things happen, my brother. He called in sick. That seems to be happening on a pretty regular basis these days. It's being looked at. He may not be with us much longer."

Kamau responded quietly, "I see." He entered the slick, well-appointed passenger compartment of the plane and began to make himself comfortable. As soon as the plane was in the air, he flipped open his cell, retrieved Adana's stored number and dialed it. She answered on the third ring.

"Hello, Kamau."

Hearing her low, sweet voice brought back memories of entering her body. He could feel his temperature rise and his body harden. He swallowed and as he spoke, his voice was filled with need for her.

"I'm on the plane. I made the departure time by one minute." His conversation was about the flight, but his thoughts were of her long, exquisite limbs wrapped around his hot, aching body. He could hear her calling his name. He could still taste her lips, could feel her hands burn into his skin. He was caught in the emotional experience he knew as Adana Terrell.

"I'm happy that you made the flight." Adana was having a similar experience on the other end of the telephone line. She was still aching for Kamau's torturously exquisite lovemaking. He had brought senses to life she had not known existed. She knew she was vulnerable. This was, after all, a man still tied in some ways to a dead wife, but just the sound of his voice sent her spiraling headlong into whatever perilous territory that awaited her. He made her feel alive, protected and thoroughly loved. For the first time in her life, she knew what it felt like to be loved by a man, a real man. She had seen it but she had never felt it.

"Kamau, I am missing you already, but I need to say that while we figure this out, neither of us should feel pressured, no matter how tempting to throw caution to the wind and run with our emotions before we know what we want to do."

"Adana, I am sorting through many things. I must be honest, the way you give yourself to me, the way you come to me leaves me more confused and more satisfied than I have ever been. Sexual encounters in my world, in my marriage, were for procreation. If pleasure was a by-product, then one considered oneself fortunate. With you, my darling Adana, there is only pleasure— pleasure so excruciating it is gloriously painful. None of that makes sense for me, and I can only share the feelings and sensations with you. Anyone else would think I have gone mad." He laughed. "Perhaps I have gone mad—you, my beautiful nymph, have driven me mad."

"You're not insane, Kamau," she teased. "Perhaps you are experiencing that chemistry we talked about months ago in Nairobi."

"Ah, yes, chemistry, that illusive commodity designed to strike a sighted man blind and turn an articulate man into a babbling idiot. The human condition requires close scrutiny. The emotional component of human affairs is laced with dangerous traps disguised as pleasure."

They both laughed. "Am I a trap, Kamau?"

"You, my darling, are pure pleasure, and if there is a hidden trap, I will risk it."

"I have no traps, Kamau. We have happened upon a rarity, a kind of connection that does not often exist. Let's just explore the connection and see where it leads us."

"That we shall do, my sweet, that we shall do. What does the rest of your evening look like?"

"Well, when you called, I had just stepped out of the bath and I am resting here on my chaise looking at my bed. The bed we used in a way that will never allow me to sleep in it the same way again."

"I'll buy you a new bed."

"Kamau, are you going to buy me a new bed every

time you sneak into town under the cover of darkness, ravish my body and leave?"

"If that is what you want. By the way, I never sneak anywhere, and we will not always meet in darkness. The continents and time zones where we choose to explore what we feel for each other can be as varied as our imaginations. Since I cannot be with you for dinner tonight, I would like to surprise you."

She said tentatively, "I don't like surprises."

"You will like this one. All that is required is that you remain relaxed in your home. The surprise will be sent to you. Do you trust me, Adana?"

The smile in her voice was evident. "I trust you."

"Then slip on something comfortable and wait for your doorbell."

Kamau and Adana said loving good-byes. Adana finished dressing in lounge wear and Kamau arranged his surprise. Forty minutes later, Adana's doorbell rang. When she answered, she found on her doorstep a tuxedoed gentleman inquiring as to whether he had the proper address. Adana answered yes, and he signaled to a small group of tux-wearing gentlemen, who entered and began setting up Adana's dining room to resemble a private, very intimate restaurant—complete with flowers, ambient lighting, champagne and the John Coltrane piece she and Kamau had listened to in Nairobi. The dish served was a rendition of the Moroccan meal Kamau had prepared for her—the first and only meal the two of them had shared. It brought tears to Adana's eyes. When she thought she could take no more, she was handed an envelope with her name engraved on the front. Inside, a calligraphied note read:

Tonight, my sweet Adana, we begin an adventure designed just for us. Enjoy the meal, my darling——may it tantalize your senses the way you titillate mine.

Kamau

At evening's end, Adana slept like a thoroughly satisfied woman with visions of Kamau Mazrui dancing in her head.

Chapter 17

Nairobi, Kenya

Salima Banda was persistent. With other clients, her persistence had paid off, making her one of the premier real estate agents in Nairobi. Kamau Mazrui was a different story. He was not cooperating with either her efforts to find him a new home or with her attempts to be coy and flirtatious. She knew she was attractive. Male suitors had never been a problem. Nothing she did, however, got through to Kamau. He was pleased, though, that she had sold his old residence for more than the listing price. She was calling once again to try to convince him to preview new houses on the market. Since he was back at work, she rang his office.

"Yes, this is Salima Banda from the Barclay Agency. May I please speak with Mr. Kamau Mazrui?"

"Hold, please."

"Ms. Banda, please forgive the wait. I was in a meeting. However, I am glad that you called. I have decided to nix the purchase of a new home. I have decided to build. What I am looking for does not yet exist, so I thank you for your help, especially with the sale of the other property. Good day, Ms. Banda."

That was his final good-bye and Salima knew it. She smiled and thought to herself, *For whatever reason, I didn't have a chance.* She gathered her things and set off to do what she did best—showcase premier properties.

Judge Garsen Mazrui and his wife, Adina, sat on the verandah of their estate, enjoying each other's company while eating a continental breakfast. After decades of marriage, Adina and Garsen still marveled at their love for each other.

"Garsen, how is Kamau doing since he has been back at work?"

"Fine, my dear. He seems fine. Seems to have a bit more life these days."

Adina Mazrui's gaze became distant, and her speech was reminiscent of one thinking aloud. "Garsen, I feel it might be time for us to broach the subject of a new marriage with him. You know Kamau is our most traditional son." She smiled. "He was always a little old man even when he was a small child. Do you remember?"

Judge Mazrui reached across the table and gently stroked his wife's delicate hand. "Yes, my love, I do remember."

Adina looked deeply into her devoted husband's eyes. "He always reminded his brothers of the traditional ways. We never had to worry about him. I think he must be feeling very unsettled these days. He needs a wife, a home, children. He needs a traditional wife, an educated woman willing to create a home for him. I want that for our son. Perhaps it's time for us to set the wheels in motion to arrange a marriage, or at least nudge him in the right direction."

"Are you sure of this, my sweet? Though Kamau is perhaps our son most enamored of tradition, he is also our most stubborn offspring." The corner of Garsen's mouth lifted in a smile. "I believe he is an incarnation of my father. If we do not approach him correctly, we will have a fight on our hands."

"Why don't you approach him in the office? Find a quiet time, perhaps after the discussion of some pressing case. He won't be on guard and will be less likely to dismiss the thought."

"Adina, you know our children. I will follow your lead. I will speak to him this afternoon."

"Thank you, my husband. I know this is the right thing to do."

The Mazrui Industries International Headquarters was a spectacular edifice. It was one of the grand landmarks of the city. The building housed every division of the extensive Mazrui holdings and was the command center for satellite offices throughout the city. Mazrui Industries was one of the largest employers in Nairobi and one of the most respected.

Kamau Mazrui sat in his office, pleased to be back in the thick of the pursuit he loved—the practice of law. With a staff of fifty attorneys and a sizable pool of administrative assistants and law clerks, Kamau's leadership kept them busy and inordinately productive.

The visible evidence of Yasmin in the offices had been removed, but there were days when Kamau could still feel her spirit—a fleeting thought, someone's passing gesture, a word spoken. He surmised that perhaps her spirit would always be with him. He found it strange because while the spirit of Yasmin floated in and out of his life periodically, thoughts of Adana Terrell permeated his very being. Lust and longing haunted him almost daily. Kamau found himself needing to speak to Adana at least once every day. It wasn't just a desire to hear her voice; it was a need. It was difficult not letting the world know. If everyone had known, it would have been so much easier to satisfy their desire to be wrapped in each other's arms, continually satiating their deepest hungers. For Kamau the timing just wasn't right. In spite of his desire for Adana, some part of him still felt disloyal to Yasmin. She had been a dutiful wife, fulfilling her obligations to him honorably, but nothing in their marriage had compared to the heat, the longing, the thrilling vibrancy and the intensity of being with Adana. Adana made him understand the phrase *making love.* She allowed him to bring pleasure to every inch of her body, and she reciprocated with an unbridled passion that rendered him desperate to take her over and over again. He questioned his sanity—did any of it make sense? In his world, long-term commitments weren't based on lust and longing. Marriages were based on things like values, family compatibility, shared spiritual beliefs and cultural sameness. Kamau knew that his parents had gone against the grain, as had Keino, his older brother, but they were not the norm. Had most people followed those paths, there would be no tradition. In exasperation, he threw his hands in the air, shook his head and went back to examining the documents on his desk. Just as he lifted his Montblanc pen to make a notation, he heard a soft knock on the door that served as the private entrance to his office. He knew it had to be family.

"Come in." He looked up to see his father enter the room.

Judge Garsen Mazrui entered with a smile on his face. It gave him joy to see his son once again in his element.

"Hello, Father, what brings you out today?"

"Well, there were a few things I needed to tie up here, and I decided to drop in on you just to see how things are going. Are you still getting reacclimated?"

Kamau leaned back in the aged leather chair that had belonged to his paternal grandfather. Judge Mazrui took a seat in a chair opposite the desk behind which Kamau sat.

"Yes, Father, I am, and the past few weeks have been good."

"Good, son, very good. You know your mother worries and it would be unthinkable for me to go home and not be able to answer her questions about your well-being."

The judge smiled, knowing that blaming his wife for being concerned about Kamau's state of being was convenient but not altogether accurate, because he was equally concerned.

"I know it was a major accomplishment to have sold your previous residence. Are you still looking for other homes?"

Kamau stroked his velvety beard, rested his chin in his hand and looked directly into his father's eyes. "I made a decision just recently to give up the search for an existing home. I've decided to build—to start new, fresh."

"Not a bad idea, my son. Sometimes in these situations it is important to move on with one's life in a new way." Judge Mazrui punched the air with his fist for emphasis. "To replenish old memories with new, vibrant ones."

A small line etched its way into Kamau's brow line. "It seems that some memories are lasting, Father. They hang on and refuse to let go."

"It is an emotional illusion, my son. The beauty that was Yasmin will no doubt always be with you, but there is a place for new beauty, new memories. That I promise you."

Judge Mazrui thought of the conversation he and his wife had shared earlier in the morning, and he asked, "My son, as you move into the second year of your loss, have you considered the wisdom of taking another wife?"

A snapshot of Adana sleeping in bed, hair tousled, uncovered breasts gently rising and falling with her soft breathing floated through Kamau's mind. His answer was slow and measured. "No, Father, I'm not thinking of taking a wife. There seem to be quite a few things I still need to sort out."

"I see. Well, you should know that your mother and I are quite willing to act as mediators in the same way we did when Yasmin was chosen for you."

"Thank you, Father. When the day comes, perhaps once again I will need to rely on your wisdom. In matters of marriage, saner heads than mine would need to prevail."

"Your mother will be pleased to know that when the time comes, you will welcome our input." He rose to leave the room. "Now I will leave you to finish what you started." He gestured to Kamau's desk, which was filled with neatly arranged stacks of legal documents. "Your mother also asked me to remind you that you need never eat alone. Our dinner hour never changes."

"Thank you, Father, and please let Mother know she is not to worry. I will come to see her soon. And, Father, thank you for everything."

"Good-bye, my son."

With good-byes said, Judge Garsen Mazrui left the room smiling to himself, thinking that now he and his beloved wife could do something tangible to bring joy back into their son Kamau's life.

Chapter 18

Virginia, USA

Adana stood in her office muttering softly, "How on earth am I going to win this case if I keep hitting road-blocks like delays, suppression of evidence and disappearing witnesses?"

She was scheduled to meet with her client, Diani Bitak, in a matter of minutes, and unfortunately she had nothing new to tell her. For the first time in a long time, Adana Terrell was stumped. She knew there was an answer lurking somewhere within her reach. She just couldn't touch it. Adana walked over and buzzed her intercom. "When Ms. Bitak arrives, show her in immediately."

"She's just walking in the door, Ms. Terrell. I'll show her right in."

"Thank you."

Diani Bitak was a quiet, unassuming woman. Her thin brown frame did not accurately depict her inner strength, just as her wire-framed glasses covering deep-set eyes could not hide, for any who cared to really look, the fine mind working overtime to make sense of a world that had seemingly gone mad. When Diani Bitak entered her office, Adana walked over to greet her, took both of Diani's hands in hers and led her to a settee where they both sat. "Diani, how are you holding up?"

"As well as can be expected. I just want this madness to be over. I have done nothing wrong. How can they do this to me?"

"Listen, Diani, you know that I am doing all that I can with the full weight of the firm's research department behind me. We are going to get you through this. I wish I could give you my exact strategy at this moment but I can't. Before we go to trial, we'll have the answer. By the way, where is Emir?"

"He is in New York on family business. One of his nephews is really being affected by all of the negative publicity being hurled at the family right now. Emir needed to be there to settle him down. My husband is a very responsible, caring man, and he is highly principled. He would never use me or anyone else for nefarious purposes. I know from your questions, Adana, that you have had some doubts, but I assure you Emir is not the weak link in all of this nonsense."

"If I believe you, Diani, that leaves us with one small problem—who is the weak link?"

"I don't know. I just know that it is not my husband."

"Well, with the cadre of people I am leading on this case, we are going to solve it, and I will be in touch with you soon with what I hope is the break we've been waiting for."

Both women rose from the settee, and Diani Bitak left the room. Adana once again sat at her desk and started going over and over every note in the thick Bitak file. If there was something she had missed, she was determined to find it. After an hour of combing through the file inch by inch, her administrative assistant buzzed her. "Ms. Terrell, long distance Nairobi, Mr. Kamau Mazrui."

Adana's calm voice did not betray what she was really feeling. "Put Mr. Mazrui through, please. . . . Kamau, how are you?"

Adana's voice was a caress to his ears. His body ached for her touch. "I am fine now. Hearing you speak my name has an interesting effect on me."

Affectionately teasing, Adana asked, "Is this effect something you enjoy, Mr. Mazrui?"

Kamau smiled and stroked his mustache. "Enjoy, now there, my dear, is an interesting word. I can safely say that when I hear you speak my name, I am in the joy of that moment."

A picture of his strong, hard legs intertwined with hers gently eased through her mind. She took a deep breath. "Ah, very good, Counselor, your quick wit is definitely swaying this jury."

He heard her take a breath. Feeling his temperature rise, Kamau steered the conversation to a less arousing subject. "Speaking of juries, how is your case coming?"

"My client was here today and I'm still stumped. I'm now inclined to agree with something you said months ago, which at the time annoyed the heck out of me."

"And what was that, my sweet?"

"You said essentially that I had wasted too much time trying to offer up Emir, Diani's husband, as the guilty culprit. Well, it turns out you were right. Further investigation really proves that he had neither motive nor opportunity. What I didn't know and just found out recently is that Emir was out of the country on business during the period that these illegal transactions took place. The company VP in charge of finances was at the helm. He is being checked out as we speak. I feel like an idiot. I really have been wasting some precious time because of my bullheadedness."

"My beautiful Ms. Terrell, you never cease to amaze me. Just when I was convinced that you could never admit to being in error, you shock me by admitting that you were a victim of tunnel vision. Thank you for showing me that side of yourself."

His deep, rich voice washed over her, reminding her of his heated embrace that was both rough and tender as he molded her to the contours of his hard, muscular body. The longing in her body eased through her lips. "Kamau, at this moment, I am more interested in showing you another side of myself."

"Ah, and so the lady is also provocative. And when, my darling woman, might I have the pleasure of seeing this other side?"

Adana could feel her body respond to the thought of seeing Kamau. "If distance were not an obstacle, I would say tonight."

Desire reached his vocal cords and his words were uttered as a velvet whisper. "Distance with us will never be an obstacle. It may provide on occasion some minor delays but never obstacles. As long as Mazrui Industries has a fleet of jets and as long as my pilot's license is still valid, we have no problems. Our only issue is finding a way to have our privacy while we explore our various sides."

She could hear his sly smile float through his words. Adana fought to hold on to her composure as Kamau continued to paint a picture of the possibilities open to them.

"Tomorrow is Friday. I could arrange for you to be flown to a beautiful little resort I know. It is not too far from you. I will go there later tonight and have things ready for us. I will promise to have us both back in our places by Sunday evening. We can steal a few hours, can't we?"

Adana's soft, low answer was, "I want to see you, and the only thing I can do here is wait and think. I'd much rather wait and think while making love to you."

"That is exactly what I wanted to hear. I will arrange everything. I will have a package delivered to your home by courier this evening. Until tomorrow, my sweet, be well."

The two said their good-byes, and Kamau began to set the wheels in motion to create a memorable reunion for his precious Adana. The experience of being with her humanized him and allowed him to explore a creative side of his personality that was so foreign it made him smile, wondering where it had been hidden. He put together the package he had promised. It included flight instructions and a gold key with a gold engraved tag that read, THE KEY TO PARADISE. He felt very proud of himself and extremely amused by the fact that he could bring so much pleasure to Adana with just the gift of himself. She left no doubt in his mind that it was him she wanted. Not his name, not his fortunes—just him. Yasmin had sometimes been so enamored with the perks of being a Mazrui that he had often wondered how she would have felt had he lost everything. He would never know, but he could surmise that it would certainly have been difficult. Though Yasmin had come from a good, respectable family and had been financially comfortable, she always demanded more from herself and everyone around her. In the end, that demanding nature took her life. With Yasmin, some part of her was always withheld—perhaps it had been her safety net, her way of shielding herself from whatever stood between her and the pursuit of what she wanted. During their marriage, Kamau had resigned himself to the perils of Yasmin's personality and had accepted the fact that she was who she was and that they would build a life, a family, around her idiosyncratic nature. Adana's freedom with him gave life an entirely new meaning.

Chapter 19

Virginia, USA

The following day, Adana was busily reading through the new information gathered about the Bitak case. The more she read, the more intriguing the information became. It was clear that somewhere in the new file, she had the missing link. Though the weeks before the trial felt like hours, she knew she was going to find the missing piece. She turned the slim Piaget timepiece on her arm to more clearly read its face and knew she had to hurry in order to be on time for the flight schedule Kamau had sent.

Adana smiled to herself as she put away files and cleared her desk. Sometimes it was hard for her to believe that she was engaged in a secret affair with one Kamau Mazrui. Her one regret was keeping it from her sisters. When she thought of her first impression of Kamau, she laughed softly—she had found him arrogant, stodgy and cold. She had since discovered that she could erase *cold* and *stodgy* from the lexicon of descriptions of Kamau. The heat she experienced in his arms could melt a glacier, and a stodgy man could never be as creative in his lovemaking as Kamau was. The arrogance she decided fit him appropriately. He was, after all, a man of the world whose physical and mental prowess had been tested in many arenas. The healthy confidence that some saw as arrogance was rightfully his, and it was that confidence and clarity about his abilities that left her feeling safe and protected in his presence. Adana closed her eyes and imagined Kamau's touch, emitting a soft ooh. She opened her eyes, shook the daydream from her head, swiveled in her chair, hit her computer keyboard and began an e-mail with final instructions for her administrative assistant. Once finished, she hurried to meet the car Kamau had arranged to carry her to the chartered flight section of the airport. He had engaged the services of companies with no ties to Mazrui Industries, wanting their secret to be safe for as long as possible.

The flight had been chartered just for Adana, and Kamau made sure that her comfort was not left to chance. There were two flight attendants employed to satisfy her every whim. An assortment of delectable foods and exquisite champagnes were shown to her on a menu designed specifically for her flight. An assortment of luxurious oversized cashmere throws and down pillows encased in silk were provided for comfortable napping as she moved through the air from one time zone to another. Kamau had made the destination a surprise. This time, the woman who disliked surprises was quite willing.

When the plane landed, the terrain seemed vaguely familiar. Adana wasn't sure why, but a feeling came over her, a certainty that it was a place she had been before. She stepped from the plane into a waiting car, and as the car was speeding down a tree-lined roadway, paradise arose in the distance. A new and unexpected warmth radiated through her. Entering paradise this time was so very different. Kamau was indeed a creative man. To return to the scene of their first passionate moments together made her weak with anticipation.

It was dusk, the most romantic part of the day for Adana. The driver stopped, opened her door and allowed her to exit the car while he retrieved her one travel bag. Adana took the golden key from her handbag and walked up the steps to the main house of the Mazrui vacation compound. The driver discreetly placed her bag next to her and left. Adana opened the door to a room flooded by candlelight. Candles and rose petals the color of red velvet marked a path beginning in the living room. Along the path were small golden easels holding calligraphied notes. The first one read, *Welcome, my darling. We are in for a treat. Relax your mind, spirit and body. Place your bags where you are, and remove your shoes, stockings and jacket (I assume you are wearing a suit—you often do).*

An easy smile stretched across Adana's face as she followed the directions, marveling at how well Kamau had observed her habits, her likes and her dislikes. Adana moved farther down the path to the next easel, feeling the smoothness of rose petals beneath her bare feet. She read, *Now, my sweet, the blouse that you are wearing must go. I am envious of its closeness to your soft, honey-colored skin.* Adana unbuttoned her silk blouse and dropped it to the floor, leaving a primrose-colored puddle atop red velvet roses.

She continued walking. When she had gone far enough, she lifted the next note from its resting place and read, *And now, my sweet, whatever garments are covering your long slender legs leading to heavenly places, please remove them. I need to be free to trace your limbs with loving touches and kisses as I wrap them around my waist.*

The sensuously suggestive game left Adana smoldering as she removed her skirt and slip and walked on unsteady legs to the next instruction.

And now, my sweet, you must remove the two items that inflame me with rage when I think of how close they are to you daily. For the rest of the time that we are together, I am going to request that when we are alone, you never again wear either garment. If I feel the need to ravish your exquisite gifts again and again, I want no barriers. Indulge me, my sweet.

Melting with every movement, Adana removed matching black silk bra and panties and left them on the waiting bed of roses. She followed the scented trail of candles to an open door, and there he was, surrounded by candlelight as the soft strains of a lone violin piped into the room. Resting in bed, his legs were covered by a silk ecru-colored sheet. His muscular torso was bare.

The rich timbre of his voice was as smooth as velvet as he greeted her. "Hello, my sweet, we are now, at this moment, just as I want us to be for however long, free, unfettered souls, bare and with never-ending desire."

Kamau lifted the silk sheet. Adana slid in next to him. Their embrace was long and slow. Together they savored the bodies they had longed to hold and touch. Kamau fingered strands of Adana's hair while whispering sweet promises of sublime loving in her ear. Adana's answer was soft, low moans as she stroked his arms, sensuously moving from strong broad shoulders down long, sinewy arms ending at tapered fingertips. Kamau's hands gently stroked Adana's face, and she kissed his palms. He blew featherlight wisps of air along her throat, stopping at her breasts, softly easing each erect nipple in and out of his heated mouth, causing her core to shatter. As Adana gripped Kamau's shoulders, riding a wave of ecstasy, Kamau skillfully and carefully explored her center to test her readiness for him. He was not disappointed. Her body called him and he answered, wrapping Adana's legs around his waist and entering her with throbbing, explosive passion. His strong hands held her soft thighs; his touch sent her into deep cries of surrender. Kamau's need was so urgent he wanted to explode. He couldn't get enough of the way in which she offered herself to him. As she arched higher and higher, his arousal became more potent. His ability to prolong their pleasure dictated that he move in long, slow, measured strokes, wringing cries of his name from Adana's trembling lips. Hearing his name brought him nearly to the brink of madness. He moved her legs farther up the length of his back and began moving into her deeper, harder, faster.

Adana moved instinctively with the power of his rhythm as though they were repeating a familiar ritual. They loved long and hard until release was the only answer. After turbulent, electric quivers raced through their bodies, they shuddered together in ecstasy. Kamau rolled over, continuing to hold Adana in his arms, not wanting to let her go. Whispering in a voice filled with the smoldering aftereffects of an intensely provocative sexual encounter, he said softly, "Oh, my sweet, you have changed everything."

Kamau touched his lips to Adana's. Looking into her love-filled eyes, he asked, "What am I going to do with you?"

She nuzzled into the soft hollow of his neck. "Make love to me as long and as often as you can. You have given me something I never thought I'd find. I just want to enjoy you." Exhausted from hungry, hard, heated loving, they slept entwined in each other's arms, the dewy moisture covering their bodies leaving a satiny sheen.

An hour later, Kamau could feel his body heating as he slept. Through a fog, he felt tender touches on his inner thighs and wisps of cool breath on his chest. He stirred, thinking he was dreaming. He reached to bring closer the woman who had inspired the dream. To his delight, he discovered Adana applying kisses to every inch of his body, causing him to show her without question that she was bringing him immense pleasure. His body was for her so thrillingly beautiful, sable-colored, smooth, perfectly sculpted. She melted as she took it all in and began to bring pleasure to Kamau in all of the ways that he had brought pleasure to her earlier. She took charge and led him to the brink, throbbing with an excruciating need for her. She straddled him and he entered her, grabbing her waist and dancing to her rhythm. It was purely sensual. They rode a new path to paradise.

The two days that followed were filled with meals prepared exclusively by Kamau, racquetball, long walks, heated debates concerning points of law and thrilling moments of lovemaking designed to create memories that would last a lifetime. Adana had complied with Kamau's request to leave her lovely undies packed, leaving them free to indulge in what had become their favorite pastime in any and every place their hearts desired and their imaginations determined. Kamau knew he would never be able to see the Mazrui family resort the same way again. Places on the property he had forgotten existed had been marked by the sweet smell, sounds, cries, laughter and passionate rhythms of Ms. Adana Terrell. He had become a new man in the time spent with the intriguing woman of whom he could not get enough. She inspired him to please her in ways he had never envisioned. They left each other after the short stay more relaxed and more at peace than either had ever been in their adult lives—and they had much to think about.

Once back at home, Adana began preparing for the week ahead. It promised to be a difficult, busy one—not unlike countless other seemingly impossible weeks she had faced as junior partner. Rushing through e-mails and organizing files, she was so engrossed in her work that the ringing of the telephone startled her. Picking it up, she saw Amara's number in Nairobi. Kamau's face floated through her mind.

"Hi, Amara."

"Hi, sis, I just felt like checking on you. How are things going? I know you have a tendency to work too hard."

"Actually, I am working too hard, but it's a case that I really feel passionately about, so the work is good."

"You sound good, more life in your voice than I've heard in a very long time."

Adana smiled. She knew the lilt that Amara heard in her voice was compliments of one Kamau Mazrui, Amara's brother-in-law. She wanted so much to tell her, but she and Kamau had agreed to keep their affair private for a time.

"I feel good, better than I have in a long time. How are things in Nairobi?"

"Good, really good. I tell you, Adana, if anyone had told me how wonderful my life would be, I would have skipped childhood and married Keino as an infant."

The sisters laughed at the humor in Amara's statement.

"Seriously, I love my life. We're planning a big bash

for the twins' second birthday. Mark your calendar because you've got to be here, and next week it appears my in-laws are throwing a huge dinner party to discreetly let it be known that Kamau is ready to get married again."

Adana's heart sped up, her throat closed and her palms started sweating. She felt momentarily light-headed. Her voice came from a distance as she asked, "Do you know the woman he is supposed to marry?"

"No, I don't think his parents do either. Kamau was always seen as the son who was and is the most wedded to traditional cultural practices. His parents chose Yasmin for him, and from what I understand, he gave them permission to select his next wife. They seem to think that it should be done now. I know they've had a few meetings with eligible families. Next week I'm sure the women will be parading through the Mazrui estate like giddy teens at a debutante ball."

As Amara laughed at her own joke, she noticed that her sister was unusually quiet. "I'm sorry, Adana, I was just rambling on. I know I'm talking too much when you get as quiet as you are."

"Oh no, I was just listening." Fighting angry tears, Adana kept talking. "It all sounds like a lot of fun, and you know I'll be there for my nephews' birthdays. Let me know what I can do to help. I'd like to be a part of the planning."

"All right, sis, I will. I'll talk to you next week. I'll let you get back to work but don't work too hard. Love you."

"Love you too." Adana placed the telephone in its cradle, picked up the empty mug from which she had been drinking tea and threw it against the meticulously painted wall of her study, shattering it into many jagged-edged pieces that landed on the carpeted floor. Adana walked in a circle, calling Kamau every ungodly name she could think of. She picked up her BlackBerry from the desk, found Kamau's cell number and called it. She didn't care what time it was; she didn't care where he was in the world. A few things had to be said.

Kamau was being chauffeured to a meeting when he got the call. The delight could be heard in his voice as he answered, "Just the voice to make my heart sing. How are you, my sweet?"

"I was doing just fine until a few minutes ago when my sister called me from Nairobi to tell me that your parents—at your request—are giving a party to choose you a wife." Kamau tried to speak, but Adana kept talking. "My sister doesn't know that I have made a fool of myself thinking that we were giving ourselves time to make a decision about us. I didn't know that you needed time to sow your wild oats before choosing a wife from one of Nairobi's eligible families. You should have told me, Kamau. You should have told me that you knew you wanted a life again in a marriage, just not with me. You didn't have to come on as this confused, grieving soul overwhelmed by unfamiliar feelings. You should have let me know. I know I said I was asking nothing from you, but I thought we were on the same page. I didn't know you had a hidden agenda. Just when I thought you were different." Adana's voice got louder. "You are just another Jeffery Scott. The only difference is the accent and the bank account. Kamau Mazrui, don't you ever speak to me again."

When Adana hung up, she was too sad to cry. Until that moment, she had not allowed herself to entertain thoughts of loving Kamau. When she ended the call, the finality of never hearing, seeing or touching him again made her realize that she loved him with all of her heart.

Kamau Mazrui had stamped not just her body but also her soul and her mind with his signature. She knew she would never belong to anyone else, and the thought of family gatherings in Nairobi with Kamau and his new wife was more than she could bear. Disappointment mingled with grief and pain rose to the surface. Her aching heart sent her to bed to numb her wounds with sleep.

Chapter 20

Nairobi, Kenya

Kamau sat in the backseat of the chauffeured car with his head in his hands. How could something so good have gone so wrong? He redialed Adana's numbers repeatedly. She had closed him out. Adana didn't let him tell her that she was the only woman in the world he wanted, that he knew when they last said good-bye that he wanted her to be his wife but was waiting for her to be more open to the idea before he discussed it. After all, it was she who had made it clear that marriage for her was not a priority. Kamau had intended to talk to her about his conversation with his father, but their love-making had clouded everything. They could only see and hear each other. He wanted to explain to her that though he had trusted his parents' judgment in the past concerning the choice of a mate, he was now very clear that he could make his own choice. He wanted to choose her. He had wanted to say it all, but Adana had closed him out. She said she never wanted to speak to him

again. She had to change her mind; he would see to it.
He had to talk to Keino. In contemporary nontraditional
matters of the heart, Keino had much experience.

Keino and Amara Mazrui sat lounging in the sitting
room adjoining their twin sons' bedroom. As often as
they could, they made a ritual of having tea and conversation while the twins took their afternoon naps. Keino
raised his teacup and before placing it to his lips, looked
at his sleeping sons and said in a voice filled with rever-
ence, "Thank you, Amara, for giving me two of my
greatest treasures."

Amara smiled. "You are welcome, my darling." Her
eyes were filled with gentleness and pride as she looked
in the direction of the contented children, whose small
chests peacefully rose and fell in rhythmic waves. "They
are wonderful, aren't they. Time has gone by so quickly.
I can't believe that in only a few weeks they will be two
years old. I'm excited about the celebration for them. I
talked to Adana and she wants to help with the plans." A
calming breath eased through Amara's throat as she
thought of her loving family. "It will be a great excuse
to have everyone together again."

She took a sip of her tea while Keino absentmindedly
fiddled with the spoon on his saucer, causing the soft
melodic hum of porcelain against metal. Amara noticed
the distant look in her husband's eyes and called to him.
"Earth to Keino. Sweetheart, you were drifting away
while I was babbling on. Is there something on your
mind?"

Keino's strong, sensual face reflected a quiet flicker
of uneasiness. "Sorry, my sweet. I received a call this
morning from Kamau. The call puzzled me—he said
he wanted to speak to me about an urgent personal

matter." The corner of Keino's mouth lifted in a tentative smile. "I can honestly say that I can count on one hand the times that Kamau has spoken to me about a personal matter, and even when he did, it was generally about someone else's personal business, not his." His voice lowered. "I just wonder what to expect. I know these have been difficult times for him."

Amara reached over and touched her husband's warm hand. "I am sure he called you because he knows that you will be helpful and that you have his best interest at heart. What time is he coming over?"

"He isn't. He suggested a round of golf at the Meru Club."

Keino looked at the finely crafted timepiece he was wearing on his wrist. "I should start moving in that direction fairly soon." Traces of concern vanished as Keino looked into his wife's eyes. "What are your plans for the afternoon, my precious wife?"

"Your mother and I are going to our favorite designer for a fitting of the outfits we are going to wear for the twins' celebration. I love your mom's taste, and I want her input on fabric. As a surprise, I am having some of the twins' outfits made to reflect your mother's Ethiopian heritage. I know she will really enjoy helping to design the Ethiopian garments for her grandsons."

Keino looked at his wife lovingly and said, "That, my darling Amara, is why I will always love you with all of my heart and soul." He got up from his chair, walked around to his wife, lifted her from where she sat and enclosed her in a warm, tender, sensual embrace that led to a kiss that left them both hungry for much more. Keino ended the kiss, whispering in Amara's ear, "Though I must go now, my beautiful one, let us not forget what we are feeling, because tonight I promise we will begin again." They kissed tenderly and Amara was left standing with a smile on her face, anticipating her husband's promise.

An hour later, Keino stood on the golf course of the Meru Gentlemen's Club, waiting for the tee time he and Kamau had reserved. He watched his young caddy ready the golfing equipment, and it brought to mind the countless summers he and his brothers had been volunteered by their father to serve as caddies. As he reminisced, he thought how wise their parents had been to make sure that in spite of their wealth and privilege, they were given experiences that fostered humility and built character.

Keino made a vow to himself in that moment that he would be sure to pass on the legacy of character-building experiences to his children. Just as he was lost in thought, he heard the familiar voice of Kamau say in his usually serious tone, "Keino, thank you for coming."

"Of course I would come. Would you ever doubt that I would come if you said you needed to see me?"

The two brothers, connected by lineage and by spirit, embraced.

"No, no, I am well aware that I can always count on family, and today I need to prevail upon the wisdom of my older brother." The look on Kamau's face was so enigmatic Keino wondered what his brother was going to say.

They began walking silently out onto the green with the caddies following methodically. Each man chose his favorite club and the game began. Kamau searched for words to begin the conversation that would allow him to share with his brother the situation that was weighing heavily on his heart. Keino waited patiently as Kamau readied his club and took the first swing. The golf club sliced the air, sending the hard, small golf ball out onto the course. It glided to a stop inches away from its intended destination.

Keino smiled. "I see I am going to have to bring my power game today." He took his stance, positioned his club for the swing, and with perfect form hit the ball, only to watch it land woefully short of the green, landing in a nearby pond. Kamau laughed out loud. The sound was so rare it almost startled Keino, but it pleased him and he jokingly said, "So you called me out here to be the brunt of your joke? You needed a laugh at my expense?"

As they walked to the next position on the course, Kamau, still laughing softly, responded, "Keino, you were not called out here to be the brunt of anybody's joke. I guess I really needed to have a reason to laugh. I am facing a situation right now that would be comical in and of itself if it weren't so tragic."

Waiting for Kamau to take his swing, Keino leaned on his golf club. He was intensely interested in what his brother had to say. "Kamau, why don't you just tell me why you asked me to meet you here. I knew it was important the moment you said that it was a personal matter."

Kamau swung again; this time his ball landed squarely in the hole. He stopped and looked directly at Keino. "I think, my brother, I have made a mess out of a potentially blissful situation."

Keino stopped his preparation to swing. Hearing his brother use the word *blissful* erased his ability to concentrate. Keino dropped his club, adjusted the brim of his hat and said to his brother, "Kamau, we can finish this game another day. I think we should dispense with golf and get down to the business at hand."

Kamau and Keino dismissed their caddies, walked to a nearby bench and sat side by side as Kamau began to bring his brother up to date on the affair he had begun with Adana.

"Do you remember the night of the last big storm in Nairobi?" Keino answered by nodding and Kamau continued. "That was also during the time that Amara's sisters came here on holiday and you made arrangements for me to consult with Adana on a case that was giving her some trouble."

Keino quietly said, "Yes, I remember."

Kamau's speech slowed and his voice became deceptively calm. "Well, that night something happened that probably should not ever have taken place, but it did and it changed everything, literally. It changed my ideas about myself, about my life and about my world."

Keino leaned forward. It was difficult for him to imagine what could cause his stoic brother the kind of anguish he saw in Kamau's face at that moment. Kamau's speech was clipped and precise as he punctuated the force of his words with a pointed finger. "I was a fool to have acted on impulse, but for the only time in my life, I felt compelled by the sight, scent and feel of a woman. I wanted no control; I only wanted the woman." Kamau clasped his hands together as if in contemplation. "That woman was Adana. She came to me so freely, so totally. No inhibitions, no guile, no traces of underlying obligation, just pure unadulterated passion. In the moment that we came together, had I owned the world, it would have been hers for the taking." His full, sensuous lips curved in a smile as he thought of Adana. Keino listened with deep understanding creasing his brow as his brother opened his heart in a way he had never heard before.

Kamau leaned back on the bench. "When I realized the mistake I had made, I apologized to Adana and we went our separate ways, and though it was difficult, we both maintained our distance until I was in the D.C. area on business and saw her being interviewed on a local news broadcast. When I watched her on that telecast, the feelings I had for her came rushing to the surface and I knew I had to see her. I could not have kept my sanity had I left the area without seeing her, so I had the driver transport me to her place. My intention had been to leave a note at her door." A frown etched its way onto Kamau's forehead, and his eyes narrowed as he remembered seeing a man he thought to be Adana's lover leaving her home. "I saw her at her door in a dressing gown escorting a man from her home. I can't explain to you the level of rage I experienced—pure irrational heated jealousy." He clasped his powerful hands together as he spoke. "Those emotions were new to me, as are the ones I am feeling even now as I talk about and think about Adana. There I was, sitting in a chauffeured car outside of her home, wanting to leave in anger, but the pull to hold her was stronger than my rage, so I called her, not knowing what I was going to say or do.

"She answered the call and invited me in. During the course of the conversation while I was in her home, the matter of the mystery guest was cleared up. The point is, it was my rage at imagining another man touching Adana that let me know that I needed her in my life, despite still feeling obligated to the memory of Yasmin. Not wanting to let go of the woman who had taught me the meaning of magic, I asked Adana for time to sort out my feelings. I did not want to defile Yasmin's memory and yet I wanted—no, I needed—to have Adana in my bed for the rest of my life.

"So for weeks we found ways to be together, promising each other that we would keep our secret until we could be clear about what we wanted to do. Unfortunately, before I could tell Adana that I am clear, that I know what I want, she spoke with Amara and got the impression—no, correction—she was told that our parents are selecting my next wife. She won't take my calls. She won't talk to me. She has closed me out. Adana now believes that all of our time together was just filler until I could select another wife. I am at a loss, Keino. You are the only person with whom I can share this extremely embarrassing, painful, nerve-wracking situation."

With a firm grip, Keino touched Kamau's shoulder. "Sometimes, my brother, these things are not as complicated as they appear. Let me be clear. You are telling me that you and Adana have been having a secret love affair?"

"Yes, that is exactly what I am telling you, and I am also telling you that during the time that we have been together, I have become attached to Adana in ways that I have never experienced with any other woman, only now she thinks I'm a fraud who was just using her until something better comes along. She doesn't understand that for me there will never be anyone better. Keino, you have got to help me through this mess. I created it thinking that I was doing the right thing giving us time away from family and questions. I thought we needed to clear our heads of any puzzling or unanswered questions concerning how we feel about each other and about the situation in which we find ourselves. Just when I thought we were making progress, all hell has broken loose and I am left standing with egg on my face. What in God's name do I do now?"

A knowing smile spread across Keino's entire face. "Kamau, I know that the picture looks bleak to you, but I am smiling because of how happy I know the entire family will be once everyone has heard the news that you and Adana are in love. This family has prayed that you would find peace after Yasmin's death. It sounds as though you are on your way, my brother. Adana could not be more perfect for you. We will all do whatever we can to help patch up this rift between you. Trust me, my brother, this can all be straightened out. I am convinced that the ancestors intervened to bring you two together, and they will not allow you to stay apart. May I enlist my wife's help?"

Kamau lifted both hands in the air. "Anything that you find necessary, I will follow your lead. I am clearly without a course to follow."

The brothers walked back to the clubhouse, where they prepared to leave. Keino assured Kamau that he would be in touch soon with a plan designed to soothe the ruffled feathers of the beautiful Adana Terrell.

Chapter 21

Addis Ababa, Ethiopia

Cassandra Terrell Selassie sat watching her son, Kebran, run around the parklike backyard of their palatial home, executing his three-year-old rendition of soccer moves. She smiled at the miniature version of her husband running gleefully across the lawn yelling, "Look, Mommy, look!" Cassandra waved from the enclosed patio. Her face beamed with pride tinged with longing as she thanked God for the privilege of being able to be a mother to Kebran, while silently wishing that she had given birth to him and pleading for a pregnancy of her own to provide Kebran with a brother or a sister to share all of the love and attention he enjoyed daily. Cassandra placed her hand on her taut abdomen and said a quick silent prayer. Sometimes her longing to experience the feeling of carrying Ras's child overwhelmed her, and she battled the demon emotions of sadness, grief and fear. Without her husband, child, international interior design business and a household of servants to manage, she would have been lost. Just as she pushed thoughts of being barren from her mind, she heard footsteps and turned to see the object of her carnal affections—her husband, Ras Selassie—enter the room. Cassandra smiled as he walked over to her and greeted her with a tender kiss. Ras stroked Cassandra's hair and asked quietly, "How has your day been, my sweet? Has our son kept you busy?" Cassandra smiled up at her husband and stroked the rich fabric on the sleeve of his elegantly tailored suit.

"My day has been uneventful. Kebran and I have had a good time. He is growing so fast, and he is learning so much so quickly. He is so bright, Ras. We are really going to have to stay ahead of him academically."

Ras beamed with the pride of a grateful father as he said, "He is amazing. I wonder often what contribution he is going to make to the world." Ras looked at Kebran running toward a rolling ball, and with a smile in his voice said, "I think I'll go outside for a while and enjoy our own miniature version of Pele, the soccer champion." Ras stepped out onto the lawn to welcoming screams of "Daddy, watch me! Watch this, Daddy!"

Kebran kicked the ball while Ras applauded loudly yelling, "Bravo, bravo!"

For a long while, Cassandra watched them, lost in her own thoughts, until a houseman came to inform her that dinner would be served within the hour. That was her signal to call Ras and Kebran in order for them to clean up and dress for dinner. Kebran walked through the door protesting the halting of his game and pleading for a few more minutes. His father reprimanded him firmly and lovingly while pointing him in the direction of his governess, who stood smiling, waiting to prepare her charge for the evening meal. When Kebran had begrudgingly kissed each of his parents and followed his governess to his room, Cassandra and Ras retired to the master suite. As they entered the room, Ras could sense a distance in Cassandra that had become all too familiar. He locked the door, walked over to Cassandra, whose back was facing him, and enveloped her in his arms.

He whispered in her ear, "My precious, your body is here, but your spirit is not with me. Where are your thoughts, my love?"

He lifted her hair and kissed her neck with touches so gentle she sighed involuntarily. He stroked her waiting breasts with skilled fingers, leaving her wanting to be loved as only he could.

Cassandra answered softly, "Ras, I want to carry your child. I want to feel our child moving in me. I want that experience, and sometimes I get frightened thinking that it may never happen." Uncontrolled tears began to flow down her face.

Ras turned his wife to face him and began lovingly kissing away her tears, reassuring her as he left a path of kisses down each cheek. "You, my darling, are not to worry. Let's just think of this as our time to enjoy Kebran and each other. This is our time, my darling. The babies will come, I promise you. One day in the not-so-distant future, I expect to hear you say, 'Ras, I'm tired of getting pregnant. I refuse to get pregnant again,' and I will have to get on my knees and beg you to give us just one more."

Ras's scenario brought a smile to Cassandra's face. She placed her arms around her husband's neck and asked in a whispery voice, "What would I do without you?"

Ras answered with a sensuous smile, "I hope you never find out."

He drew her into a long, deep kiss. Cassandra could feel her body pulsating to the rhythm of Ras's desire. She could feel him wanting her. Ras led Cassandra to their bed and they silently undressed each other, exchanging appreciative looks and intermittent kisses. By the time the last garment was discarded, Cassandra was begging to be loved and Ras willingly obliged. He filled her with his love and with a hard, wanton heat that shook her soul. Ras smothered her erotic eruptions with deep kisses that left her body heated, tingling and screaming for more. The loving became the cathartic release of Cassandra's fear and worry. Her husband's powerful elixir heated her body and calmed her soul.

Chapter 22

Virginia, USA

Adana found herself working even harder than usual, her nights and days running together. She sat at home extending her workday by hammering out the particulars involving the Bitak case. She had written and rewritten her opening statement so many times the words began to blur on the page. With crucial pieces of her defense missing, her persuasive arguments declaring Diani's innocence had a hollow ring to them. She opened her desk drawer to retrieve a new pen, and there in the drawer was the handwritten note Kamau had written and personally delivered the night he had come to her home. Picking up the fine linen card on which the note was penned, Adana was reminded of the elegance of the man. Though to the naked eye the paper seemed perfectly fashioned without flaw, a sensitive touch revealed small imperfections that made one well aware of the intricate price it must have paid to become as elegant and as beautiful as it was. Her throat started to constrict thinking of how much she cared for Kamau and how much she was going to miss his gentle touch, the taste and feel of his full, sensuous lips and the strength of his arms enfolding her in an embrace that seemed to take her very soul. Their fiery lovemaking floated through her mind as she held the handwritten note, wrapped her arms around her torso and sighed deeply, remembering how Kamau, whose façade was one of stoic distance, had made love to her with an abandon that she was sure no one would believe. He had surely stamped every inch of her body with his signature. Adana knew her senses would never again be awakened so thoroughly and so magically. She returned the note to the desk drawer, walked to her bedroom, ran a bath and prepared to soak until the warm scented water lulled her to the precipice of sleep.

Chapter 23

Nairobi, Kenya

Kaleb Mazrui was pacing the floor in his brother Kamau's office. Kaleb's persona as the perpetual family jokester was gone, and in its place was the face and demeanor of a man highly perplexed by a situation that hinted at possible legal trouble for Mazrui Industries.

Kamau leaned back in his chair and peered at Kaleb through steely, deeply penetrating eyes. "Kaleb, tell me once again what you just said, only this time stick to the facts—no embellishments." Kaleb's pacing was threatening to wear a permanent path along the elegant carpet that covered highly polished ebony wood floors.

Impatiently Kaleb replied, "I said as succinctly as I know how that Mohammed's mystery disappearances from the flight schedule seem to have been brought on by more than illness. Last night a call came through from security. A random locker search found documents connecting Mohammed to a very elaborate smuggling ring. According to the documents, which we are sure were left behind accidentally, he was slated to use our planes to transport arms to a number of destinations both in Africa and in the Middle East. The documents record dates, times and personnel. Fortunately for Mazrui Industries, Mohammed is a bungling fool, otherwise we never would have known. We were well aware of his shortcomings, but his competence as a pilot overshadowed his other issues. Now it seems those issues have caught up with him. My concern is making sure Mazrui Industries is not implicated in these goings-on and making sure our ability to operate is not compromised."

"Kaleb, when you say Mohammed has issues, I need you to elaborate. What do you mean?"

"Mohammed is notoriously addicted to the gaming tables. He has a reputation of losing small fortunes in a night of frenzied betting. My guess is he got in trouble with money launderers and wound up having to sell his soul to save his life. A man in that position will do anything."

"You are right. Where is Mohammed now?"

"The authorities are searching. At this moment both he and his wife are missing."

"Do they have children?"

"No. Why do you ask?"

"I am sure they would be much easier to track if they are on the run with children in tow or if they have had to stop in order to make provisions for children. Having children could be problematic and could work in favor of the authorities. If they have no children, then the flight risk is much greater because Mohammed is, after all, a pilot who has logged in countless hours around the globe. They could be anywhere. In any case, Kaleb, you were correct to come to me. I shall immediately start doing damage control on this end. I need you to alert our parents so that they are made aware before the news hits the media. Let them know that I am going to make sure that the Mazrui name is not smeared in all of this."

"I shall and I'll be in touch with any new developments."

Kaleb left the office, clearly focused on his mission. Kamau rested his elbows on his desk and stroked his bearded chin, thinking that for some odd reason, there was something very familiar about what Kaleb had told him. He didn't know why this seemed familiar, and at that moment he couldn't connect any relevant dots, but he was convinced he would.

Keino struggled with the way in which he would share with Amara the news about Adana and Kamau. He knew that Amara would find the news both unsettling and exhilarating. He had no idea what would happen when Amara called Adana. The sisters loved each other dearly, and because he knew that in the past they had shared everything, Adana's secret had the potential to cause a severe rift in the fabric of their relationship. In spite of that fact or maybe because of it, Keino knew with certainty that he had to enlist his wife's aid in order to bring Adana and Kamau together again.

Keino found his wife in her sitting room arranging long-stemmed birds-of-paradise in a crystal vase. When he entered the room, Amara looked up and smiled.

"Hi, sweetheart, you're home early. Are you finished for the day?"

"I am home early because I need to speak to you."

Amara noticed a flicker of worry ease across her husband's face. She placed the last floral stem in the vase and stood staring at Keino with a look mixed with anxiety and bewilderment. Given the look on Keino's face, Amara wasn't sure what to expect. Keino took her by the hand and led her to a love seat where they sat side by side. Amara's heart was hammering in her chest, and her pulse was racing.

"Keino, you're scaring me. Is something wrong? Has something happened to someone in the family?"

"My love, slow down. I can assure you that everyone is physically fine. I need your help and I need your patience while I say what needs to be said."

Amara took a deep breath. "Okay, just please tell me whatever it is. The suspense is going to drive me crazy."

Keino lovingly pressed a kiss in the palm of her hand. "Amara, I should start by saying that although you may find some of what you hear unsettling, there are parts I'm sure that will warm your heart."

"Keino, just tell me."

"Today Kamau shared something with me that he has not told another human being. He and Adana are—or should I say *were*—secret lovers and had been for quite some time."

Amara's eyes registered disbelief. She was momentarily dazed, not sure she had heard correctly. Her eyes narrowed as she studied her husband's face feature by feature, looking for answers to the confusing questions going on in her head.

"Did you say secret lovers? Kamau and Adana?" She blinked and focused her gaze on Keino again. "Did you say Kamau Mazrui, your brother, and my sister, Adana Terrell, are secret lovers?"

"Yes, my darling. They were until you inadvertently told Adana that Mother and Father are in the process of helping Kamau select a new wife. When Adana heard you say that, she let Kamau have it. She won't see him; she won't return his calls—nothing. She has shut him out completely, and Kamau is at his wit's end trying to reach her to explain that it was all a very big mistake."

Amara stood up. "Let me get this straight. My sister

has been secretly involved with your brother and they hid it from all of us."

Keino nodded, causing Amara to erupt in a low laugh that masked confusion and disbelief. Keino rose from his seat, stood next to her and encased her in his arms. Her laughter turned to tears, and she buried her face in the hollow of his neck, spilling warm tears on the fine linen of his shirt.

"My love, there is no need to cry. All will be well."

Amara's sobs were quiet. "I know. I'm just so stunned. I don't know how to react. I would never have thought that Adana would keep a secret like that from her family. She must have had a really good reason, and if she did have a good reason, then it makes me sad that she has been going through this alone. Adana is so headstrong and so hell-bent on doing things her way. She must have felt so hurt when I told her that Kamau was thinking of getting married. My God, she must have been crushed." Keino removed his handkerchief and wiped the lingering tears from his wife's eyes. "Keino, is Kamau looking for a wife or not?"

"Kamau's mind is only on Adana and evidently has been ever since they started seeing each other. Unfortunately, our parents took a conversation Father and Kamau had and started putting the wheels in motion to help Kamau get his life back on track. Kamau had no idea they were going to rush ahead. He thought Father understood that he would ask for help if he needed it. Now, Kamau thinks he has lost the love of his life."

"Keino, did he tell you he loves her?"

"Not in those words but I understood what he meant."

"What are we going to do to help him? I feel so bad. My idle conversation has caused quite a mess. What should we do, Keino? How can we fix this? They at least need a chance to talk."

"Well, my sweet, my first order of business had to be to fill you in on the problem as Kamau presented it to me. Now we can get down to the business of working this out." Keino reached for his wife, stroked her face and kissed her cheek. "How are you now, my love? Is your mind settling down? Do you need more time to collect yourself before we begin to focus on how to help Adana and Kamau?"

"I'm fine. The news was just a shock to my system, that's all. So many mixed emotions. At first I just didn't know what to think or to say, but now all I can think about is what Adana must be feeling. My poor sister, I've got to get to her to console her in some way. I know she's hurting. Adana appears to the world a lot tougher than she really is. She is actually very vulnerable. She is strong but she has a very tender heart. I should call her now."

"Wait, my love, let us sort out a plan and then you call, all right?"

"All right."

Kamau looked at the mountain of paperwork on his desk requiring his time and attention. He considered the fact that many times in his adult life work had been his safe haven. He felt particularly drawn to it out of necessity. Adana's absence from his life had left him craving just the sound of her voice. He found himself replaying messages of hers he had saved. Though the subject matter had been mundane, the tone for him always lent itself to erotic visions of the woman constantly in his thoughts.

Restlessness and anxiety rode through him in constant waves. Picking up the telephone, Kamau dialed Adana's number for what felt like the hundredth time. He pressed each number slowly and deliberately, willing Adana to answer the ringing telephone. A thin veil of anguish covered his face as Adana's disembodied voice wafted through the telephone wires. There seemed to be little that he could do to assuage the feelings of heart-wrenching apprehension that engulfed him when he thought of never seeing her again. Her absence had convinced him that his world was missing an essential piece without her. Little satisfied him—not his culinary exploits in the kitchen, not his heroic executions on the racquetball court, not his favorite jazz recordings, not his pipe, not a snifter of his favorite brandy nor a glass of his favorite port. Even the practice of law had lost its luster without Adana in his life. Yasmin's death had left him racked with sadness, but Adana's departure had left him without a life. It was clear he didn't just want her back; he *needed* her back. He was sure that if he was ever to be whole again, he had to be with Adana.

Leaving the mountain of paper on his desk, Kamau stood up abruptly, retrieved his briefcase and left his office. With a parting word to his assistant concerning his unavailability, he headed to his car, got behind the wheel and drove in the direction of the Mazrui family mausoleum. Kamau parked the car and walked to the site where Yasmin was buried. He ran his hand along the cool stone, fingering the words etched in the marble. He knew it was the last time he would come to mourn Yasmin. He didn't know the moment it had happened, but he knew that phase of his life had closed and a new chapter had started.

"All right, my darling, now that we have a plan, perhaps you should call Adana." Looking at his timepiece, Keino commented, "She is probably preparing for work. Now may be a good time to call. I shall leave you alone to converse with your sister."

Keino left the room and Amara dialed Adana's number.

Waiting for the familiar ring, Amara wasn't sure what she'd say to her sister. Her feelings about the situation were a mass of confused elements. Amara took a deep breath just in time to hear Adana say, "Hello, Amara, this is a pleasant surprise. In my business it's always a treat to hear a friendly voice."

"When this conversation is over, I hope you will still think of me as a friendly voice."

Slightly distracted with seemingly never-ending work-related details, Adana answered, "I can't imagine anything that would cause me to think of you as an unfriendly voice."

"I called to talk about something that I think is not going to be pleasant for either of us."

Instantly Adana was no longer distracted. Her attention was riveted on the phrase *not going to be pleasant*. "Oh my God, Amara, did something happen to someone in the family?"

Amara rushed to reassure her sister. "No, nothing like that. No, Adana, this is just a little closer to home. It has to do with you and my brother-in-law, Kamau Mazrui. I think you know him." Amara said sarcastically, "Am I right?"

Adana was still for a few moments before saying, "Amara, where is this conversation leading? What are you talking about?"

"I am talking about the fact that I just learned today, a few moments ago, that you and Kamau have been having a secret affair. Adana, you didn't have to hide. You know we all would have accepted your decision to date Kamau. How could we object? He's a great guy. Why were you hiding? Now my big mouth has caused all of this confusion, and you're not speaking to a man who sounds like he's in love with you. Adana, what is going on?"

Adana slumped in her chair and took an audibly deep

breath. "I guess in a way I'm glad you found out. The hardest part in all of this was not being able to talk to you, Afiya and Cassandra. There were so many times when I wanted to share the joy, the wonder and the magic of that man. Kamau Mazrui made me question everything, and just when I thought I was clear and had settled on a course, you told me about Kamau selecting a wife and I just lost it. I was so hurt. I felt so betrayed. I was more angry with Kamau than I ever was with Jeffery. I never felt about Jeffery the way I feel about Kamau. Honestly, Amara, I didn't know I could feel like that. He made me rethink everything I ever thought about a relationship between a man and a woman. I was starting to crave his touch, his taste. I think he was becoming my air."

Amara listened as her sister poured out her heart, expressing emotions she had kept bottled up for months. As Adana spoke, Amara was sure she was hearing her sister express pure unadulterated love for a man for the first time in her life.

Adana kept talking, not caring at all how transparent she was as she expressed her feelings about Kamau. "I just couldn't believe that he would ever betray me. I couldn't believe I had misread him that completely. What kind of an idiot am I? Have I been in the courtroom so long I can only read criminal minds? Am I totally out of touch with the rest of humanity? The only bright spot in this whole fiasco was that since no one knew, I wouldn't get pitying looks from all of you, and you, Afiya and Cassandra wouldn't have to go behind my back and devise ways to cheer up 'poor Adana.' Now look! Here I am, the laughing stock again! Who told you? How on earth did you find out?"

"Adana, slow down. I also need to clear up some things. First of all, you were not betrayed. This was all a really big misunderstanding. My father-in-law misunderstood the intention of a conversation he and Kamau had, and he and my mother-in-law got a little ahead of themselves trying to help Kamau. Kamau has since straightened the whole thing out, but when he couldn't reach you to explain, he went to Keino as a last resort. The way Keino explained their conversation, that man loves you, Adana. Put him out of his misery and call him. Now the two of you don't have to hide. It sounds like both of you were trying to play both ends against the middle just in case something went wrong. Both of you know better than most that with affairs of the heart, something can always go wrong. The joy is when you really love each other, really love like you've never loved before, then the bond is too strong to be broken, and sometimes if you are really lucky, adversity only makes the bond stronger."

"Amara, I can't try again. That slap in the face was a serious wake-up call. I was tiptoeing through the tulips. I had forgotten that this is the real world. Life happens, and if you aren't careful, it will roll all over you. I wasn't paying attention. I let my guard down for a minute and got flattened like a pancake. No thank you, I don't need to go back for more."

"Did you hear anything I said? Adana, stop letting your fear of being hurt determine the quality of your life. When you come to the birthday celebration, the time will be perfect to talk to Kamau to hear him out. I feel so responsible. If I hadn't been sharing family gossip, none of this mess would have happened. Please, Adana, you got it all wrong. Call him."

"No, I won't call. Maybe it's all for the best. I am still coming to the birthday party for my nephews, but I don't need to talk to Kamau. You don't understand, Amara. I was losing myself in a man, in Kamau Mazrui, and I didn't even know it until you mentioned that he was going to select a wife. I don't need that pain again, Amara. I don't need it. I can't live like that, waiting for the other shoe to drop. I need to go back to my predictable, solitary life. I have my work; I have my family, my friends—that's enough. I don't need Kamau."

"Adana, you and I both know that none of those things can give you what Kamau does. You don't have to tell me. I know there is no substitute for that kind of love. Believe me, I know."

"I'm not you, Amara. I am not setting myself up again. I'll see you in a few days. Bye."

Amara was left with the telephone in her hand and Adana's words ringing in her head. Adana placed her telephone in its cradle and went back to her ever-present distraction—a mountain of work.

As Keino approached the sitting room, he heard silence. Peeking his head in, he saw Amara standing with the telephone in her hand. He walked in slowly, placed his arms around his wife, removed the phone from her hand, set it in the cradle and said softly, "I take it your conversation did not go as well as you had hoped."

"No, it didn't. Adana is so frightened. She is hell-bent on saving herself from hurt, but I can hear in her voice that she is hurting anyway. I don't know what else to do."

"You have done as much as you can, my sweet."

"This is all my fault."

"Amara, you know you did nothing wrong. Had you known what you were saying would have this effect, you would not have said it. Now stop berating yourself. No one loves your sister more than you, and you would not ever hurt her intentionally. She knows that."

Keino continued to console her. As Amara melted into the warmth of her husband's embrace, she said, "I think you should call Kamau tonight to prepare him, and I should call my sisters to see if they have any ideas about how to smooth this over."

"Before we make any calls, my sweet, I made a promise to you before I left today, and I am nothing if not a man of my word."

Amara was smiling a slow, satisfied smile. "Keino, you can't be serious. Our siblings are fighting for their emotional lives and here you are talking about taking me to bed."

Keino gently touched his lips to Amara's and started unbuttoning her pearl-white peasant blouse, revealing lacy lingerie designed to whet his appetite for the treasures that awaited his touch. She sighed and whimpered, "Keino, we shouldn't."

His voice was a husky whisper. "We should, my love, we should."

Keino led Amara by the hand, locked the door to the study, lifted her in his arms and carried her to the waiting sofa. Amara extended her limbs dreamily, smiling at her husband as he placed long, slow strokes along the length of her white silk chiffon palazzo pants. Keino felt the material warm beneath his touch. He slid the pants easily down his wife's smooth, firm legs. His fingers burned her tingling skin. Keino's expert touch was all Amara needed to forget everyone and everything except the moment in which they existed. Keino unsnapped and unzipped his trousers and eased them, along with his silk boxers, down his muscular legs. Amara shimmied out of her lace bikinis, and they were left to steal a few unbridled moments of passion. Keino gently pulled Amara a few inches down the length of the sofa and lowered his body over hers; his voice was warm and dark. It mellowed her like a sip of rich cognac. He whispered, "I want to be inside of you." The fire of his touch spread to her heart.

Her eyes fluttered. "I am waiting."

Keino thrust into her as she moaned aloud with erotic pleasure. He covered her mouth with heated kisses, using them to arouse and at the same time muffle his wife's sounds of searing ecstasy so as not to capture the attention of the household staff. The thrill of being discovered added to the excitement of the midday sexual encounter. There was no foreplay, just all-consuming, raw, explosive passion. A husband, a wife, a man, a woman locked in a web of unrestrained lovemaking. Keino's thrusts were long, deep and rapid. Amara's hips matched every thrust. They rode waves of electrifying heat until the delicious explosion of orgasmic waves released them, and they collapsed into each other's arms. Keino looked into his wife's eyes.

She stared back and said with a tilted grin, "You are so naughty."

Keino's sexy reply was, "You are so good." He ran one finger down the long length of her thigh. She shivered. He said slowly, "Now we can make our calls."

Chapter 24

Senegal

A lazy Saturday afternoon found Afiya Terrell Diop sitting contentedly watching her husband, Ibra, as he gently rocked their baby daughter, Fara, to sleep. The two of them created a perfect picture of peace and beauty. With a sculpted, bare, ebony chocolate-colored torso; long, muscular arms; strong legs covered in gauzy sapphire-colored drawstring pants; and long, meticulously groomed, sable-colored locks hanging gently on his shoulders, Ibra gazed down admiringly at his precious daughter. His thoughts were of her perfection and of future days when his preoccupation would be the examination of countless suitors vying for her affections. He conceded that his daughter was indeed a combination of the physical best of both her parents. She brought him joy beyond anything he could have imagined. Just as a smiling Afiya shifted in her chair, Ibra looked directly into his wife's eyes and said in a low, husky tone, "She is as beautiful as her mother."

"Thank you, sweetheart. I love watching the two of you. Every little girl should have a father who loves her dearly." With a faraway look in her eyes, Afiya continued. "I don't know how my father did it, but he made all of his daughters feel so special. We each felt as though we had the key to his heart." She sighed. "Later today I need to call and check on everyone. It will be so good to see them all next week at the birthday celebration."

Ibra stroked Fara's soft, pecan-colored cheek. "My sweet, I am sure that with each miraculous birth, your father's heart was taken over and over again."

Ibra rose, holding his sleeping daughter, and walked into her playroom, where he placed her down in an opulently appointed crib for an afternoon nap. When he returned to the master bedroom, he found Afiya at her desk, examining slides of newly acquired paintings to be displayed in her Virginia gallery. Ibra walked up behind her chair and began gently massaging her bare shoulders. He noted that the cinnamon-colored halter top and matching sheer broomstick skirt almost matched her skin tone perfectly, leaving an illusion of a nude figure, beautifully proportioned, lost in thought. Ibra stopped his gentle massage for a moment.

Afiya said distractedly while easily rotating her neck in semicircles, "Ibra, don't stop; that felt so good."

Ibra unpinned Afiya's locks, allowing them to fall from the topknot in which she had placed them. He eased his hands gently through the tendrils of hair, causing Afiya's body to tingle. She sighed and leaned her head back, relaxing into the soothing ministrations of her husband's strong hands. Speaking only with his actions, Ibra went from Afiya's head to her neck, where he untied her halter top. As the ties fell like obedient minions doing their master's bidding, Ibra continued to massage Afiya's shoulders and upper arms. She closed her eyes and moved deeper into each stroke. He eased the halter down and tenderly caressed both of Afiya's soft, warm breasts, leaving her senses reeling as he fondled the highly sensitive nipples, pulling, playing, turning them with exquisite precision between his fingers and thumbs, causing her center to throb with pulsating rhythms. Sounds of pleasure flowed from her lips. Ibra turned her chair to face him and got on his knees. He lifted her sheer skirt to her waist, and beginning with her bare feet, applied the same tender massage from Afiya's toes to her hips.

Afiya, eyes closed, senses colliding, grabbed her husband's shoulders tightly, attempting to stifle her desire to scream. The stifled screams became muted whimpers. Ibra gently pulled Afiya to the floor and began kissing her in all of the places his hands had touched. Afiya reciprocated; loving her husband was for her a pleasure of which she never tired. On the floor of their expansive master suite, even the exquisite Persian rug felt the power of their love. With legs and locks intertwined, Afiya and Ibra moved to their own rhythms, loving as they always did, with tender desperation, wanting to touch each other's souls. When the raw act of possession had subsided and the flames of passion had become embers, the two lay nuzzled in each other's arms, their clothes strewn across the floor beside them. Ibra smiled and kissed the top of Afiya's head. He spoke with desire still on his lips. "Promise me, Afiya, that we will always love like this, no matter what."

She stroked his muscular back. "Ibra, nothing can stop our rhythm, not even your mother." With that quip, they both broke into uncontrollable laughter.

* * *

The following week, the family gathered in Nairobi to celebrate the second birthday of Amara and Keino's twin sons, Garsen Markos and Joseph Terrence. Though in Kenyan Kikuyu tradition the firstborn son is named after the father's father and the second-born son is named after the mother's father, Amara and Keino added to tradition. Garsen Markos was named for his Kenyan paternal grandfather and his Ethiopian maternal great-grandfather. Joseph Terrence was named for his African American maternal grandfather and maternal great-grandfather. There was no special reason to celebrate the twins' second birthday so lavishly, but Amara wanted to use the day as an excuse to bring her large beloved family together. For the event she was even able to coerce her maternal grandmother, Lillian Gardener Chatfield, and her paternal grandparents, Lancaster and Savannah Terrell, into coming. Having them chauffeured and flown in on Mazrui private jets had helped to eliminate the reasons given by all three grandparents for not wanting to bother with the excruciating details of traveling, especially when the travel destination was another continent.

Everyone oohed and aahed over the identical sons—small replicas of their father.

The grounds of Keino and Amara's home were decorated with whimsical sophistication. Events planner Camille Evanti had outdone herself again. The celebration had all of the elegance of an upscale wedding reception, with the touches of whimsy that represented the children. The children's area was designed to be reminiscent of a carnival equipped with rides and games and food fashioned especially for toddlers. The twins' friends and cousins joined them as strategically placed nannies maintained watchful eyes, and the children's parents indulged themselves with delicious food from several continents and a select few of the finest wines and other beverages from around the world. Throughout the canopied sections of the grounds, crystal twinkled in the sunlight, white linen shown brilliantly and laughter and conversation rang joyously in the air.

Keino had warned Kamau that Amara's conversation with Adana had been unsuccessful. Kamau was disappointed but he was clear that he was not going to allow her obstinacy to stop him from making another attempt to convince her that they had been victims of a horrible comedy of errors. He had to convince her. He was not prepared to take no for an answer. He was not prepared to leave Keino and Amara's home without having settled the rift between the woman he loved and himself. He was not willing to give her up. He had watched her throughout the day, and he had felt her watching him. Kamau was just waiting for the opportune moment to get Adana alone. He would wait. There was ample time.

Adana was sitting near her two grandmothers, listening to them catch up. She loved her family but she wanted the day to end. She wanted to get as far away from Kamau as she could. Every time she caught a glimpse of him, her heart sank. She kept telling herself even if Amara was right about the misunderstanding, he could still hurt her again. She just didn't want to take that chance. She tried to tell her heart, but every time she saw him, the rhythm of her breathing changed, and a fine mist of perspiration covered her body even though she was sheltered from the Nairobi sun. Her body ached just remembering his touch. She had to get away. She turned to her grandmothers. "Mimi, Grams, I'm going to walk around a bit. I'll see you both later."

The matriarchs smiled, nodded in her direction and continued their conversation. Adana headed for the lanai on the other side of the home, away from the festivities.

Kamau saw her walking. He waited a few seconds, made a graceful exit from the table where he was sitting with his brothers Kaleb, Aman and their wives, and followed Adana. He found her slowly walking back and forth on the lanai. Her head was slightly lowered, and her arms were folded.

Kamau called her name as only he could. "Adana."

She looked up, saw him and with a look of pure anguish in her eyes, she turned to walk away.

Kamau reached out and grabbed her arm. "Adana, please don't go. Sit down and listen to me."

"I won't sit down. I can't listen to you. I can't listen to you tell me how I've misunderstood your intentions. Kamau Mazrui, I don't care about your intentions, your explanations, your half-truths. I don't care about you."

Adana attempted to walk away again. Kamau quickly stepped in front of her, firmly grabbed both of her shoulders and held her in place facing him. The fire she saw in his eyes was new to her.

"Adana Terrell, do not ever again tell me that you don't care about me. You care—you care in ways no other woman ever has." His voice lowered and deepened. "I know you care every time your long, smooth legs wrap like silk around my body. I know you care when the rhythms of our hearts beat as one. I know you care when my touch causes your body to tingle beneath my hands."

Adana's eyes glistened with tears as she watched the play of emotions on Kamau's face. His dark smoldering eyes slowly closed as he gently brought her to him and worshipfully explored her mouth with his lips. Adana, fighting torturous pleasure, gave in to the man she desired with every fiber of her being. And then she stopped.

"Kamau, I'm afraid."

"Adana, you have my heart. For as long as you will allow me, I will be your port in any storm. Give me that chance, Adana. Is your heart as full of me as mine is of you?"

"Yes. I wish I could say no, but yes."

"Then my beautiful one, there is nothing to fear."

Adana stared into Kamau's eyes, looking for signs of indecision. "What about your torn allegiance, your loyalty to the memory of Yasmin?"

"God and the ancestors have intervened. You were placed in my path to show me that life can be new again. Give us a chance, Adana, on your terms. I have sorted it out in my mind over and over, and what is clear is that I need you in my life. I know what I want. I know what tradition dictates, but my heart requires that I relinquish control and move at your pace in your way. Doing things my way has not exactly led us to the ending either of us envisioned."

"I was so hurt when I heard you were choosing a wife—I just felt so betrayed. You became the Jeffery Scott experience all over again. Kamau, you were so perfect; you were everything I ever imagined I wanted in a partner. You made me feel things I have never felt."

"I am still that man. You bring out the best in me, Adana. When I touch you, lightning strikes, my imagination runs wild and I become a man I've never known myself to be. You inspire me to bring you pleasure in every imaginable way. I need you, Adana. So what do you need me to do so that we can move on with our lives?"

"If we are going to start fresh, the first thing I want is for us to not hide from our families. I think that was one of the hardest things I've ever done. I don't like deceiving my family, especially when it comes to my personal life. When it comes to work, a certain level of discretion is understood, but our personal lives have always been open books."

"Good, I can solve that problem immediately."

Kamau took Adana's hand and led her back onto the grounds filled with family and friends. He walked up to Keino and whispered in his ear. Keino nodded and walked away, intending to perform the task Kamau had requested. Kamau and Adana stood chatting comfortably, sipping champagne as knowing glances were sent their way by family and friends.

At the end of the evening as the guests left to go to their respective homes, Judge Garsen and Adina Mazrui, Keino and Amara, Ras and Cassandra, Ibra and Afiya, Drs. James and Ana Terrell, Kaleb, Aman and their wives, and the grandparents all entered Keino and Amara's library and sat comfortably around the room. All eyes were on Kamau as he stood and gestured to Adana to sit in the chair nearest where he was standing. Kamau stepped forward slightly; his voice was deep and resonant.

"Family, thank you for remaining a while longer at my request. I am sure you are all wondering why I convened this meeting; therefore, I will not keep you in suspense." The room was still. A pin could have been heard as it dropped. "For two years now, this family has rallied around me and supported me in ways beyond description. Knowing that I have been a source of worry and concern for many of you has been difficult for me to bear. I want you to know that I will be forever grateful. A few months ago, I was not clear which path my life was taking. I was thrown off course until a very strong-willed, exceptionally persuasive litigator who is also, I might add, an extremely beautiful woman, was placed in my path. It did not take long for me to understand that I needed time to convince Attorney Adana Terrell that our legal collaboration could lead to much more.

"Unfortunately, my plan for our getting to know each other has backfired. It was my suggestion, and Adana indulged me, that we spend time away from friends and family because I had already caused you enough worry and concern. I selfishly thought only of how my life would be affected by our choice to discreetly explore a relationship. It did not occur to me that Adana would or could be adversely affected; she has been, and so I need to rectify here, in front of family, any misperceptions that might be lingering in your minds. First, it is my intention to openly court Adana for all the world to see." Kamau turned directly to Adana's father and mother. "Drs. Terrell, I assure you my intentions are honorable."

Adana's father nodded in Kamau's direction. Her mother smiled knowingly. Kamau continued, speaking directly to his parents. "Father, Mother, though your wisdom is never discounted, this time my choice of a life partner will rest solely on my shoulders, and whether or not that union will look like the tradition we know will be a decision made as time unfolds."

There were smiles and murmurs around the room as Kamau extended his hand to Adana. She grasped his hand, rose from her chair and stood next to him. She thought how amazing it was that Kamau had the ability to make her feel protected, sheltered and autonomous all at the same time. He regarded her strengths as equal to his own while being very clear that in their relationship their strengths had their designated places and complementary designs. Adana's reverie was interrupted by the sound of Judge Garsen Mazrui's booming voice.

"Well, Dr. Terrell, it appears that once again one of my sons has found a precious jewel among your daughters."

"So it would seem. My only observation at this point

is that your sons and my daughters appear to have excellent powers of discernment."

Warm laughter filled the room as family members approached Adana and Kamau with warm sentiments of approval. Cassandra whispered in Adana's ear, "Make it last forever."

Afiya whispered, "I told you he would come."

Amara whispered, "I'm just so happy for you."

Adana's mother said openly, "This is answered prayer; now I know there is a chance that one day I might be able to say all four of my daughters are married."

"Mother, don't get ahead of yourself. Did you hear Kamau? He said his intentions to court me are honorable. He didn't ask for my hand in marriage."

"I know what I pray for, and any step in that direction is progress in my mind."

"Mom, you are absolutely incorrigible. What am I going to do with you?"

"Leave me alone and let me do what I do."

Adana kissed her mother's smooth cheek and smiled. As Ana Terrell walked away to speak to Kamau, Adina Mazrui softly took Adana's hand and led her into an adjoining room. "Adana, my dear, I needed to be alone with you for a moment. I try very hard to stay out of my children's lives unless asked, but it is not always an easy task. I need to start by saying I am happy beyond words that my son has found you. I have worried incessantly about his emotional well-being since Yasmin's death. Of all of my sons, Kamau is the most traditional."

Adana's mouth lifted in a tilted smile as she said, "So I've been told by almost everyone who knows him."

"I am saying it only because when Kamau made his announcement tonight, two things were troubling—the decision to court openly as opposed to marrying and the statement he made about the possibility of a nontraditional liaison. I was puzzled because neither of those things sounds like my son. Are you opposed to marriage?"

Adana sighed. "I have been convinced of two things. One, that I didn't think I'd ever find a compatible mate, and two, that if I did, I didn't know whether I'd have the stuff required to build a good marriage. To be very truthful, the idea of taking on a marriage is unsettling to the point of being frightening."

"I see, and since Kamau knows your feelings on this matter, that determined how he phrased his statement to us." Adina Mazrui clasped Adana's hands tightly. "My son must care for you beyond measure to take the stance he has taken. Understand clearly, my dear, what it took for him to do what he did tonight. I want you to understand that if my son never says I love you using those words, he said it tonight. Handle his love carefully, my dear, and be very clear who he is before you relegate him to living a life for which he was neither born nor is he emotionally well suited."

Adina Mazrui gave Adana a tight hug, and they walked back into the loving arms of the family. Adina's words were still resonating in Adana's mind.

As the other family members retired to their respective homes or to guest rooms in Keino and Amara's home, Kamau and Adana sat on the lanai. A warm breeze flowed softly over them. Adana sat with her head resting on Kamau's shoulder. His strong arm embraced her.

"Kamau, thank you for tonight. I realize that operating outside of traditional norms is difficult for you."

Kamau pulled Adana a little closer. "I have found, my sweet one, over the past few weeks that there is nothing more difficult than being without you. I will do whatever it takes to make you feel at ease with the fact that I want you and only you to share the rest of my life in a way that makes sense to you."

Adana looked directly into Kamau's eyes and without speaking traced the velvety hair on his face, beginning with the mustache outlining his top lip, then spilling over to the beard that covered his chin. He sat still, reveling in the softness of her touch. He watched her until the desire in his eyes stilled her hand. Kamau placed Adana's hand in his and covered her lips with a mouth burning with lustful heat.

"Adana, I thought the things you make me feel were only fanciful musings. Now I know they are real."

Adana felt transported; she breathed lightly between parted lips. She knew Kamau had forever unlocked her heart and soul. He held her hands and gazed into her eyes. "Adana, I don't want to leave you tonight."

She shook her head. "We don't have a choice, Kamau. Even I am not willing to ignore tradition and parade our private affair in front of everybody we know. It's one thing for them to speculate about how intimate we are. It is altogether another thing for us to be that open. You know I'm much too private for that and so are you."

Kamau's skin shone as brilliantly as black velvet in the moonlight as he spoke. "Adana, my love, I am a very private man who prides himself on having mastered the art of discretion. Just go to your room and leave the rest to me." Kamau cupped Adana's chin tenderly in his warm hand and quickly kissed her waiting lips. "Now go, love. I will soon join you."

Adana rose from her seat and started walking. She looked back over her shoulder and smiled; Kamau nodded and winked. She continued walking into the house. It appeared that everyone had retired for the evening. The house was still except for the unobtrusive bustling of servants readjusting the house for the following day. Adana quickly slipped into the guest room she occupied, closed the door behind her and breathed a deep sigh filled with heated anticipation. She undressed slowly, savoring the time she and Kamau had spent together. She rested her body in the large down-filled bed. The Egyptian cotton sheets caressed her like a layer of fine silk. She embraced the fluffy pillows, closed her eyes and waited. As she was drifting off, she was startled into consciousness by a tender kiss on her cheek. She whispered, "Kamau, I must have dozed off. I didn't hear you come in." Adana lifted her arms, inviting Kamau to join her in bed.

"In a moment, my sweet. I must make sure we are secure. I slipped through the door of the balcony leading to your room." He locked the door, quickly discarded his clothes and slid into bed with Adana. They were both hungry for the connection of which they had been deprived. Kamau felt Adana's body tremble beneath his fingertips. He softly said, "Adana, I have waited for so long. I have missed your scent, your taste, your touch. I have needed you." He stroked her hair and held her face, kissing her deeply, leaving her reaching for more. She surrendered completely.

Kamau drained all of her doubts and fears. Aroused beyond the peak of desire, she tried to communicate her need with every stroke of her hands, every movement of her lips, tongue, legs. She whispered erotic phrases in his ear, arousing them both until her desire left her begging, "Kamau, Kamau, I need you inside me. I need you . . . I need you."

His voice was low, smooth and deep. "In time, my sweet. I want to prolong the experience of loving you. At this moment you are my water after a long and deep thirst. You are my food after my body has been ravished by hunger. At this moment you are my air. I want to breathe in all of you." He began at the top of her head and touched every visible inch of her body with lips used solely for her pleasure. Adana writhed with her senses spinning as she inhaled his scent, reminding her of a cool ocean breeze. Kamau's name sang through her lips only to be captured again and again by the man she found herself loving more than she thought possible.

His voice was husky with need. "Adana, never leave me again." His lips parted hers as his hands explored her thighs and moved up gingerly, radiating pleasure throughout her body.

Adana pressed her open lips to Kamau's and in a suffocated whisper answered him. "I can't leave you. You have my heart, my mind, my soul. I need you, Kamau, I need you." Her soft voice became silk to his ears. Their instinctively powerful responses to each other were tinged with hints of maddening obsession. Adana buried her face in his throat, placing kisses that caused Kamau's breath to leave his body as a stifled moan. Adana continued layering kisses on his chest, neck and shoulders. Kamau's moans were low, deep and heated with arousal. His hands spoke for him, claiming every inch of Adana's body. His hands traced the length of her spine and slipped up her velvety smooth arms. He explored the hollows of her back. Adana placed her arms around his neck. Kamau encircled each of her waiting breasts, first with nimble fingers and then with warm moist lips.

Adana's limbs trembled as she clung to him. His touches became almost unbearable as they went from tender to urgent. His hardness aroused them both. Her soft curves molded to his dark, strong body. She could feel his uneven breathing on her cheek as he held her close. He grasped her waist and slid into the seat of her hot, waiting femininity. She arched her body, pulling him in farther, deeper. The separation had been too long. His mouth grazed her earlobe. Breath left her body and became long, surrendering whimpers. The passion was uncontrolled, intoxicating. They were consumed by the love they made. Kamau's raw sensuality when loving her left Adana hungry for his arousal, and his hardness electrified her, causing moans of ecstasy to slip through her lips.

What they had awakened in each other could never be undone. They made love until only sheer exhaustion could stop them. Bodies bare and still moist from the exquisite harmony of their lovemaking, they lay with legs intertwined, hearts racing and minds spinning. Neither had ever experienced before what they had found in each other. Kamau gathered Adana against his warm, still, very much aroused body. He gently kissed her swollen lips, and she drank in his sweetness as she caressed the strong tendons of his burnished onyx back. Kamau buried his large, strong hands in Adana's hair and deepened the kiss. Her taut nipples strained against his muscular chest. Unceremoniously he took her again, feeling like a madman with an insatiable compulsion. She welcomed him in as she rode her own wave of madness, wanting Kamau to enter her every pore and never leave. The loving was hard, fast, a raw act of possession. The end left them both silently committed to forever fueling the flames of their desires. Kamau encircled Adana in his arms and ran his thumb deliciously up and down her palm as he stared into her glistening eyes.

When he spoke again, his deep-timbered voice was a velvet murmur. "You know, my angel, I must leave this room before we are discovered."

Adana's quiet answer was, "Yes, I know."

"I am not going to stay the night. I'll drive back to the compound. It would be too difficult tonight to sleep in the same house with you and not have you in my bed."

Adana turned her face away. "I understand."

Kamau gently turned her face back toward him and

saw tears glistening in her eyes. "Please, my precious, tell me why you are crying."

Adana took a deep breath. "I am so afraid, Kamau. So afraid of everything you make me feel. When you touch me, I lose myself in you. I have never in my life given anyone that kind of power over my emotions. I've given you too much, Kamau. I've given you too much."

"My beautiful, incredibly brilliant Adana, in this instance your mind will mislead you. Follow your heart, my darling. I think for both of us this is a classic case of what you Americans call chemistry. I have as much to lose as you do, and for the magic that we make, I am willing to risk it all. Now let me dry your eyes, tuck you in for a few hours of rest, and tomorrow in the bright light of a new day, you can tell me how to make you feel comfortable in the role of Kamau Mazrui's woman. My woman. Your wish, my darling one, will be my command."

Adana's face radiated with a peaceful smile. Kamau gave her a quick, soft kiss. "We will talk tomorrow, my precious." He dressed, let himself out through the French doors leading to the balcony and made his way quietly to his car.

Keino was taking a midnight stroll on his expansive grounds, something he often did when business weighed heavily on his mind. He saw his brother leaving the balcony of the guest room where Adana was staying. Kamau did not see him. Keino looked puzzled for a split second and then the reality of what he had seen hit him. Rendered speechless in his surprise, Keino laughed quietly to himself, thinking that once again a Terrell sister had brought a man literally to his knees. Keino murmured under his breath, "I do understand, Kamau. I do understand." He then walked into his home and into the bedroom where he had shared with his loving wife many of his own intensely passionate moments.

The following morning, the Mazrui clan gathered for breakfast before company planes were to deposit family members at their various homes across the borders of continents and countries. Throughout the course of the family breakfast, Kamau plied Adana with tender touches at every opportunity, whether it was to clasp her hand with his or to lightly touch her shoulder or to place his hand on the small of her back as they walked. Every touch reminded Adana of how well he had loved her the night before. Their stolen looks and shared whispers were not lost on anyone. Adina Mazrui in particular noted that she had never seen her son publicly display his affection for a woman—not even Yasmin. Adana relaxed into the festivities, feeling relieved that she no longer had to hide the man who made her feel more alive than she had ever felt. Her sisters and her parents couldn't get enough of seeing Adana more content than they had ever seen her. For all involved, the day seemed bright and full of promise.

Chapter 25

Kamau and Adana, back home on separate continents, busied themselves with full calendars, desks loaded with case files, countless unanswered e-mails, court appearances and a long-distance love affair that required nurturing. They were never far from each other's thoughts.

Adana was leaving what was for her another exasperating partners meeting. As she was about to enter her office, her assistant announced, "Ms. Terrell, you had a call from Mr. Kamau Mazrui. I told him you were in a meeting. He said he would like you to call him at your convenience. His accent is so wonderful to listen to. If I might ask, where is he from?"

Adana smiled, thinking, *He is more wonderful than you know*. She picked up a stack of messages and answered her assistant while reading through them. "He was born in Kenya, but that accent is no doubt the result of being a world citizen. Thank you for the messages. Hold all of my calls unless it's family. I need to clear my desk today."

"Yes, Ms. Terrell."

Adana walked into her office, sat at her desk, added

the messages to the other stacks of paper in front of her and dialed Kamau's private cell.

He picked up on the second ring. "My angel, how are you?"

"I feel better now that I am talking to you."

"Why did you not feel well before?"

"I work in a situation that is stressful to say the least. The stress of the job is one thing but to deal with the pressures of being constantly scrutinized by your own team is sometimes like living in hell."

"It goes without saying, my sweet, that your skills are greatly needed on the continent of Africa in general and more specifically in Nairobi, Kenya, at the Law Firm of Mazrui Industries."

A thoughtful smile curved Adana's mouth. Kamau could hear it in her voice. "Kamau Mazrui, you are asking me to go from the frying pan into the fire. Would dealing with an office full of African men be any different than working in an office full of American or European men?"

"Yes, it would be different. Contrary to popular opinion, in ancient Africa during the height of civilizations in Egypt, Sudan, Mali, Songhai and Ghana, there was no inequity between the sexes. The advent of Europeans sent our worlds spinning out of control, and we have not yet recovered; however, because of that history, we can be brought back to our senses rather quickly. I am a living example."

Adana laughed out loud. "Kamau, you can be so funny, especially when you are not trying to be."

"Nothing I said was meant to be amusing."

"I know, darling, I know. I just wish that things were as simple as you just laid them out. They're not and you know it."

"I know no such thing, and I believe it bears further

discussion. What I don't want is for you, my woman, my angel, to be in any way dissatisfied if I can resolve the problem."

"You know I love that trait of yours that rushes to rescue and protect me. Until I met you, I didn't realize I needed it. I'm getting used to the fact that your first instinct seems to be to take care of me. I am so used to doing it all myself."

"Yes, my angel, though I acknowledge that you are an immensely strong, capable woman, every strong woman needs a strong man. I am yours, my sweet. I am yours. Speaking of being yours, and as proof that you are constantly on my mind, last night as I was going through files concerning one of our missing pilots, who appears to have been involved in a smuggling ring, I ran across something that might interest you, because I think there is a connection to your Bitak case."

Adana's eyes widened, her mouth opening soundlessly. She stood up from her chair and started walking the length of her desk. "Oh my God, Kamau, I need a break in this case. I really need a break in this case. What did you uncover?"

"I can't be certain until we do further research, but names from your files kept flashing through my mind as I thumbed through Mohammed's personnel folder. As it turns out, Mohammed is married to Ali Sanussi's sister. That is the same Ali Sanussi who is married to your client. Mohammed and his wife are running from the authorities as we speak."

An anxious Adana blurted out, "Kamau, how does that connect to my case?"

"Where there's smoke, there is often fire. Our researchers did complete backgrounds on Mohammed and his wife in order to speed up the investigation. It turns out that she was working temporarily at her sister-in-law's firm when very suspicious financial transactions were made to some offshore accounts. My instincts tell me that if we follow that money, we will find our culprits."

"Oh, Kamau, I don't know how to thank you." Adana sat down again. "I have been so worried about this case. I knew all along that it had to be someone close to Diani but I had the wrong person."

"Don't thank me yet. This is all pure speculation."

"Yes, but it's better than what I had, and it gets me closer to the guilty party." Adana took a deep breath. "Are you ever going to get tired of coming to my rescue?"

"I always want the privilege of being the lead warrior in all of your battles."

"Kamau"—she hesitated—"thank you."

"Save your thanks, my sweet, until I have really earned it. I am coming to Washington in three days. We will strategize then about how to proceed. We will have a chance to combine business with pleasure. If it will work for you, I'd like to fly in a day earlier before my meetings."

"I'll make it work. Why don't you plan to come directly to my house, and we can enjoy a day and a night of undisturbed bliss."

"I like the way that sounds. Until then, my angel, think of me."

"Sometimes it feels as though that's all I do. Good-bye, Kamau."

"Good-bye, my angel."

Adana felt like dancing. A break in the Bitak case and the anticipation of seeing Kamau made an otherwise bleak day a cause for celebration. She thought to herself, *Afiya, my mystical sister, would love the magic synchronicity of how all of these things have fallen into place.*

Over the days that followed, Adana worked long hours to clear her desk and her calendar so that clients would not suffer while she enjoyed time with the man she had grown to love. Adana went about juggling the demands of work with the mundane rituals involved in keeping her personal life in order. She wanted everything to be perfect for Kamau when he arrived. Her desire was to make sure her house was equipped with everything the two of them would need without having to leave the house. Their time together was precious for both of them. Adana's days became blurs as she worked, shopped and stocked her kitchen with Kamau's favorite delectables, and little by little, she rearranged her bedroom suite to resemble a luxurious spa. She was exhausted but exhilarated.

On the day before Kamau's arrival, Adana rushed to shop for a few additional items at one of her favorite gourmet food haunts called Epicurean Delights. She loved the store. Every item was beautifully displayed. It reminded her of a European delicacy shop with every imaginable edible treat from many parts of the world. Adana strolled through the aisles, fingering the attractive packaging and reading the labels of items she found appealing. Since she knew that Kamau was a serious gourmand, she wanted to find things for him to try that would whet his palate but surprise him as well. Clearly that would be quite a task since Kamau's knowledge of foods was extensive. She found her way to the African delicacies section and looked at a wide array of finger foods she thought might please Kamau. The thought of feeding him before, after or during lovemaking brought a radiant smile to her lips. Adana almost laughed out loud when she thought about how surprised people would be if they knew how adventurous she and Kamau were in bed. Shaking her head, still smiling, she thought the prim, proper, staid couple the world saw was not the couple they became when behind closed doors. They

truly ignited fires in each other that had never been lit
before in either of them.

She picked up a sparkling cellophane-wrapped basket
of North African dates. They were dark and smooth like
Kamau's burnished skin. Mangoes were next. She imagined peeling them and feeding Kamau as the flowing
nectar eased down his chin to be removed by the flick of
her tongue. Adana never thought she'd have time in her
life for real romance. Something deep inside her had
always wanted it, but she never thought it would really
happen. Now she stood amid the fragrant, exquisitely
arranged international foods, daydreaming about the
man she thought she'd never find. With a bit more lightness in her step, Adana picked out a package of gebna
(Egyptian Brie), and dozens of smoked prawns flown in
from the Gulf of Benin. She made her way to the check-
out counter, paid for her purchases and headed home.

It was early evening when Kamau arrived. He walked
through the door wearing what was for him casual dress,
which meant he was not wearing a tie, though he was
impeccably dressed as always. Adana could not help but
stare. No matter how many times she had seen him since
their affair had begun, he mesmerized her. The light
charcoal-colored suit with barely visible silver threads
hung stylishly on the body she knew to be as close to
perfection as the human form could be. Her eye traveled
to the folded three-cornered handkerchief in his breast
pocket, which matched the white linen collar of his blue
pinstriped shirt. The collar was open, reminding her of
the heavenly places hiding behind the fabric.

Kamau's thoughts mirrored Adana's. It occurred to
him that his memories of her did not compare to
the Adana he saw standing before him. She was lovely.
Her smooth, bare shoulders begged to be touched as
they were revealed from the off-shouldered black lace

peasant blouse she wore. The modesty piece worn under the black lace covered only her breasts, leaving midriff and satiny arms peeking through inches of lace, reminding Kamau of a body that molded to his as though made to his exact specifications. Kamau closed the door behind him and dropped his bags on the floor. They were both silent as Adana walked into his arms. They savored the satisfaction of being together again. Adana placed a kiss on Kamau's neck. He kissed her forehead and slowly moved one hand over the surface of her black silk flared pants, which covered her perfectly round derriere. Their lips touched gently, both understanding that what they felt in that moment was more than sexual desire; peace and contentment flowed between them like warm honey.

Adana took Kamau's hand and led him into the kitchen. He sat in one of the chairs positioned at the kitchen table and pulled her onto his lap. His eyes were dark and magnetic as he looked at her. She stared back with a haunting serenity that touched his heart. His strong fingers laced their way through her hair as his hands guided her lips to his. The kiss was slow and gentle. He kissed the pulsing hollow at the base of her throat.

Lifting his head, looking into Adana's eyes and speaking for the first time, Kamau asked, "How are you today, my angel?"

Adana kissed his neck. "I am fine now that you are here. I've been looking forward to spending time with you."

Kamau ran his finger in a feathery stroke from Adana's neck down one bare shoulder. "I have missed you as well, my angel. The right words are difficult to find when I try to express what you mean to me."

"Kamau, you don't need words." She smiled. "Your unspoken communication tells me everything I need to know." She kissed his lips lightly and said, "I have a wonderful bottle of wine that I think you will enjoy. We'll have a glass before dinner."

Adana stood and walked to retrieve the wine. Kamau took off his suit coat, placed it on the back of the chair and said, "Let me help you." He reached for the bottle.

Adana placed it in his hands, then turned, opened her cabinet and took down two long-stemmed glasses. Kamau fingered the bottle in his hands, reading the label. "This, my precious, is a magnificent bottle of wine. Chambave Rouge is rare. Where did you find this?"

"Actually, I didn't. A client sent it to me as a gift. I was told very few cases were made."

"That is true. This, my darling, is liquid gold. A perfect choice for our time together."

Kamau uncorked the bottle and poured the tantalizing liquid into the waiting glasses. Adana lifted her glass and savored the rich taste of the wine. She looked at the glass and said, "This really is wonderful."

Kamau took a sip. "Exquisite, exquisite. Now, before we make our plans for dinner, let me share with you a few new developments concerning the Bitak case."

"New developments? Are these developments going to help clear my client?"

"Be patient, my sweet. I think you will be pleased with where this is all leading."

The two lovers sat at the table, glasses in hand, poised for conversation. Adana's eyes were riveted on Kamau, braced for his every word.

"Mazrui Industries retains a cadre of investigators for a myriad of purposes. As you might imagine, our vast holdings bear watching, and from time to time we are caught in sticky situations that require extensive research. Our recent problem with the missing pilot is just such a case. Sometimes ferreting out the culprit or culprits in these cases leads us to things for which we were not searching." Kamau took another sip. "We have found a piece of evidence that I believe will help strengthen your case."

Adana fingered the stem of her glass. "This I've really got to hear."

"It seems, my sweet, that our former pilot Mohammed Bashir and his wife, Saba, Sanussi's sister, have been, and perhaps still are, involved with an arms smuggling ring connecting some of the major political extremists in Africa and the Middle East. Thanks to those forgotten documents that Mohammed left behind, we have been able to follow the money all the way to Geneva."

"Switzerland?"

"Switzerland. If the ringleaders of this escapade knew how inept one of their operatives is, his life would not be worth much. At this point, our job is to get proof of the money before the trail can be destroyed. In order to do that, my sweet, I am going to need you to accompany me to Geneva, where I have friends who can be of assistance in this matter. I could send my investigators, but the process would take longer, and I need to stop Mohammed and you need to clear your client."

Adana was stunned. "Switzerland . . . Go with you to Geneva, Switzerland?"

"Yes, my angel, as soon as I finish my meetings here, we can leave. You have only a few weeks left to close out this case. If you are able to get your hands on the needed documents in order to clear your client, it will certainly be worth the trip." Kamau took another sip of wine.

Adana smiled incredulously. "Kamau Mazrui, you never cease to amaze me. Yes, I'll go to Switzerland with you." She drank the last of her wine. "I knew there was a reason I worked so furiously to clear my desk. I thought it was so that my head could be clear to focus on us. I had no idea I'd be focusing on us in Switzerland."

Adana's reaction amused Kamau. Seeing the amusement in his eyes, she laughed. He joined her with his deep, rich laughter and said, "Switzerland it is."

Kamau finished his wine and had them driven to a very intimate upscale restaurant. The menu was Moroccan and the restaurant itself had been on Kamau's "to do" list for a while. He couldn't think of a better way to enjoy the chef's culinary skills than in the company of his beloved Adana. As they rode in Kamau's hired car, it was not possible for them to resist stolen kisses, touches and long soulful looks. Kamau was determined to talk to Adana in more depth about his thoughts concerning their relationship. He didn't want to push her or frighten her, but he had promised himself that he would never again have thoughts about the two of them that he did not share with her. They walked into the restaurant and were immediately shown to a secluded corner. The restaurant was small and magnificently well appointed, an excellent place for Kamau to add to his culinary repertoire, to incorporate new flavors to his own creatively prepared meals.

Adana remarked, "We must have come at just the right time." She glanced at her slender gold wristwatch. "I haven't been here before, but it's rare that a restaurant of this caliber is empty at dinnertime."

"It is, my angel, if the chef was hired for the evening, just to cook for us."

A corner of Adana's mouth lifted in a smile. "Mazrui men certainly know how to wine and dine a lady."

"Angel, one of the purposes of wealth, aside from securing the lives of family, is to enjoy whatever there is in life one deems pleasurable. If I have learned nothing else, it is that life is short and fleeting. Moments must be seized. I have never understood more clearly the Latin phrase *carpe diem*. All pleasures of the moment must be seized without undue concern for the future. It is true we have only this moment."

Adana was halted by the tone of his voice. There was quiet power as if holding raw emotion in check. The waiter came. Kamau asked Adana if he could order for them. She consented. When the waiter left the table, Adana looked at the magnificent man sitting across from her. He placed his warm hands on top of hers. His eyes caught and held her sparkling ones. Tenderly her eyes melted into his. "Kamau, I can feel the wheels turning in your mind. There has been a shift in your mood since you got here. Is this case really weighing on you?"

"Not the case, my angel." He cleared his throat. "I need to talk to you."

A thread of anxiety lasered through Adana. "Is there more about the case that you haven't told me?"

Kamau's tone was layered with a hint of exasperation. "Adana, the case is important but we are more important. I need to say some things to you, and I need you to listen very carefully." His eyes probed her soul.

Her eyes searched his face, trying to reach into his thoughts. She spoke softly. "Okay, Kamau, I'm listening."

"Angel, my beautiful Adana, you have introduced me to a side of myself I have never known. You have made me feel things I had only contemplated in theory. You are all I will ever need or want for the rest of my life." He paused. "I know I said that I would allow us to be together on your terms in your way, but I was wrong. I am the son of my father, my grandfather and all of those men who came before them for whom tradition was everything. I want—no, I need—to proclaim to the world that you are my woman, not just because we told our families that we are seeing each other and not just because we are able to snatch a few transcontinental moments, but because you are in actuality my woman in name and in function. I am not ever again going to sneak into a room in my brother's house, or anywhere else where you are staying in order to be with you, because I need you so badly I feel I'll go mad without you. I need you to be my wife, Adana." His voice deepened. "I need you to be my wife. I need you in a home that is ours, a bed that is ours. I need you every day, and I'm not sure what I will do if you say you don't want the same thing."

Adana's eyes glistened with unshed tears. She swallowed and took a breath. "Kamau, you mean everything to me, but you know how I feel about marriage. I don't know if marriage is for me. I don't know if I have what it takes to make it work. I like our arrangement. Yes, we could see each other more often but marriage is a big step, Kamau. You would have to put up with all of my strangeness on a daily basis. That's more than anyone should have to deal with." She smiled tentatively.

Kamau stared at her with vacant eyes. "Adana, marriage is not a board game. It is a lifelong undertaking where two people commit themselves and their families to building a lasting union. A foundation for children and generations of progeny. I want us to make that commitment."

"Kamau, if I'm not ready for marriage, what makes you think I'm ready for children?"

"I'm ready, Adana, and I know you are even though you have convinced yourself otherwise. I need you to trust me, Adana. Trust me."

"Kamau, you're asking me to trust you with my life— my life."

"Yes, I am, my sweet. I am asking you to trust me with your life. To trust me with helping you build a new life. I will allow you time until we have returned from Geneva. When we return, I will need an answer. If you say yes, I promise that I will give you all that I am for the rest of your life."

The waiter came as if on cue. Kamau handed Adana his handkerchief. She dabbed her teary eyes. He touched her hand. "Are you going to be all right, my angel?"

A soft, loving curve touched her lips. "I'm fine, really I'm fine."

Her words were only half true. The conversation had changed everything. They continued their meal with quiet, thoughtful conversation about a variety of topics. Never far from either of their minds was the topic of marriage. After a while, the chef joined them to discuss culinary approaches to international foods. Adana sat lost in thought while Kamau and the chef shared secrets about the artistry of preparing fine foods.

After dinner, they rode home in silence, with Kamau giving Adana the time he knew she needed to sort through her thoughts. Their only communications were the soft touches and strokes they exchanged while being chauffeured along the highway.

Once they entered Adana's home, Adana began to feel an urgent uneasiness she had not experienced before, a disturbing finality. She felt as though her heart were bursting with anguish, and her thinking became tortured. Kamau could feel her mood shift. He knew his statements earlier in the evening were the cause. He knew she had to fight her own mental battles, but he was not going to allow that to deprive them of the pleasure of each other. He led her by the hand to the bedroom and without words undressed her and then himself. He scooped her up in his arms and carried her to the bed. She lay in the drowsy warmth of her bed, thinking, *How can I give him up?* Her thoughts scattered.

Feeling the warmth and strength of each other's bodies, their reactions were swift, almost violent. Their responses were powerful, pounding, hammering, driving, intense. Adana tried to pull from Kamau all of the reassurance she needed. Kamau tried, as if by magic, to reach Adana's heart.

When the demanding lovemaking had spilled over into a dizzying afterglow, Kamau kissed Adana gently and said, "Trust me, my angel. Trust me with your life." The two fell asleep in each other's arms.

Their last day together was spent in quiet solitude. They fed each other the wonderful delicacies Adana had found, drank exquisite wines and made love as though they would never see each other again. Late in the day, Kamau left for his meetings, saying that in four days he and Adana would fly to Geneva. He left Adana with much to sort through.

As Saturday morning peeked slowly onto the horizon, Adana stretched in her bed, opened her eyes and took a deep breath. She had slept but the sleep had been restless, filled with disturbing dreams of Kamau's stern face admonishing her to trust him and her running furiously until exhaustion overtook her. She lifted herself out of bed, went into the adjoining bath, cleaned her face, brushed her teeth, slipped on a robe and made her way to the kitchen. She couldn't get away from him. As soon as she opened her cabinet, she saw the mixture of spices she had purchased for Kamau's tea. Her smile had a tinge of sadness as she retrieved the spices and made herself a cup of tea. Adana wondered aloud, "What am I going to do?" She had no obvious answer. Her heart and her mind were in serious conflict. She finished her tea, placed the saucer, cup and spoon in the sink and decided to get on with her day. She had errands to run and lunch at her parents' home at noon.

* * *

She finished her errands. The distractions of the day had not been enough to quiet the anxiety Adana was feeling about having to respond to Kamau's question about marriage. She wished he could just leave well enough alone. What they had was for her as close to perfection as she ever thought she'd come. She battled continually in her mind with the pros and cons of marriage. Always the lawyer, she had certainly made her case for the opposing side. The routine and monotony of marriage would kill the spontaneity, the adventure. Kamau, she was sure, would grow tired of her flip-flops between confidence and insecurity. She knew she was a workaholic, and she didn't see that changing, and more importantly, though in some ways she relished family and tradition as much as Kamau, there were ways in which her behavior was not at all traditional. She wondered if he could really live with that. He had been so frank and open with her about his need to honor the traditions of his ancestors. Could she live with that?

As she approached her parents' home, she was grateful for the picture of well-maintained comfort the house presented. It calmed her nerves. As she turned into the driveway, her parents' prizewinning flowers were there to greet her. She parked in front of the garage, got out of the car, walked to the door and used her key. "Mom, Dad, I'm here."

"Come on back, baby. We're in the den."

It was her father's mellow baritone. Adana walked through to the den and found her father reading an article from the *Wall Street Journal* and her mother reading a collection of short stories by J. California Cooper. They both looked up as she entered the room. "You two are as relaxed as usual."

With a smile in her voice, Ana Terrell responded to her daughter. "Sweetheart, when you've been married as long as we have, you've earned a little relaxation. How are you, darling? It's good to see you."

Ana Terrell put her book on the table next to her, looked admiringly at her oldest daughter and continued talking. "I've just about got lunch ready for us. You and your dad can talk while I finish. I'll call you two when it's ready." She kissed Adana and left the room.

"All right, Mom."

James Terrell folded his paper and placed it on the floor next to his recliner. Adana sat in the chair next to him, crossed her trousered legs, looked directly at her father and said pointedly, "Okay, Dad, what does Mom want you to talk to me about?"

James Terrell broke into gales of deep, throaty laughter. As his laughter subsided, he said, "Sweet pea, from the time you were born, that keen sense of observation when it comes to reading people has been turned up full volume."

"I just know my mother, and whenever she thinks she's not making progress with me, if there's something she wants to know, then she calls in the big guns. You, Daddy, are Mom's equivalent of the big guns, especially when it comes to me. It has always been that way."

"Well, Adana, in all seriousness, your mother always felt that since you and I are so similar in temperament, I would be more successful when it came to getting you to confide in me."

"Has she been right?"

"I don't know—you tell me. Do you feel comfortable confiding in your old dad?"

"I am grateful that I feel comfortable with both my parents. Now what does Mom want me to pour my heart out about?"

They both laughed.

"Your mother, as always, is concerned about you and so am I. We read the papers, watch the news. We know you are under a lot of pressure, and you're not one to discuss the pressures, and we don't know how you relieve the stress." He took a breath. "We both thought that when you found a love interest, that would bring some lightness into your life, but you picked a young man who seems to be as intense as you are."

Now it was Adana's turn to laugh so hard tears sprang to her eyes. Through peals of laughter, she asked, "Does he seem that intense, Daddy?"

"I'd hate to meet him in a dark alley unless I had my posse with me."

Adana laughed uncontrollably. She didn't know when she had laughed so hard. Once her laughter was just a gentle ripple, she said, "Daddy, you are too funny. I'm going to tell Kamau that you think he's scary."

James Terrell's soft laughter was a full-hearted sound as he said, "As long as he doesn't scare you, sweet pea, then he's okay with me."

"He doesn't frighten me, Daddy." A dreamy look entered her eyes. "He makes me feel very safe."

James knew that look. He had seen it before three other times. "I take it this is serious."

"Serious, yes, Dad. It's serious enough for me. Kamau wants to make it more permanent, but I'm not sure I'm ready."

Ana Terrell walked into the room just as Adana was saying *not sure I'm ready.* Ana asked, "Ready for what? What do you need to get ready for?"

"Nothing, Mom. I was just telling Dad that Kamau wants our relationship to be more permanent, but I'm not sure I'm ready."

Ana Terrell sat down. "Adana Terrell, are you saying that Kamau asked you to marry him?"

"Yes, Mom, he asked me to marry him."

"What did you say? Did you say no?"

"I didn't say anything. He's giving me time. I have to have an answer when we return from Switzerland."

Ana almost shouted, "Switzerland. We didn't know you were going to Switzerland."

"Relax, Mom, I just found out. It's a business trip in connection with this case that I'm working on. You know the Mazruis are connected everywhere, and Kamau has people in Switzerland that I need to meet in order to get some vital information for the Bitak case."

Her mother's eyes squinted as they often did when she was thinking. She asked, "Now, Adana, tell me why you didn't give him an answer."

"Mom, at the time I couldn't. I like our relationship just as it is. I don't even know if I'm marriage material. I look at you and Dad and at Cassandra and Ras, Keino and Amara, and Afiya and Ibra, and I just don't know if I can do it. My God, look at Gram and Papa. I don't know if I can do it."

"Do what, sweetheart? What is it you think you need to do?"

"I don't know. I wish I could tell you."

Her father asked, "Do you love him, sweet pea?"

"Yes, Daddy, I love him."

"Do you have any doubts about loving him?"

"No, I am very sure that I love him and that he loves me. I've never felt the way that he makes me feel."

Ana Terrell's voice softened and her eyes narrowed. "Adana, listen to me, sweetie, and as you listen, I want you to hear your mother talking, not the psychologist." She leaned over and clasped both of Adana's hands in hers. "From the time you were a little girl, you kept me wondering about you. You were always my distant little puzzle. You were and still are my moody, introspective baby. I have watched you all of your life, and this is what I know. You, my darling daughter, have a deep, deep well of love to give and for whatever reason, you fear the love that you need to complete your life. You do need it, you know. You need love intensely, Adana. Without it you are not whole."

Adana's eyes watered as tears began to fall. "You want the love, my darling, but you want guarantees. You want love to have the same predictability as one of your business deals. It's never going to be that way, and the truth is when one of your business deals goes awry, you handle it, and you would handle a glitch in love the same way. You've done it. It didn't kill you. You survived. You thrived. I know you've got these warring voices going on in your head, and I'm sure you've made your lists of pros and cons, but the bottom line is you can only do two things. One, choose well, and two, trust and let go. You've chosen well. Kamau Mazrui is perfect for you. He is brilliant, financially secure and you practice the same profession. He is as intense as you are, he's willing to jump through hoops to be with you and, to top it all off, he is absolutely exquisite to look at." She smiled. "Almost as fine as your father." Adana smiled through her tears as her mother said, "Trust him, baby, trust him."

Adana collapsed into her mother's arms. Her father stood and placed one hand on each of them, smiling a warm, contented smile.

Chapter 26

Nairobi, Kenya

No matter how they tried, any conversation between Kamau and Ras could never escape having a fine thread of contention running through it. They were first cousins and loved each other like brothers but had been like oil and water since they were children. They sat in Kamau's office discussing Ras's architectural designs for Kamau's future home.

Kamau's voice had a steely edge. "Ras, these plans are not what we discussed."

Ras's voice rose an octave. "Kamau, where is your head? These plans are exactly what we discussed, and fortunately for me, I have the notes and a recording of our meeting to prove it. Look, Kamau, if you have changed your mind and now these plans don't suit you, just say that. Don't tell me I am presenting you with the wrong plans."

The room was silent. Ras stared at Kamau. Kamau stared at the plans. Kamau looked up and started speaking, spacing his words evenly. "Ras, these days I have a few things on my mind that are distracting me. I do not intend to question your veracity. If it appeared that way, it was not my intention."

Ras answered in a low, composed voice. "One of these days, perhaps we will be able to have a conversation that does not require a shouting match. Now, what would you like to do with these designs?"

"I will study them when I return from Switzerland next week. My business there should not take very long."

In a more lighthearted tone, Ras said, "Ah, Switzerland. Boarding school memories. Is this business pleasure or serious business?"

"Serious business."

"I should have known, cousin. Well, at least fly down a few slopes for me while you are there."

"I'll see what I can do."

The cousins embraced and Ras asked before leaving, "Are you coming to Keino's for dinner tonight?"

"Possibly, I am not sure."

"Then if I don't see you tonight, we will talk when you return."

Ras walked out and closed the door behind him.

Kamau knew he was on edge because of the ultimatum he had given Adana. He knew he wanted to live with her openly, and he wasn't willing to defy tradition if it meant living with Adana without the benefit of marriage. Where would that leave him if she said no? He knew it would leave him with a loss as significant as the loss of Yasmin. He wasn't sure how he could face the devastation of a loss like that again. First things first. He would get to Switzerland, sort out the case of the missing pilot, perhaps get the needed Bitak information and then he and Adana would once and for all, one way or another, make a life-altering decision.

The morning arrived for Adana and Kamau to leave for Geneva. A car had been sent for Adana, and she was transported to where Kamau was waiting for her so that they could fly together. Seeing each other again was a rush for both of them. Adana felt her body start to smolder as she watched him walk toward her with a sensuous gait that set her soul on fire. Kamau radiated virility as he walked with a hint of arrogance in a navy blue pinstriped suit, white linen shirt and burgundy tie. He could feel the heat between them as he boldly and seductively appraised her body. He had truly missed her. She was beautiful and sexier than he cared to admit, wearing a black knit jacket trimmed in black leather, sumptuous black leather pants, gold earrings and a necklace matching the small gold belt buckle around her tiny waist. Anticipation had heightened the mood of the moment; the air around them was electrified. Their memories of each other were intensely vivid. Kamau gently touched Adana's lips with his own. She sank into the kiss, savoring every moment.

His greeting was a husky, "Hello."

She whispered, "How are you?"

He kissed her hand, stared into her eyes and said, "I am fine now. Let us get aboard the plane."

They boarded, made themselves comfortable and were soon en route to Geneva.

When he spoke again, Kamau's voice was tender, almost a murmur. "Adana, I need to prepare you for the way in which we will function once we are on the ground in Switzerland."

"All right, I'm listening." Her voice was shakier than she would have liked.

Kamau continued in a voice filled with depth and authority. "The people with whom we shall have our meetings are private bankers who have dealt with sensitive accounts for years. One of these people, Marc Lazard, is an old school chum, and he will grant us access to the people and places where we can get the documentation we need in order to indict Mohammed and Saba. Marc has suggested, so as not to arouse undue suspicion, that we present ourselves as husband and wife. He felt it would be much easier to gain entrée if we pose as just an ordinary married couple on holiday, rather than two lawyers snooping around. Also for those bankers who are going to be willing to take us into their confidences, it will be much more discreet for them to say they are sorting out services for a married couple interested in sheltering assets than to say they are talking to foreign lawyers. Once we are in their offices, they no longer have to be discreet. They can then share information because they will know we have been referred by Marc. There will also be a number of private parties where we need to be seen in order to cement the image of us as a married couple for the movers and shakers who like to scope out newly arriving investors."

"Wow, Kamau, this is quite a play we're undertaking."

"Yes, it is, my angel. Are you up to it?"

"I think I can handle pretending to be your wife."

"I notice that the operative word is *pretending*."

"Kamau, please, let's just complete what we're going to Geneva to do. Let's handle one thing at a time, please."

"As you wish, my sweet, as you wish."

Kamau reached into his coat pocket and removed a small black velvet box. Adana was looking out the window, lost in thought, when he took her hand and said, "In order to make this masquerade more plausible, I bought something for you to wear. If you were my wife, this would be your ring, the token of my affection for you." He removed from the box an eleven-carat sapphire ring. The setting was a glittery tulip with diamond-encrusted petals. The ring had been made to order, and when he slipped it on her finger, the fit was perfect.

For a moment Adana was rendered speechless until she could recapture a voice that seemed to come from far away. "Kamau, it is so beautiful. It is so beautiful." She turned the ring, watching it catch every shard of light streaming through the window.

Kamau looked at her lovingly. "It is not nearly as beautiful as you are, my sweet."

"How did you know my ring size?"

"I have made it my business, my angel, to know all of your sizes. Enjoy the ring."

For the remainder of the flight, Adana and Kamau enjoyed food, wine and intense conversation about the case, international politics, their families—everything except their relationship. They both knew that that conversation would be saved for another time and place.

When they landed in Geneva, they were whisked away by limousine to the hotel Kamau had reserved for their stay. As they drove through the city, Adana was struck by its beauty and its serenity. It occurred to her that the city's lakeside setting gave it a calm exterior that was in direct opposition to the undercurrent of unscrupulous behaviors visited upon the city by a select group of unsavory characters. She was pulled from her quiet thoughts by Kamau's soothing voice.

"We are here, my angel."

The limo stopped in front of what was clearly a deluxe luxury hotel. The architecture, inspired by baroque traditions, was splendid, understated elegance. As Kamau escorted Adana into the hotel, they were greeted with polished utterances of "Welcome to La Reserve Palace Royal."

Adana's response was a polite "Thank you." Kamau tipped his head slightly and continued walking, displaying for the world to see the royal lineage from which he had come. When they reached the registration desk, Kamau, with one hand resting comfortably on the small of Adana's back, spoke to the desk clerk. "I am Kamau Mazrui. My wife, Adana, and I have a reservation for the presidential suite."

"Ah, yes, Mr. and Mrs. Mazrui, your suite is ready. I will have your luggage sent up."

"Thank you."

Adana was still processing hearing herself referred to as Mrs. Mazrui. She looked at the exquisitely crafted ring on her finger and remembered that for a time she was to act as if Kamau were her husband. As they rode the private elevator to their suite, Kamau watched Adana looking at the ring and asked with an underlying sensuality coloring every word, "My wife, are you happy with your ring?"

Not to be outdone and more than willing to join the game, her answer was, "Yes, my husband. It is quite beautiful. You have excellent taste."

Kamau smiled at Adana's quickness and at the fact that she did not seem the least bit uncomfortable uttering the words *my husband.* When they entered the suite, Adana was momentarily taken aback. She had traveled extensively and had always frequented lovely hotels, but this was her first trip to Switzerland and her first time in a presidential suite. Kamau Mazrui really knew how to live, but then didn't his entire family?

"Kamau, this is beautiful." Adana started walking slowly from room to room. "Did we really need all of this space?"

"When I travel, my angel, I prefer all of the comforts of home whenever possible."

Kamau took his platinum cell phone from his breast

pocket and began to make a call. "Excuse me, my sweet, I must return this call. It concerns our business here."

"Go right ahead. I'll continue looking around."

While Kamau completed his conversation, Adana went from room to room, shaking her head and smiling at the opulence and elegance surrounding her. The suite overlooked Lake Geneva. There was a sitting room and a dining room both arranged to accommodate at least twenty, a master bedroom with a private bath and sauna, a separate room housing a Turkish bath and a Jacuzzi, a full kitchen and two executive bedrooms with their own bathrooms. Every room had a view of the lake. The suite was magnificent. Kamau made everything for her larger than life. Every new experience with him heightened her senses and caused her to rethink the solitary way in which she had chosen to live her life.

Kamau found her standing in the master bedroom, which looked as though it had been decorated for the Saudi royal family. He was closing his telephone as he walked in.

"That was Marc ringing me to confirm that our first meeting is in thirty minutes. We'll just have time to freshen up quickly and rush over." He walked up behind Adana, encased her in his arms and spoke softly into her ear. "That is a good sign. If he has been as efficient in getting our other meetings scheduled, then we will be able to wrap up our business rather quickly."

He kissed her cheek, tapped her lightly on her bottom and walked away to prepare to leave. Adana stood feeling a mixture of emotions. Though she wanted to close out the Bitak case with her client being deemed innocent, she was not anxious to tear herself away from Kamau and the beautiful environment he had provided for them.

After Adana and Kamau briefly strategized for their

meeting, Kamau called for the driver and they were driven to an impressive office complex on the shoreline of Lake Léman, which had the famous shooting fountain Jet d'Eau visible in the distance. They were shown into Marc Lazard's plush office. An effusive Marc Lazard stood to greet them. Marc was an athletically built man with a full crop of blond hair and twinkling green eyes. His skin was so tanned it made one wonder how he had time to work and at the same time keep his skin golden brown. It was clearly a gift of the sun and not of artificial device.

"Kamau, how are you? It has been so long since you've paid us a visit, and this is your lovely wife." He winked slyly. "You always were selective to a fault finding the rarest of gems while the rest of us were constantly picking up pebbles." The three of them laughed at Marc's quip.

"Yes, Marc, this is the lovely woman to whom I am committed for the rest of my life, Adana."

Kamau's statement was not lost on Adana nor Marc. She smiled and said, "I am very happy to meet you, Marc. I really appreciate your willingness to help us with this very sticky situation."

Marc smiled his megawatt smile. "There are many sticky situations in this city." He waved his hand in the direction of two chairs in front of his desk. "Have a seat, you two, have a seat."

Kamau and Adana made themselves comfortable. Marc walked over to his liquor cabinet and started pouring himself a drink. He lifted the crystal decanter and asked, "Would anyone like to join me?"

Kamau quickly looked at his watch and noted that the stresses of the job must have been weighing on his friend, because it was a bit early in the day for spirits.

Adana shook her head no and Kamau said, "I want no distractions as I listen to everything you have to say."

Marc sat down, glass in hand. "As you know, Geneva is a city where trillions in art, gold and cash are hidden. It has been estimated that one-third of the world's internationally invested private wealth is stashed in vaults around this city."

Adana asked very pointedly, "How are the accounts logged?"

"The largest accounts are referenced by serial codes that reference other serial codes that reference serial codes ad nauseam. Names are known only to the quiet few. While this city is home to the seat of the United Nations, it is also home to the bank accounts of some of the world's most notorious characters fleeing scandals and safeguarding colossal illicit fortunes."

Kamau interjected, "It is the strategic quiet few to whom we need to be introduced."

"I am way ahead of you, my friend. I've done my research and I've been in this city long enough to know how to circumvent the mystery system of all mystery systems."

He took a drink. "There is a seasoned private banker here from Société Générale. Her name is Paulina Cruz. She knows where a number of bodies are buried. The things she does not know she can find out easily enough. There is one thing working tremendously in your favor. The copies of the docs you sent me were filled with numbers I know to be serial codes; with those codes, Paulina can discreetly track down your culprit in a day. Your Mohammed must have been either stressed to the max or incredibly stupid to leave such an obvious trail."

"A bit of both, I'm afraid. We are grateful that he could fly a plane better than he handles being an operative in a terrorist cell. If they were all as inept, they would have been wiped out long ago."

"Hear, hear." Marc lifted his glass and finished off his premier brandy. Marc Lazard handed Kamau a card with the place and the appointment time for the scheduled meeting with Paulina Cruz. Kamau and Adana said their good-byes and left to meet Ms. Cruz.

The place was a discreet bankers' club where prominent bankers and their sometimes high-profile clients met to discuss business away from the prying eyes of the pedestrian populace. It was a beautifully renovated old château near a man-made lake. They were shown into a private meeting room that had been set aside for them. They took seats at a round conference table and waited.

Kamau shot his cuffs and spoke in a deep quiet tone. "I am pleased so far with the way in which Marc has orchestrated our meetings. It appears that Mohammed's ineptitude will be a great plus in our search to get to the truth of this ridiculous madness."

Looking at Kamau across the table, Adana could hear and understand every word, but her body was reacting not to his words but to his powerful demeanor, his sensual strength and his sable beauty. She felt the ring on her left hand as she turned it with her thumb, wondering to herself, *Am I capable of being his wife?*

When she spoke, her voice was soft and low. "Things are moving much more rapidly than I thought they would. I'm grateful. Diani Bitak does not deserve to be convicted of a crime she did not commit."

Just as Adana finished her sentence, Paulina Cruz entered the room apologizing for her lack of promptness. Kamau rose to greet her. After introductions were made, Ms. Cruz placed her briefcase on the table, opened it and retrieved a stack of documents. Paulina Cruz was the consummate businesswoman. Her raven-colored hair was pulled back in a spinster's bun revealing porcelain skin and cold blue eyes ringed by tortoiseshell glasses that picked up the brown in the tailored pantsuit she wore. Her voice was a natural tenor.

"Marc shared your documents with me and told me of your dilemma. I think I can help you. Marc and I have a relationship that is cemented by years in this business. I once worked in New York as part of a special team under the auspices of an international bank that set up offshore accounts in the Cayman Islands, and other less-well-known places, and so I am very aware of how the game is played."

Adana asked pointedly, "Ms. Cruz, what is in this for you? What makes you want to risk your livelihood for someone you don't know?"

"Let's just say I want to even the playing field. I've watched enough wolves in sheep's clothing get away with murder." She looked over her glasses directly into Adana's eyes. "Sometimes literally. This is where we stand. Thus far I've been able to track millions through the numbers from your docs. Those serial numbers lead to dummy accounts for real estate, blue chip stocks, shell corporations and fronts for many illicit activities, not the least of which are gains from unlawful arms sales. It appears Geneva is the purifying reservoir for your guy's dirty laundry."

Kamau interjected, "Since Geneva is far from the scrutiny of SEC regulations, do you have enough evidence that Adana can use to extricate her client from the backlash of Mohammed and Saba's activities?"

"Oh yes. Mohammed's carelessness paid big dividends. I have it all right here." She handed a stack to Adana. "I hope this helps."

Paulina placed the other documents back in her briefcase. They all rose from their seats, shook hands, said their good-byes and Paulina left the building with Adana and Kamau following shortly thereafter. Once in the limo, Adana couldn't contain her joy and relief. As she perused the documents, she knew she had every bit of evidence needed to clear Diani Bitak. She slipped the documents back into her briefcase, turned to Kamau, placed her arms around his neck and kissed him tenderly. His body reacted instantly. "Thank you, Kamau. I don't know how I'll ever be able to tell you how grateful I am."

Kamau lovingly stroked the side of her face as he said, "You never have to thank me for doing what I know I was born to do, and that is to protect and care for you for the rest of my life."

His kiss captured her lips just as she uttered, "Oh, Kamau." With eyes closed, they kissed until they felt the blood coursing through their veins like a heated stream. The pit of her stomach fluttered and rippled. His heart hammered. The harsh uneven rhythm of their breathing reminded each of them of the hot, torturously passionate loving that had become second nature to them. Kamau brought a halt to their passionate encounter minutes before the driver stopped in front of their hotel. The chauffeur opened the door, and they walked into the hotel with Kamau resting his heated palm on the small of Adana's back. The strength and the weight of his hand, like the strength of the man, pulled her in, and in that instant Adana realized that she never ever wanted to be separated from that strength. She felt the ring on her hand, looked at the man walking beside her and knew she never wanted to leave him. When they entered the suite, Kamau kissed Adana's cheek and turned to go in order to dress for dinner.

Adana grabbed his hand. "Kamau, come in here and sit with me. We need to talk."

He looked at her lovingly and stroked her arms. "If we want to meet Marc, his wife and his business associates, we don't have much time."

With a gentle plea in her voice, Adana said, "Please, let's make our apologies. We have all of the information we need, and Marc will understand."

Kamau stood still as the realization dawned on him that something was troubling Adana. "Of course, my sweet, I can telephone Marc. Tell me what is bothering you."

"I'm not bothered." She smiled. "But I'm clear. For the first time since I've known you, I'm not afraid to say I love you, Kamau Mazrui. I want to be your wife. I want to spend my life with you. You have been God's gift to me, and I can't let you go."

Kamau was stunned. As conventional as he knew Adana to be in her everyday life, her ideas about how she would fit a romantic relationship into her life had been anything but conventional, and now she was agreeing to be his wife. Kamau held her and kissed her with a deep, lingering kiss.

Adana whispered, "Does this mean you'll marry me?"

"Yes, my darling Adana. You have answered my prayers. I did not want to live a life without you. I need you not just in my bed but also as a permanent fixture in my life. What changed your mind?"

"You just being you changed my mind. When I'm with you, all of my fears vanish. I also had a conversation with my mom that helped me put some things in perspective."

They kissed again, tenderly, and sat snuggled on the sofa to plan their future nuptials. Smiling, Kamau asked, "And now, my sweet, tell me how long I have to wait in order to make you my bride?"

Smiling back with a mischievous twinkle in her eye, Adana responded, "Not long—how about tomorrow?"

Kamau uttered a surprised, "What, tomorrow?" His speech slowed. "Adana, don't you want the fanfare and ceremony that goes with being a bride for the first time?"

"No. I don't want the fanfare. I want the life I am going to live when I become your wife. Now that I know what I want, I just want to move forward. Just our parents, and your uncle the Coptic priest can marry us. We can have the ceremony here. The setting is beautiful and the timing is right."

Kamau threw his head back and laughed loudly and deeply. "Adana, my sweet, your wish is my command. Let us each get our parents on the phone, and I shall make flight arrangements. Tomorrow at seven p.m. in this time zone we will be married."

Chapter 27

The arrangements were made with all of the precision and efficiency characteristic of Kamau and Adana. The following evening amid candlelight and formally attired guests, Adana and Kamau were married quietly and privately in the Presidential Suite. Violinists played as their elated parents looked on. After champagne toasts and a banquet fit for kings and queens, their parents and Kamau's uncle were flown home and the newlyweds were alone again in their suite.

A contented Kamau Mazrui asked as he embraced Adana, "Well, Mrs. Mazrui, did you enjoy becoming my wife?"

Slipping her arms around his neck, Adana answered, "I enjoyed becoming your wife, but more importantly I am going to enjoy just being your wife."

In a slow, smoky voice, Kamau said, "Well, in that case let us begin by having you perform your most important wifely duty."

A smiling Adana asked, "And what might that be, Mr. Mazrui?"

"Loving me as only you can—totally, fearlessly, passionately."

"Gladly, my darling, gladly."

And so the loving dance with which they had become so familiar began. Kamau led Adana by the hand in the direction of the bed in which they would celebrate their marriage. Kamau pushed a button on a remote, and the room filled with the musical sounds of "Moonlight Sonata." Their experience of each other had for each of them transcended time and space. Kamau gently, methodically, as though performing a sacred ritual, removed every garment Adana wore, beginning with the crimson spaghetti-strapped gown she had chosen as her wedding dress. He left her standing wearing only the intricately textured baroque-pearl necklace he had given her as a wedding gift. Adana walked to the bed, removed its satin duvet and comforter, and folded back silk sheets, preparing the bed so that she and Kamau could love each other for the first time as husband and wife.

Kamau positioned himself in a chair across the room and set about removing his formal clothing. With his tuxedo jacket and tie discarded, and his tailored shirt unbuttoned to his waist, he began to remove his socks and shoes until he looked across the room at his flawlessly formed wife. Her nude, honey-colored body was exquisite. As she moved around the bed, the background music took on a different dimension for Kamau. Her arms long, slender and supple, her legs slender, toned and maddeningly long, moved with a fluidity and grace that took Beethoven's piece to new heights. Her round, firm breasts with milk-chocolate-colored erect nipples were waiting to be caressed by his warm, succulent mouth. The baroque pearls moved lightly with her, gently caressing the cleavage where Kamau longed to place his head. His body reacted almost violently. Adana looked up, directly into her husband's eyes. She saw desire tinged with the sensation of pain. She could feel the heat from his eyes course down the length of her body. As he aroused her passion with merely a look, his own desire grew stronger. He began again removing his clothes as methodically as he had removed hers.

Adana walked across the room to her husband. He stopped; his hands stilled. His eyes followed every placement of her narrow feet on the plush carpet. He memorized every slow movement of her hips as she came nearer and nearer to where he sat. The pearls moved slightly, positioning themselves between breasts that almost hypnotized him. When she reached his chair, she knelt and began where he had left off removing his shoes and socks. After removing his socks, she gently kissed the arch of each of Kamau's perfectly formed, smooth, onyx-colored feet. The gesture sent spiraling shock waves through his veins. They were silent. Her center was melting in anticipation. He was visibly ready to love her with all of the urgency flooding his senses. They moved in sync, removing the remainder of Kamau's garments. Adana placed long, lingering kisses on every spot of his body left bare. Kamau lifted her off her feet and carried her to the bed. As he carried her, Adana placed searing kisses and nibbles along his throat, causing him to release surrendering moans.

They both felt the cool smoothness of the silk sheets as they were enveloped in the lushness of the bed. With feathery touches, Adana stroked the length of Kamau's body. The power and strength of his taut frame electrified her. He was aroused to the peak of desire, causing her to moan aloud with erotic pleasure. Kamau caught her sounds on his lips as he kissed repeatedly her outcries of delight. Adana writhed beneath Kamau, clutching handfuls of the silky sheets and then stroking Kamau's hard, smooth back. She heard him whisper, "I am savoring you, my love, I am savoring you," as he fingered her melting center with all of the care and finesse of a master violinist fingering the strings of his instrument. His hardness and his skillful manipulations of her body sent her senses spinning. His name erupted from her lips over and over again until he answered her. His entry was long and slow, and her body responded with quaking tremors. She rose to meet him. He lifted her soft, smooth hips with his strong, dark hands, and they moved to the music of the universe, magically gliding through space.

Kamau could never get enough of Adana in the throes of passion. She became wild and free, exploding in his arms. Every inch of him was for her a treasure to be unearthed and explored. He teased each of her hardened nipples first with catlike licks of his tongue and then with strong sucking motions, causing both their bodies to move to rhythms only they could hear. With moans of ecstasy and a heart bursting with love and torturous desire, Adana kissed Kamau's neck and shoulders, tasting the sweet mixture of his clean body and his fragrant signature cologne.

His strong hands combed through her hair as he in turn kissed her lips until they were swollen with pleasure. His touch was tender and demanding. She wanted him to have all of her. She wanted to disappear into the crevices of his soul. She lifted higher, and he moved in deeper, deeper until they felt as though they were one. The rhythms went from pulsating, long and hard, to slow, lingering and controlled. His hardness, her softness met in uncontrolled passion.

Without warning but ever so delicately, he removed himself from the only earthly heaven he had ever known and began layering kisses down the length of her body. His senses were reeling with the intoxication of her cottony soft skin and her scent, a mixture of heated passion and sweet perfume. Parting her long, shapely legs, he inhaled the ambrosial nectar of her body while tantalizing the seat of her femininity with mind-numbing sensations.

Adana cried out in tortured delirium until her body shattered with tremors that came in mounting, crashing waves. Her nails dug into Kamau's hard, strong back as she rode out the delicious quakes. He left her body burning. He watched the sensations ripple through her as she lay soft and bare with only a fine dewy mist and the baroque pearls to cover her. Kamau found her more captivating than ever. She was his love.

Adana opened her eyes and saw Kamau watching her savor the pleasure he had given her.

He spoke in slow, deep, rich tones. "Welcome back, my love, welcome back."

She smiled and spoke in a breathy whisper. "I did leave this earth, didn't I?" She stretched her long limbs. "But don't I always when you make love to me?"

Kamau moved his hands sensuously along Adana's highly sensitized body. His touch was divine. Her body craved his hands. "Adana, I want you to know that I have never in my life loved a woman the way I love you, and I never will again. I love you, Adana. With all that I am, I love you."

A teary-eyed Adana kissed his lips and spoke with a voice filled with emotion. "I love you, Kamau, with every fiber of my being. You have taught me the meaning of love. You are the first man I've loved and you will be the last. I love you so. I love you so."

Their desire to cement the love they had expressed overrode everything else. Their bodies were aching with searing need. Without prelude, Kamau ravished his wife. She welcomed his entry, pulling him farther into an abyss of pleasure as he moved with rhythms that were reminiscent of ceremonial drums. The rawness of the sensuality brought them to greater heights as they shattered and shattered, leaving them both with the deep sense of peace that was to be the hallmark of their marriage.

The morning after their marriage, Adana and Kamau lay awake, intertwined in each other's arms. Kamau kissed his bride's forehead and whispered softly, "With you I will never again want for anything. With you I am complete."

Adana placed her arms around Kamau's neck. A suggestive smile caressed her lips. "You make me so happy." She touched his full, sensuous mouth with her fingertips. "You are my magic man, my magic potion. You make me drunk with pleasure." Her bare breasts stroked his hard, muscular chest, easing up and down with the movement of her arms.

Kamau laughed and then began kissing his wife with the abandon they both relished. Adana melted into her husband and without thought answered all of his silent demands. When the kiss had momentarily satiated their hunger for each other, Adana heard Kamau's deep baritone filled with the timbre of early morning and underlying sensuality. "You know, my love, we were married so hastily we never discussed when you would like to move to Nairobi."

"No, we didn't." Adana took a deep breath. She stared into Kamau's eyes. "I know you are allowing me transition time."

He stroked her back and softly kissed the tip of her nose. "Of course, my sweet. There is much to be done, and because there is so much to consider, I thought now may well be the perfect time to start sorting it all out."

Adana's voice got softer. "I don't want to sell my house. Maybe down the road but not now."

"I understand." Kamau held her closer. "It can be our base when we are in the area. We will probably be there fairly often." His eyes caught and held hers. "And now, my sweet, what about my offer for you to join the Mazrui law firm? Have you given the offer any thought?"

Adana slowly moved one of her legs down the length of Kamau's body, causing an inaudible breath to ease up from his throat, breaking his concentration for a brief moment. Her eyes narrowed as she answered. "I have thought about it, and I know for sure that I am not satisfied where I am. I have to fight too many battles on too many fronts before I even get to the courtroom. It would be nice to really practice my profession without having every decision scrutinized to the nth degree. I'm just not sure, though, what hurdles I'll have to climb at Mazrui." She smiled and playfully poked Kamau in his unyielding chest. "I'm well aware of how chauvinistic African men can be."

Kamau gently stroked her hair as he spoke. "I have said more than once, my angel, regardless of the perceived chauvinistic streak people may see, every African man worth his salt understands that a queen must always be paid homage. You, my darling, are a queen, and every man at our firm is worth his salt. You will have no problems based on your gender or your ethnicity." He kissed her cheek.

"You make it sound so simple."

"It is simple, my sweet. It is simple. Say yes and I'll start putting the wheels in motion."

"First I have to get through this case, and then I can give the partners a formal resignation. Joining the Mazrui firm would make life easier for me, and oddly enough, I think we would work well together."

In planning the move, it occurred to Adana that they had no place to live in Nairobi. Her focus changed almost instantly. "What about a house, Kamau? Where will we live while we're in Nairobi?"

Kamau's hand stroked Adana's soft, warm breast, causing her breathing to slow and her eyes to flutter. He spoke softly. "I had scrapped plans to purchase a new home and had decided to build. To start fresh. I would still like to do that, only now, of course, add your input because it will be our home, not just mine. If that sounds like too much of an undertaking for now, we can always go back to the original idea and just buy a house to use temporarily."

Adana slowly stroked Kamau's back. "I like the idea of building, starting fresh." She placed a feathery kiss on his lips. "The two of us living like vagabonds at the family compound should add adventure to our lives."

Kamau laughed. "For us, being vagabonds will be a novel experience, and I am going to enjoy every moment of it." He kissed his bride in a series of slow, lingering kisses.

Adana, feeling a contentment she had never experienced, said, "I'll start packing right after the trial."

Kamau hugged her and gently stroked the derriere he wanted to proclaim as a national treasure. "I will clear my calendar so that I can be with you when you present your case."

"I'd like that."

Feeling as though much had been accomplished, Kamau asked, "Are you ready for breakfast?"

Adana stretched her long limbs. Kamau ran his hands along the length of her torso. She responded, "I am a little hungry."

Kamau asked with a mischievous smile on his face, "Can we risk breakfast in bed?"

Adana smiled at her husband. "Bed is the perfect place. After we've finished our food, we can feast on each other." They both laughed. Adana nestled in Kamau's arms as he made the call to room service.

When the food arrived, Kamau slipped into his robe, went into the living room and waited while the breakfast cart with an assortment of fruits and pastries was positioned for them to be served. Kamau dismissed the waiter and prepared a tray to take back to the bed where Adana waited, missing the warmth of her husband.

Kamau entered the room. She smiled, thinking she would never get enough of seeing him in all of his magnificence. The silk magenta robe with flecks of gold made his onyx-colored skin glow like highly polished ebony wood. It occurred to her that if Kamau were her food, hunger would be a distant memory. Kamau placed the tray in the middle of the bed, removed his robe, slid in bed beside Adana and said, "And now, my angel, we share our first breakfast as husband and wife." He lifted a kiwi slice and placed it on Adana's waiting tongue. He kissed her cheek and asked, "Is it sweet?"

Adana picked up a slice, swallowed and said, "Very."

Kamau opened his mouth. She placed a kiwi slice in his mouth and kissed a corner of his upturned smile. Kamau tore a croissant in half, placed a torn half in his teeth and offered it to her. She threw her head back, giggled like a schoolgirl and then, dreamy-eyed, began to nibble on the end of the croissant until their lips met. They playfully fed each other until the desire for food was replaced with the desire to be in each other's arms.

The following morning, one of the Mazrui company jets flew Adana and Kamau to their separate destinations. Their parting was bittersweet. Kamau held his wife and asked, "Do you need me to conference in when you tell your sisters about our marriage?"

Adana smiled. "No, sweetheart, I can handle my sisters. Besides, it's good news. They may be a little miffed that they weren't allowed time to fly out for the ceremony, but they'll understand."

His dark eyes narrowed and lasered into hers. "Are you sure?"

Adana found his concern, as always, touching and endearing. A gentle laugh eased through her words. "I am sure. Do you need me to help you tell your brothers and Ras and Ibra?"

It was Kamau's turn to smile, the wickedly sexy gesture that sometimes left Adana breathless. He responded, "Touché, my beautiful one, touché."

Their final kiss telegraphed the message that they did not want to be separated for long. Kamau made sure that Adana was safely seated in the hired car. He watched it drive away until it was out of sight; then he reboarded the plane and flew home, looking forward to the time when Adana would join him.

Adana rode in silence with a smile of contentment on her face. In her briefcase was the information that would clear her client, and on her finger she wore a symbol of her new life. Had she been a more effusive person, she would have been singing and laughing out loud, but she was Adana, always appropriate in her demeanor. She smiled when she thought of the fact that only her husband knew for sure that there was a side of her that could throw caution to the wind and release all inhibitions. She mouthed his name, closed her eyes and envisioned his sable face, velvety mustache and beard, perfectly straight white teeth and sensual smile. Her pulse quickened; along with a familiar aching in her limbs, a smoldering heat eased through her body. A soft sound eased up through her throat.

She was brought back to reality by the chauffeur's question. "Did you say something, ma'am?"

Adana collected herself. "Oh no, I was just thinking aloud." She smiled, took a deep breath and opened her briefcase to once again study the Bitak file.

When Adana reached her home, she knew her first order of business was to get her sisters on the phone and then share with her client some much-needed good news about the case. Adana placed her bags at the front door, walked up the stairs to her bedroom, undressed, put on a silk caftan and prepared to make her calls.

She checked the time. There was never a perfect time across two continents and four countries, but she thought to herself, *There is no time like the present.* By the time she had settled in, it was a little past noon. It was a calm Sunday afternoon.

Adana stilled herself and prepared to share with her sisters the most important decision she had ever made. The first number she dialed was Amara in Nairobi, Kenya. The housekeeper brought Amara the telephone announcing, "Mrs. Mazrui, your sister Adana is on the line."

"Thank you." Amara's eyes sparkled anticipating hearing her sister's voice. "Adana, how are you? How did things go in Switzerland?"

"Everything went really well. Hold on a moment, I want to get Afiya and Cassandra on the line."

"Okay."

Adana dialed her other sisters and found them both at home going about their days, following their particular routines. As the sisters gathered, Adana brought all of the preliminary greetings to a halt with "I wanted you all on the phone so that I can share something with you."

The silence on the other phone lines became so

intense not even breathing could be heard. Adana sensed the tension brought on by the anticipation of the unknown and spoke again, trying to put her sisters at ease. She laughed softly. "Everybody can breathe now. The news I'm sharing is good. Nothing catastrophic has happened."

Afiya chimed in, "Cut the suspense. I'm always ready for good news."

Playfully Adana asked, "Is everybody sitting down?"

Now it was Cassandra's turn to show impatience. "Adana, stop stringing us along. What is it?"

Amara, always the peacemaker, interjected, "Hey, you two, she said she would tell us. Now give her a chance to get to it."

Adana could barely contain herself as she decided to play with her sisters' curiosity just a little longer.

"Thanks, Amara, I just want you three to know that in a few weeks, I'm moving to Nairobi."

Afiya screamed happily, "What? Why? What brought that on?"

"Well, I've accepted a job offer from Mazrui Industries to be a part of their law firm."

Joy could be heard in Cassandra's voice as she said, "Adana, that is wonderful, and at least you'll be a few countries away instead of on another continent."

Amara added, "Adana, you can stay with us until you get settled."

Now Adana was really smiling on the other end of the phone. "Thanks, Amara, but I'm going to move in with Kamau. As a matter of fact, I think Kamau's bed is where I want to spend the rest of my days."

Silence once again. Each sister in her own way was attempting to reconcile what Adana had said with the prim, proper, discreet Adana each one knew her sister to be.

Amara spoke first. "I see, so let me get this straight. You, Miss I Don't Want Anybody in My Business and Mr. Reclusive Kamau Mazrui are going to openly live together, defying convention. I don't believe it."

"Well, I think I have a right to live with and sleep with my husband."

As the stunned sisters were rendered speechless, Adana collapsed in laughter. She laughed so hard tears literally streamed down her face. After a moment, her sisters joined her in laughter. They were caught off guard by a mixture of surprise, joy and complete amazement.

Afiya recovered more quickly than the others. "Adana, when did you two get married, and why didn't you tell us?"

Cassandra added, "You know we would have been there."

Amara asked, "Were you all alone?"

Adana reassured her sisters. "It happened really quickly. I made up my mind almost in a flash, and once I had made the decision, I didn't want to have time to allow my insecurities to take over and cause me to run from the man of my dreams. He really is, you know. He really is everything I never thought I'd find. I love him more than life. I never thought I'd hear myself say it, but I love him as though he is life. He makes me believe in magic."

"Wow!"

"Have mercy!"

"Oh my God!"

All three sisters individually exclaimed their approval and surprise.

Amara asked, "Have you told Mom and Dad?"

"They know already. The only people we had at the ceremony were our parents and Kamau's uncle, who officiated. It was beautiful and intimate, and we swore our parents to secrecy."

Cassandra chimed in, "For this act of rebellion we forgive you."

They all laughed as Amara said, "It's a good thing I love you, Adana, because we are now doubly related. You are my sister and my sister-in-law. I like it. It has a great ring to it." The sisters said their loving good-byes and went about their generally contented lives.

Chapter 28

Nairobi, Kenya

Kamau had called his brothers from the plane and asked them to meet him at the compound upon his return. When he arrived, they were waiting. Kaleb was walking off his nervous energy, smiling easily and making friendly irreverent quips about each of his brothers. Aman sat peacefully, legs crossed, staring at Kaleb as though Kaleb had landed from another planet. Aman never understood anyone's need to joke about much of anything. His life as a cardiac surgeon left him well aware of the seriousness and the tenuousness of life. Keino sat with a physical posture not unlike his brother Aman, but with a smile on his face that matched Kaleb's. Keino enjoyed Kaleb's humor. It always lifted his spirits.

Kamau entered the expansive main room of the family resort, dropped his luggage, looked at his brothers, smiled crookedly and said, "Thank you for meeting me. There is something I need to say."

Kaleb stopped his comedic act and, recognizing the seriousness of Kamau's tone, sat down.

Kamau paused, took a seat, adjusted the cuffs of his shirt, crossed his legs and began speaking. "Before I go any further, I told both Ibra and Ras that I would conference them in so that they can hear this conversation."

Kamau then made the necessary technological connections, and both Ras and Ibra greeted the Mazrui brothers. Kamau started again with deeply felt, controlled emotion. "Over the past two years, all of you have been powerful forces in my life. You form a network of strong, formidable men, brothers on whom I can depend no matter what the circumstances. I want you to understand that I am not sure I would be sitting here were it not for your not-so-gentle prodding and your eternal vigilance even when I said I didn't want it or need it. I needed to survive so that I could have a new life. In many ways a better life."

Silence thick enough to cut hung in the room. All of the men were well aware of the fact that they were witnessing an uncommon event—Kamau articulating aloud a heartfelt emotion.

"Two days ago, in Switzerland, I did something I never thought I would do. I married the woman who has my heart and my soul. I did it with little fanfare, only our parents and Uncle Menelik were present. Uncle officiated. We both apologize for not allowing time for the entire family to celebrate with us, but Adana, the woman who is now my wife"—he loved the sound of the words *my wife*—"helped me to see the wisdom of going with what we felt at the moment. Though not at all traditional, it was the right thing to do." He smiled. "Adana Terrell is now Adana Mazrui."

Enthusiastic congratulatory remarks went around the room. Kaleb opened with, "Kamau, I always told everyone who would listen that *sneaky* was your middle name."

Keino interjected, "Kaleb, you know Kamau can always be trusted."

"I didn't say he couldn't be trusted. He can be trusted, all right—trusted to keep his mouth closed, do what he wants to do and tell us later. That, my brother, is sneaky."

Everyone bellowed with laughter, even Aman, pleased that his brother's life was back on track, simulating order and purpose.

Keino grabbed Kamau, hugged him tightly and said, "You made the right choice."

Ras and Ibra, vowing to see everyone soon, expressed their good wishes and hung up knowing that conversations in their respective homes that evening would be filled with joy and plans to see the newlyweds.

Chapter 29

Addis Ababa, Ethiopia

Cassandra was so excited. Adana was really married. The sister they all thought would be content to work, enjoy her home, her family and friends, and maybe an occasional male companion. Adana was married. Cassandra's eyes sparkled and her smile radiated from ear to ear. They were all going to so enjoy sharing stories about husbands and children. Thoughts of children were for Cassandra bittersweet. Little Master Kebran was the delight of her life, and she wanted more. She hoped a visit to her doctor later that afternoon would ease her mind.

Ras and Cassandra's palatial home was unusually quiet when Ras entered at dusk. His day had been long. The highlight of the day had been the conversation he and Cassandra had shared about Kamau and Adana's surprise marriage. The house was too quiet. No servants about, no playful noises from Kebran. He placed his briefcase and a copy of the *Wall Street Journal* he had been reading on the circular table in the foyer. He called out, "Cassandra." No answer. He called louder, "Cassandra?"

Ras searched his brain, trying to remember whether Cassandra had told him about plans she had for the evening. He walked into the family room and there she was on the sofa, deep in the most peaceful sleep he thought he'd ever seen. Her breathing was soft and calm. She was wearing a jewel-toned silk caftan. The scarlet painted toes of her bare feet peeked from beneath it. Ras lifted Cassandra's tousled hair, and in her sleep she could feel the heady sensation of his lips against her neck.

She stirred beneath the kiss. Her eyes opened in a dreamy smile. "Hi, sweetheart. I tried to wait for you but I fell asleep."

"I see." With his eyes he telegraphed feelings of longing and appreciation. "Where is everyone? The house is rarely this quiet."

"Oh." She eased into catlike movements with her arms and legs. "I gave everyone the night off, and your parents wanted Kebran to visit them for a couple of days." She moved her mouth over his, softly and sensually, and asked, "Do you think we can handle being home alone?"

Ras's answer was to ease the silky caftan up the length of his wife's torso, feeling her soft bare skin while plying her with slow, drugging kisses that left her mouth burning with fire.

As if stealing sacred moments, Cassandra began to help her husband undress in order to leave the cares of the day behind and find solace in her. It took little for them to ignite flames of passion in each other. His hands were strong and warm, and the soft core of her body was heated. As Ras rained kisses over her bare skin, a shudder began at her toes and was released through passionate whimpers from her throat. She eased her hands over every inch of Ras's long, strong, bronze muscular body. She could feel the slight tremors of his muscles beneath her fingers.

He whispered, "You are just what I needed after a long, trying day. I need you."

Cassandra's breathless answer was, "I'm here, I'm yours and I'm—" The last word was swallowed in Ras's electrifying kiss as he slowly entered her, connecting them in a way that brought them the pleasure they craved. There was no resistance, no restrictions to the invitations they presented each other. Their rhythms were in sync. The gliding, the surging, the waves pulling them in and leading them to the place they wanted to be.

Wrapped in her husband's arms, covered with the afterglow of intense lovemaking, Cassandra said in a silky voice, "My sweet husband, you do that so well. If I had to, I'd pay you."

Taken by surprise by Cassandra's mischievous remark, Ras fell into a warm, deep, rich laughter. He gently tapped his wife's bottom and said, "Cassandra Selassie, you are a naughty woman." With a hint of impishness in his voice, he added, "And don't you ever change."

"Well, I'm going to change a little."

"Really?"

"I'm going to expand, my darling, in many ways."

"Is that so? Tell me about this expansion."

"First, I think my outlook on life is going to expand and then my personal duties are going to expand." Ras was gazing at Cassandra with a puzzled look, wondering what on earth she was talking about, when he heard her say, "And my body is going to expand."

He looked at her intently and asked, "Cassandra, what are you talking about?"

"I'm talking about what happens when you get pregnant." Cassandra's smile was glowing.

Ras was silenced with disbelief and confusion, and then he remembered that Cassandra had seen the doctor that afternoon. He grabbed her and held her close. He could feel her tears falling on his neck. He whispered, "Prayers are answered. We are blessed beyond measure."

"Yes, my darling. We are so blessed." They collapsed in each other's arms, silently giving thanks.

Chapter 30

Arlington, Virginia

After a final conversation with her client, reassuring her that all was well, Adana sat in her study going over her opening argument for what felt like the hundredth time. She crossed out a word that seemed too ambiguous. She added a quote from Oliver Wendell Holmes, scratched it and decided to go with Thurgood Marshall. It had been painstakingly tedious to summon up the proper phrasing along with logically and legally sound arguments she hoped would sway the jury in her client's favor, but after hours of revisions, Adana felt certain that she had what she needed. She took a deep breath, placed her favorite Montblanc on the legal pad containing her notes and said out loud, "That's it, Adana. You've finally got it. Now let's see what a jury has to say."

She looked at the delicate timepiece on her arm and checked to see how much time she had before Kamau's call. They had been apart for a week and had arranged to communicate by telephone every evening. Their time had been spent conferring with Ras about plans for the new house and discussing the Bitak case and the Mazrui firm caseload and the ways in which Adana might best merge her talents into the firm. No conversation between the two had been complete without the expression of how much they wanted and needed each other. Adana poured herself a glass of sherry, sat down and savored its mellow, sweet, nutty flavor. Just as she tipped her head back and closed her eyes, exhaling the cares of the day, her telephone rang. Knowing it was Kamau, she picked it up and answered with a deliberately sultry, "Hello, my husband."

Kamau's smooth silky reply touched her ears. "That has such a nice ring to it. I can't wait to see you tomorrow. Are you feeling ready?"

Jokingly, Adana asked, "Am I feeling ready for you, or am I feeling ready to try the case? Tell me, my darling, to which question do you need an answer?"

Kamau's smile could be heard in his voice. "I hope you are ready for both. They will be equally challenging, though in very different ways."

"In both cases, my darling, I am ready. I am up for the challenge."

"I am certain that you are. I will arrive very early in the morning. Five a.m., to be exact. I want us to have a moment alone before court. I wanted to fly in earlier today but work interfered. I won't go home. I will leave the office this evening and go directly to the plane."

"Kamau, you are going to be exhausted. You know you don't really have to be here."

"Yes, I really have to be there, and you know that flying on a Mazrui aircraft is like being in a luxury hotel in the sky. My father made sure of that years ago. I'll be fine. I am planning to stay at least four days."

His voice dropped, and Adana could hear the thoughts

cascading through his mind as he spoke. "The longest number of days we've spent as husband and wife. I look forward to the end of these periods apart."

"So do I."

"As soon as things are wrapped up in Virginia, would you like some time away, just the two of us?"

Adana hesitated. "Maybe later. To tell you the truth, I am looking forward to our time alone at the compound. Time alone at the Mazrui paradise is honeymoon enough for anyone. We can relive every sensual experience we ever had there"—she laughed—"and create some new ones."

"Ah, my angel, you make me want to tell them to fuel up the jet right now. I am not sure we will have enough time in the morning to cool our passions."

"Kamau, I don't think our passions will ever cool. Hearing your voice sends my mind into wicked places and my body into a meltdown. I can't wait to see you. When you get here, use the key that I sent. I have a surprise for you."

"I have my key and I look forward to the surprise. Good night, my love."

"Good night, sweetheart."

After the conversation, Kamau threw himself back into work. Adana took a long, leisurely bath and planned the finishing touches of her surprise.

Kamau's night had been long. The comfort of the plane hadn't stopped his longing for Adana. When the plane touched down, he was relieved. He deplaned and was whisked off in a hired car to once again hold his wife in his arms.

Kamau opened the front door, dropped his bags where he stood and locked the door behind him. Almost immediately his senses were captivated by the heady, erotic aroma of sandalwood. The ambrosial, spicy scent made him think of warm passionate nights nestled in Adana's arms. He started walking and was stopped mid-stride by a professionally created sign that read, ENTER AT YOUR OWN RISK.

Kamau smiled and whispered, "I'll risk it."

The votive candles lining the stairs floating in crystal pools of water left no doubt as to the place from which the sensual fragrance emanated. He kept walking and heard the sounds of "Moonlight Sonata," the same arrangement he and Adana had made love to on their wedding night. Kamau followed the sounds that led him to the master bedroom. The sight he beheld almost took his breath away. Adana was poised in the middle of the bed, reclining on top of gold-colored silk sheets and propped up by stacks of matching silk-encased pillows, looking as though she were the willing subject of a skilled artist. She was wearing only the necklace of baroque pearls Kamau had given her as a wedding gift. He stood in the doorway with one hand lifted, touching the upper part of the door frame, smiling. His eyes moved seductively over her body. Adana's body's reaction to his seductive stare was a tingling in the pit of her stomach. He stood there exuding arrogance, power and raw sexuality. The air in the room left when he entered it.

His voice was filled with the essence of vintage cognac and smoldering fire as he said, "Those pearls have never been more beautifully displayed."

A smiling Adana responded in a low, soft voice, "Thank you, my long lost husband."

"Is this my surprise?"

"No, I am your gift. The surprise comes later."

"I see, my wife is also a woman of many mysteries."

"Yes, I am, but I know you have the key to unlock them all."

"Show me the lock."

"You'll have to search me, my darling husband."

"Gladly."

Only Adana's eyes moved as she watched her husband discard every garment he wore and slide into bed next to her. His large, strong hands encircled her slim waist and her long, lithe thighs brushed his hard muscular ones as they ravished each other's mouths. His kiss was strong and searching, leaving her mouth burning with desire. She kissed the hollow of his throat; he reclaimed her lips and moved his mouth over hers, devouring its softness and its sweetness. The touch of Kamau's lips was a delicious sensation as he used his mouth to explore Adana's honey-colored limbs. Breath left her body in erotic whimpers, and her legs parted slightly as if on command. Adana felt Kamau's lips touch her center like a whisper. His name rung itself from her throat over and over again. She heard him answer, "Yes, my darling, yes."

Kamau's mouth moved to Adana's hardened nipples. He fondled her, alternating nimble fingers with tantalizing tongue. His hands explored the silken skin of Adana's belly as she writhed beneath his touch. Kamau's hands found every pleasure point. He whispered words in her ear he had never uttered before, arousing her more and more. Kamau gently eased Adana down farther onto the bed. He explored the soft lines of her waist and hips. She caressed the length of his back and slipped her hands up and down his arms ever so slowly as her tongue traced a path down his neck. Kamau moaned and grabbed Adana with an urgency that spoke to his need. Adana responded by wrapping her legs around his waist as he entered her, satisfying them both. Their mouths and bodies moved together in syncopated rhythms. Their desire for each other overrode everything else. The hardness of Kamau's body electrified her. Adana's softness ignited in Kamau a searing need to take her repeatedly. The room swirled with surrendering moans and ravenous desires. The end was Adana's scream as Kamau's name eased through her lips and hung in the air. They held each other close and slept the most peaceful sleep either of them had had in days.

Two hours later, feeling extremely well rested and rejuvenated, Kamau lay awake, stroking Adana's perfectly round bottom while kissing her neck. Her eyes fluttered open and she smiled, remembering that her husband was in bed with her for the first time in days. She mischievously moved her derriere in a way that made Kamau instantly show his appreciation.

Laughing gently, Adana chided her husband, "If we keep this up, Mr. Mazrui, I won't make it to court."

"I promise you will. Just let me hold you a while longer."

Adana acquiesced and placed her arms around Kamau's neck, burying her face in his chest. He parted her legs ever so gently and entered her as smoothly as a kite gliding in the wind. She released a breath, and they danced a slow, melodic dance set by the rhythms of their beating hearts.

When they had once again satisfied each other as only they could, Adana's fingers trailed down Kamau's beard as she asked, "Now are you ready for your surprise?"

"I am ready, my sweet."

Adana got out of bed and slipped on one of her ever-present caftans. Kamau, still in bed, raised himself up on one elbow and followed her with adoring eyes. Adana walked over to her walk-in closet that ran the length of one bedroom wall and said with a dramatic flourish of her hand, "And now, ladies and gentlemen, for Kamau

Mazrui, the man who has everything, a gift that he will use many times over."

Adana opened the closet doors, and Kamau was stunned as he realized that half of the closet contained men's clothing.

He got out of bed and walked to the closet. "Adana, what have you done?"

"What I have done, my darling husband, is to make sure that when we are in Virginia, you are not naked"— she smiled—"like you are now. I had your tailor give me all of your sizes, and he helped me to select a few items so that when you come to Virginia, you really are coming home. He helped me select everything—shoes, socks, shirts, suits, underwear, pj's . . . you name it, it's here."

Kamau was almost speechless. He hugged Adana tightly and said, "Thank you, my love. No one has ever done anything quite so thoughtful for me."

"You are so very welcome, my darling. Let's go win this case."

Chapter 31

Kamau and Adana shared a light breakfast after which
Kamau took a hot shower and Adana soaked in a fragrant tub. When they were dressed, they were the picture
of perfection, both in charcoal gray suits. Kamau called
for a chauffeured car so that Adana could focus on her
case and he could focus on Adana.

When they arrived at the courthouse, the press corps
was waiting. Journalists were vying for position, trying
to be the first to get a whiff of new information about the
case. Adana was poised and graceful as the whisper mill
swirled around her with media people wondering about
the devastatingly handsome, imposing gentleman escorting her into the court. The air surrounding them was
electrified. Adana maintained a laserlike focus as she
and Kamau walked like visiting royalty into the courtroom and sat at the defense table. As Adana introduced
her client, Diani Bitak, to Kamau, Ms. Bitak greeted him
warmly and appreciatively, having been told by Adana
about the role he had played in mounting her defense. As
Kamau and Diani were talking, Adana could feel Jeffery
Scott entering the room, staring at her.

Jeffery was wondering about the expensively attired, no-nonsense-looking guy sitting next to Adana—a new partner? Not likely; he would have heard. A bodyguard? No, he couldn't afford those clothes on a bodyguard's salary. Something about him telegraphed power. He wondered what Adana had up her sleeve.

She glanced in his direction and found that her instinctive feeling that Jeffery was watching her was correct. They nodded acknowledgments just in time to hear the bailiff announce the arrival of the judge. Adana thought to herself, *Let the games begin.*

The first day's jury selection had gone without a hitch. Adana had challenged two of Jeffery's selections, giving her what she felt to be a group of fair-minded jurors who would look past their preconceived notions and see that her client had been framed. Jeffery was not as pleased but never doubted his ability to win the case. After the jury selection, the judge had instructed the attorneys that opening arguments would begin the next day. Adana leaned over and once again reassured her client that they were on the right track and that with any luck the trial would go rather quickly. Ms. Bitak thanked her again and left the courtroom with a harried look on her face. As Diani Bitak was walking away, Jeffery Scott approached the defense table.

"Well, Counselor, it looks as though you may have won this round. You couldn't have done better if you had handpicked the jury."

Kamau stood, observing. He recognized Jeffery as the man he had seen weeks before, leaving Adana's home—the opposing counsel who desired his wife. Adana finished placing documents in her briefcase.

"Well, Jeffery, as they say, you win some, you lose some."

"Knowing you, Adana, I can look forward to another surprise attack."

Jeffery looked in Kamau's direction. "Since this is a new face, do we need to rehash some of our pretrial motions?"

"You can stop your fishing expedition, Jeffery." Adana straightened up, adjusted the hem of her suit jacket, looked at Kamau, smiled and said, "Jeffery Scott, I'd like you to meet Kamau Mazrui, esquire from Mazrui Industries, Nairobi, Kenya—my husband."

Jeffery swallowed, did a double take but recovered quickly. He extended a hand. Kamau, with an expressionless face, shook Jeffery's extended hand as a matter of propriety while Jeffery offered congratulatory sentiments and then made a hasty retreat.

Kamau stroked his wife's back and whispered, "Are you all right?"

Adana's answer was laced with a smile. "I've never been better."

The following morning, Adana's parents were in the courtroom waiting, with a throng of others, to hear opening arguments. Adana was masterful; her legal arguments were designed to appeal to the sense of rightness and fairness she hoped was in every juror. Jeffery was equally masterful, calling forth the demonic twins of fear and insecurity. He knew those emotions existed in every man and every woman, and he played them for all they were worth, painting a picture of Diani Bitak as a conspirator, laundering money and hiding criminals who were destined to destroy life, liberty and the pursuit of happiness for American citizens. Adana acknowledged silently that Jeffery had pulled out all the stops. Proving her case was not going to be a cakewalk, but her confidence never wavered.

The trial lasted for twelve days. Kamau flew back and forth, missing very few days. Near the end of Adana's presentation of her case, Jeffery started challenging witnesses out of desperation. Adana's placement on the stand of a forensic accountant who traced the laundering of the money through Swiss banks in a way that the jury could understand and the last-minute confession from Mohammed after his capture were nails in the coffin of Jeffery's case. Jeffery fought hard in his efforts to rebut Adana's case, but when the defense rested, Kamau reached across the table and touched Adana's hand—then she knew she had won. It took the jury two hours to return a not-guilty verdict. Diani Bitak and her husband embraced each other with tears streaming down both their faces. They thanked Adana profusely and left the courtroom. Adana's partners were present to hear the verdict and both congratulated her, telling her they knew she could do it. She smiled and thanked them, knowing it would be the last time they would meet in a courtroom as partners. Kamau was ever present, touching her back, her arm, her hand. His touch made her feel so safe, and she was clear that she would not have won the case without his help. They were a formidable team.

Jeffery offered a perfunctory congratulations and walked away. He hated to lose, and at that moment Adana was a reminder that he had lost two very important battles—the courtroom battle and the battle for Adana to share his life.

After leaving court, Kamau, Adana and her parents shared a victory dinner at one of the Terrells' favorite restaurants.

Ana addressed her newest son-in-law. "Kamau, you must be exhausted. Commuting across continents for days can't be easy."

"I am used to the travel, and this was for a very good cause." Kamau looked lovingly at Adana, held her hand and kissed it.

"Daughter, you were magnificent," James Terrell spoke with immense pride as he praised his daughter.

"Such skill, such a command of the facts, and you never let a single witness off the hook."

"Well, Daddy, I think you are just a little biased, but this was a case about which I felt strongly, so I really tried to give it my all—and Kamau's contacts helped me to get to the real essence of the case. I'm really glad it's over so that we can start to get settled."

Ana interjected a motherly "What are your plans, sweetheart? I know you're leaving us, but when?"

Adana looked at Kamau and then her parents. "We've decided to leave in the morning. I'd already told my partners some time ago that when this case was finished I'd be taking some time off. What they don't know is that I'm going to tender my resignation and join the Mazrui firm. Kamau and I will be staying at the compound until our home is built. I'm not selling my place here. We will use it when we're in town."

Kamau, looking directly at both parents, said, "Drs. Terrell, please be assured that Adana will be well cared for. She is the love of my life. No harm will come to her. I know there is some sadness because you are losing your last daughter, but understand that you are gaining a large, loving, loyal family. You have been enfolded once again into the Mazrui clan, and everything we own is at your disposal."

James Terrell's response was a short, emotional "Thank you, son." Ana Terrell's was a teary-eyed nod. Dr. James Terrell had known from the moment he met Kamau Mazrui that Kamau was the man for his firstborn. He had no doubt that she was in good hands.

Chapter 32

Nairobi, Kenya—
Three Months Later

Cassandra and Afiya flew in to Nairobi for a sister gathering hosted by Adana at the Mazrui compound. Living in the same city, Amara was chauffeured in. The sisters were lounging around the pool sipping various libations, laughing, talking and generally enjoying each other. Afiya teased, "Well, Mrs. Kamau Mazrui, how does it feel to be a married woman?"

"I'd say it's a lifestyle change that suits me perfectly."

Amara added playfully, "It's those Mazrui men. Honey, they keep you all hot and bothered. They make you want to never leave the bedroom."

Adana quipped, "Or any other room."

The four sisters burst into laughter. Afiya recovered, still panting, fanning herself with her hand. "Sisters, from where I sit, all of that sexual magnetism didn't just stop at the Mazrui brothers—it afflicted their relatives and friends."

Cassandra chimed in, "Amen to that. I am a serious witness. By the way, Adana, Mom told me to ask you if you are reviving your cooking skills. She says she forgets to ask every time she talks to you. You know she taught us all and thinks that cooking talent shouldn't go to waste, even if you have household help."

Adana plastered a sly grin on her face. "Ladies, my husband has no need for me to cook." She paused. "At least not in the kitchen." After a quick double take, the sisters once again collapsed into uproarious laughter.

Afiya held up both hands while still laughing and said, "Stop, stop, stop, I can't take any more. My stomach is sore from laughing."

Adana responded, "Okay, okay, let's give our funny bones a rest. News flash—Kamau and I just got word from Ras yesterday that in another month we can move into our new home."

"That's great." Amara was excited at the prospect of having her sister almost next door.

Adana added, "Kamau and I have also been looking at properties in the south of France. He really wants to fulfill his dream of a five-star restaurant where he can really test his culinary skills. We found a villa surrounded by beautiful vineyards. It needs work, so, Cassandra, we'll be calling on your interior design skills."

Cassandra paused and looked at her sisters. She smiled as she said, "As long as I don't go into labor on the grounds, I'll do it."

"What?"

"Did you say labor?"

"How far along are you?"

"When did you find out?"

The sisters bombarded her with questions. Cassandra laughed. "I knew we were coming here, and I wanted to see your faces when I told you. I'm three months and

I'm so happy. Ras is beside himself. If he had his way, my feet would never touch the ground."

Each in turn, Afiya, Amara and Adana embraced their sister and expressed to her all of the love they felt.

Amara said, "We knew it would happen for you, Cassandra. We are so happy for you. Have you told all of the future grandparents?"

"Ras and I told them just before I flew here so that they wouldn't have to wait so long to talk to you about it. You know Mom hates to keep secrets."

Afiya laughed. "That's because she can't but she's forced to because she's a psychologist. You know Mom secretly loves to gossip." They all laughed, knowing their mother would take issue with Afiya's statement. The Terrell sisters, now all married women, were basking in the glow of their lives. When they returned to their respective homes, they were all grateful for the bond they shared.

Chapter 33

One Month Later

When Kamau Mazrui entered his new home, he once again felt the peace and contentment that always enveloped him when he stepped over the threshold. He knew it wasn't the structure, though it was magnificent, nor was it the ambience or the plush furnishings in their elegant placements around the spacious rooms. No, it was the tone set by his wife. Her mixture of fire and calm, her attention to all of the details of his life, her ability to read his moods and their ability to be both together and alone at the same time. And most importantly her ability to reach his soul when she made love to him. As Kamau moved farther into the foyer, his houseman greeted him and took his briefcase.

"Good evening, Mr. Mazrui."

"Good evening, Vusi. Is my wife in her sitting room?"

"No, sir, she is sitting in the garden."

"Thank you."

"Dinner will be ready, sir, in approximately thirty minutes."

Kamau acknowledged the houseman's comment with a nod and walked in the direction of the garden to find his lovely wife. As Kamau walked, he loosened his tie, removed it and unbuttoned his collar. He saw Adana walking slowly along a path lined with a variety of flowering shrubbery. The variety of colors provided a beautiful backdrop for Adana as she walked along wearing a flowing taupe-colored skirt and matching cropped off-shoulder blouse. Her feet, shod in gold-colored jeweled sandals, seemed to barely touch the ground, making her appear to float.

"Hello, my wife." Kamau's greeting caused Adana to turn, smile and start walking toward him. When they met in the middle of the path, they embraced like long-lost lovers. Adana encircled her husband's neck with her long, delicate arms. Kamau encircled her slender waist with his strong, muscular arms, molding them together, allowing them to relive the pleasure they always associated with each other.

"I really missed you today."

Kamau gently kissed Adana's forehead. "I look forward to your move to the office. I hope you've had a wonderful rest period, because your expertise will definitely be used."

She stroked his face. "Soon, my love, soon. I've made arrangements to have my office furniture transported. You know my desk was a gift from Cassandra. I want it with me. It should be here in a few days. It won't take me long to get settled. Are things going well at the office?"

"Things are good. Are you enjoying our new home?"

"Yes, sweetheart. It is beautiful and Cassandra's decorative skills certainly helped to make it reflect our personalities. I must say I am having to adjust to having servants. I now understand Amara's initial hesitation to use household help."

"Don't worry, my love. You will adjust to being treated royally. You are my queen, and you deserve adoration in every form that I can provide."

Adana laughed a soft, gentle laugh. "Spoken like a true king and my precious husband."

The two turned and walked arm in arm into their home and into a life for which they were truly grateful.

Epilogue

A year later, Kamau and Adana Mazrui stood in a loving embrace in the south of France, in the dining room of their villa, looking out over the vineyards that stretched for miles on their property. Kamau's pursuit of epicurean delights had led them to the purchase of a timeless villa, which they remodeled and converted into an exclusive restaurant. Though the restaurant was completely staffed with internationally known culinary artists, Kamau was still able to indulge himself whenever the creative sparks required him to test his culinary skills.

Adana and Kamau worked together at Mazrui Industries like a well-oiled machine. Their drive, competence and efficiency left them room to spend six months of the year in France, enjoying the pleasures of exquisite foods, wines, family and friends. Family visits were long, plentiful and loving.

Judge Garsen and Mrs. Adina Mazrui and Drs. Ana and James Terrell were elated that their most stubborn offspring had found each other and seemed destined for happiness. They wondered if they'd see grandchildren from the union. Kamau and Adana were sure to keep them guessing—but not for long.

Kamau was lost in thought, staring at the profile of Adana's smooth face. Feeling the warm penetration of her husband's stare, Adana turned to face him. A radiant smile was heard in her voice as she said, "Kamau, you're doing it again."

He looked into her eyes. "What am I doing, my love?"

Adana ran one finger gently along Kamau's velvety mustache. "You're staring at me."

He pulled her closer and lovingly stroked her back. "There are many things you cause me to do over which I have no control. I am drawn to you like a magnet to steel."

He touched her cheek and gently ran the back of his hand down the side of her face, causing tingling sensations to radiate from the core of her body. She sighed. He captured the sigh with a tender, sensual kiss. Her arms, knowing their place, wrapped around Kamau's neck as she deepened the kiss. He slowed the passionate encounter by placing a trail of light feathery kisses down the length of Adana's long, lovely neck. She whimpered, causing his body to react instantly. He smiled knowingly and said, "My beautiful Adana Mazrui, wife of my heart, it was not long ago that I was struggling for meaning in my life. I had no idea what was waiting for me. My elders would say that you are my blessing from God and the ancestors. I am so grateful. I am married to a woman whom only the divine spirit could have fashioned for me." His voice lowered. "There were times when I felt like a ship without a rudder. You changed all of that."

Adana's voice was laced with emotion as she said, "And you, my strong, loving husband, have become my port in every storm. You wash away all of my fears, and you make me feel so wanted. I love you so."

Kamau took his wife's hand. "Wanting you, my darling, will be for me a lifelong preoccupation."

They both laughed as Kamau led Adana into the residential wing of the villa into the master bedroom. She sat on the canopied bed and watched as Kamau opened the French doors leading to a private garden he had designed to provide privacy and beauty as they indulged in all of the ways they found to please each other.

Unbuttoning his shirt, Kamau turned and started walking toward Adana. She felt a light breeze ease through the room and caress her face. She closed her eyes and eased her head back to catch wisps of air. As she tilted her head, her breasts rose, the full, erect peaks waiting to be taken as only Kamau could. He discarded his shirt and joined her on the bed. Adana felt Kamau ease his mouth onto her blouse, and with skillfully measured nips, he suckled her through the silken fabric. His hot, wet mouth pulled at the highly aroused nipples, causing Adana to whisper his name over and over again, hardening his body and deepening his love.

The reaction of Kamau's body fueled Adana's passion for him. Her fingers, as if on a course of their own, found the button holding his trousers and eased the zipper down, slowly mimicking the rhythm of Kamau's mouth as he teased and fondled her breasts. She eased his trousers and silk boxers down over his hard, firm backside, causing him to respond with a sharp intake of air as a light breeze and the softness of Adana's smooth hands ran over his ebony-colored skin. His pull on her nipples deepened through the fabric of the blouse. Adana arched up, burning with sweet tremors that melted her core. Her nails dug into his back as he pushed his pants down the length of his legs and onto the floor. Feeling the heat of Kamau's bare body, Adana's lips quivered as she uttered erotic sounds that deepened Kamau's arousal. He could hear the need in her voice. Her desire for him grew stronger, erasing time and space. Stroking his strong, muscular legs, she wanted him to absorb her into his soul.

"Kamau, love me now, make love to me."

His deep voice was labored and filled with raw passion. "Soon, my wife, soon."

He unbuttoned her blouse slowly, giving himself time to savor the moment. His control was masterful as Adana tortured him with erotic words, nibbles, pecks and strokes. He removed her blouse and took his time layering erotic kisses down her bare body, savoring what he had missed while the objects of his desire had been covered.

Adana started to slip her thin flared skirt down her legs. Kamau stilled her hands, allowing her only to feel the part of him her body was craving through gauzy pleated fabric. It was deliciously infuriating. When he had driven her to the brink, writhing and pleading, he lifted her skirt and removed thin lacy panties. Adana's mind fragmented as Kamau's hands and lips hungrily explored her body. He brought her uncontrollable joy. Cries of passion and ecstasy rose repeatedly from her throat. As she arched up and Kamau grabbed her skirt to remove it, the turbulence of his desire caused him to pull with a force that split the delicate fabric. His "I am sorry, my sweet" was lost on Adana as she moved the fabric aside and found the place beneath her husband she most desired. She wrapped her long, smooth legs around his back. He needed no invitation to slip into her hard and fast. They were consumed by their need for each other.

Each time he entered his wife, Kamau found insatiable pleasure. Together they created unspeakable joy.

They rode a tidal wave of smoldering, maddening, raw, reckless passion that held them captive. Kamau held Adana in his arms like a priceless jewel as they followed their familiar rhythms into an ecstasy that led to the sleep of contented lovers.

Want more Chilufiya Safaa?
Turn the page for a sizzling excerpt from
The Art of Love.
Available now wherever books are sold!

Chapter 1

South Carolina

Afiya Terrell sat lounging lazily on her grandparents' wraparound porch. The wide, whitewashed swing on which she sat swayed easily in the South Carolina breeze. A faint gust of wind swirled past her floor-length, gauzy lemon yellow flared skirt, lifting it just enough to reveal perfectly pedicured, delicate, and flawlessly formed bare feet. Afiya held her head back, catching snatches of the air as it eased across her pecan-colored face. Her refined, shiny, carefully locked hair was upswept in a tangle of exquisitely shaped tendrils, with a few curling wistfully from her temples to her haughty chin.

Afiya had come to visit her paternal grandparents as a respite from the hustle and bustle of city life and from her complicated life as an entrepreneurial gallery owner. Willows, as the Terrell ancestral home was called, was a place that held precious memories for Afiya and her three sisters, Amara, Cassandra, and Adana. Cassandra had even named her interior design firm Willows in honor of the paternal homestead, and Afiya had named her gallery Devore Gallery in honor of her grandmother's paternal ancestors. Almost from birth, they had spent extended periods of time on the land. The acreage was vast, and their grandparents, Lancaster and Savannah Terrell, indulged their grandchildren, and so the girls, during their visits as little ones and as adolescents, had been allowed to run freely from sunup to sundown, with endless activities that ran the gamut from swimming in the lake bordering the property to horseback riding, berry picking, feeding chickens, and, of course, playing the never-ending games of jump rope, jacks, dolls, and paper dolls. The memories were good. Afiya found her way to Willows as often as she could. There was a peace and tranquility on her grandparents' land that she could not duplicate anywhere else she had ever been in the world.

Just as she felt the wispy touch of another breeze caress her bare shoulders, covered only by the string ties of her lemon yellow halter top, she heard hinges sing as a screen door opened, and simultaneously, her paternal grandmother, Savannah Devore Terrell, with a lyrical inflection, called out her name.

"Fiya." Savannah always dropped the *A* from her granddaughter's name. "Baby, would you like some cool lemonade? I'll make it just the way you like it, with a sprig of peppermint from my garden and frozen mango cubes."

Afiya lifted her head and responded to her grandmother quietly and easily.

"Gram, that sounds so good. Should I come in and help you?"

Savannah smiled, looking at her granddaughter while, out of habit, wiping her palms on her trademark crisp, ruffle-trimmed apron. She spoke with a warm Southern accent that was both refined and comforting.

"Well, I suppose that would be a nice way of spending time with one of my precious granddaughters. We don't get to spend nearly enough time these days. I'm so glad you came to stay awhile."

Afiya lifted herself up from the swing and followed her grandmother into the house. Though she loved both her grandmothers, Savannah Devore Terrell was her heart. There was a special connection between them. The home of the elder Terrells was spacious and as comfortable as a plush down comforter on a cold winter night. The farmhouse had been constructed in the 1800s and continued to be lovingly maintained by the Terrell clan. Afiya and her sisters had recently remodeled the entire kitchen as a gift, giving Savannah Devore Terrell more room and more state-of-the-art appliances than she knew what to do with or would ever use.

Afiya entered the kitchen and started opening the beautifully carved walnut cabinets while asking, "Gram, where do you keep your juicer? Tell me where it is, and I can juice the lemons for you."

Savannah Terrell, a stunning woman in her late seventies, looked at her granddaughter and, laughing gently, said, with feigned indignation, "Now, Fiya, you know I haven't seen that gadget since you girls bought it for me. I still know how to get juice from a lemon without hooking up some machine."

Afiya laughed out loud while humorously chastising her grandmother. "Gram, you just won't let people make life easier for you, will you? We buy you all of the things you call gadgets so that you can have more time to just enjoy your life and not spend it on all of these time-consuming tasks. If we let you, you would try to work yourself to death." Afiya stopped and asked more seriously, "Gram, do you understand the logic of what I'm trying to say?"

With a sparkle in her almond-shaped eyes, set in a face covered in nut brown, beautifully unwrinkled skin, Savannah Terrell answered, "Oh, I understand the logic, but it's not logic I'm looking for when I'm doing the things I love, especially in my kitchen. My kitchen is my little piece of heaven on earth, and when I'm in it, I want to experience the sensations of touch, taste, and smell, and any gadget that gets in the way of my senses I can do without."

With a slow, easy smile, she continued. "Now, sweetie, I know that's not logical, but that's your grandma."

Afiya shook her head, smiled, grabbed her grandmother, hugged her, and said, "Let me help you squeeze the lemons." She released her grandmother and gave her a soft kiss on the cheek, and the two women began working in companionable silence.

Savannah moved about her new-millennium kitchen, performing tasks in ways that had been handed down for generations. She walked to her window box herb garden and picked a handful of mint sprigs. She rolled the stems in her hands and lifted them to her nostrils and inhaled deeply the pungent fragrance of the deep green, vein-etched leaves. The sweet, acidic odor brought to her mind wonderful memories of hot summer days and warm nights filled with peace and love. She rinsed the leaves, the color of well-watered grass, under cold running tap water and enjoyed the spray that flowed along her wrists and hands.

When she finished washing the mint leaves, Savannah retrieved a muslin cloth from a nearby drawer and spread it out on her newly constructed, gray-colored, granite-topped counter. Her delicate hands moved slowly across the length of the fabric, flattening it out with each firm stroke. Each leaf was placed gently on the sparkling white cloth, and with soft pats, the sprigs of greenery were methodically dried. The matriarch of the Terrell family then opened her refrigerator and carefully lifted from it a glass pitcher that had been her grandmother's. The pitcher was filled with the water and sugar needed for the lemonade base. Savannah placed it on the counter directly in front of her and touched its round belly with her flat palm to gauge its temperature. She decided it was just cold enough.

Afiya continued squeezing lemons while watching her grandmother execute tasks she had seen her perform countless times. Afiya marveled at her grandmother's strength and focus. She hoped that she would herself develop those traits by the time she reached the eighth decade of her life.

While Afiya continued squeezing lemons and peripherally feeling the movements of her grandmother, Savannah reached into her freezer and brought out mango-juice cubes, which had been frozen with tiny slices of strawberries to add more color and flavor to the lemony brew. Afiya added the freshly squeezed and strained lemon juice to the pitcher, and with one of her grandmother's ever-present wooden spoons, she quietly stirred the mixture until the tartness of the lemon juice and the sweetness of the sugar formed nectar waiting to soothe thirsty palates. Savannah brought out two tall crystal glasses and placed a decorative stack of the mango ice cubes in each, before gently pouring a slowly cascading ripple of the pale yellow liquid in each. She then removed two white linen napkins from one of her cabinets and placed them on a silver tray, along with the pitcher of lemonade and the glasses. She added a sprig of mint to each glass, picked up the tray, and walked outside to the porch. Afiya followed. They sat at a round white wicker table topped with glass. The comfortable wicker chairs in which they sat had mauve and teal chintz seat cushions. The women mirrored each other as they savored the delicious aromas emitting from their glasses.

Afiya took a sip and spoke in a slower version of her usually lightning-quick cadence.

"Gram, as usual you were right. I think this is just what we needed. This must be what they mean when they say we should stop and smell the roses."

"Yes, sweetheart, there are days when all we need to do is just slow down." Savannah looked at her granddaughter with a pensive stare, took a slow sip from her glass, then set it down gingerly and asked, without prelude, "Fiya, are the ancestors still talking to you? Are you still having prophetic dreams?"

Before Afiya could answer, her grandmother continued, speaking as though she were thinking aloud. "From the moment of your birth, I could see that you had been blessed." She smiled. "Or cursed, depending upon your point of view. I knew that you had the gift that I have and that your great-grandmother had." Now she looked more deeply into Afiya's eyes. "How are you handling your gift?"

Afiya's smile was long and slow as she responded, "Fine, Gram. I'm okay. The ancestors are still talking to me, and I'm still dreaming. It all still happens without my asking. It's as if the divine knows when I need to be guided, and my angels appear. Always on time."

"Good, good. Just keep praying daily, asking for guidance, and you will always be protected and wisely led."

As Afiya indicated her agreement with her grandmother by an affirmative nod of her head, they both heard a booming masculine voice announce, "I'm home."

Lancaster Terrell was a big-boned, tall man, with sandy hair sprinkled liberally with silver strands. He had been fishing and had entered the house through the back door. His wife of fifty years answered by calling to him in her usually affectionate way. "Lan, we're on the front porch."

Lancaster walked out onto the porch, beaming. "Here are two of my favorite girls." He walked over and pecked Afiya on the cheek, then leaned over to his wife and asked, with a sly grin, "Vannah, did you miss me while I was gone?"

With a hint of the flirt her husband knew her to be hanging on her lips, Savannah responded, "Man, I didn't have time to miss you, and you smell fishy."

He stroked his wife's shoulder-length salt-and-pepper hair as he said, "Woman, I remember a time when you couldn't stand to have me out of your sight. It didn't matter what I smelled like."

Savannah laughed and said to the love of her life, "Lancaster Terrell, that was a long time ago." Her husband feigned a wounded look, and Afiya and her grandmother met his fake countenance with gales of laughter.

Savannah, after a moment, took pity on her dutiful husband, and with a smile tracing the lips he loved, she said, "Lan, you know I always miss you."

This time his grin stretched from ear to ear as he answered, "I knew you did."

"Lan, what am I going to do with you?" said Savannah. Before he could respond, she asked, "Did you and Jake catch any fish?"

"Woman, you know Jake couldn't catch a fish if they walked up to his line. I just don't know why that man can't fish, and when he invites himself on my fishing trips, he runs my fish away, too."

Afiya laughed and asked, "Poppy, if Mr. Jake is such a bad fisherman, why have you two been fishing buddies for over forty years?"

"Oh, I just took pity on the man years ago," replied Lancaster. "I thought I could teach him something, but, by God, he's the slowest learner I've ever seen."

This time all three of them laughed at Lancaster's depiction of one of his dearest friends, a man for whom he would give his life. Savannah interjected, "Lan, I'm going to tell Jake you said he can't fish. Now go wash up, and I'll fix you some nice cold lemonade."

As Lancaster walked away, he hollered over his shoulder, "You won't be telling him anything he doesn't already know."